BETWEEN
YESTERDAY AND
TOMORROW

MARGARET DUARTE

Omie
PRESS

Book Cover design Yocla Designs by Clarissa

Publisher's Cataloging-in-Publication Data

Names: Duarte, Margaret, author.

Title: Between yesterday and tomorrow / Margaret Duarte.

Description: Elk Grove, CA : Omie Press, 2018. | Series: Enter the between, bk. 3.

Identifiers: LCCN 2018933165 | ISBN 978-0-9860688-6-7 (pbk.) | ISBN 978-0-9860688-7-4 (Kindle ebook)

Subjects: LCSH: Women--Fiction. | Self-actualization (Psychology)--Fiction. | Alcoholism--Fiction. | Spiritual life--Fiction. | BISAC: FICTION / Visionary & Metaphysical. | FICTION / Fantasy / Paranormal. | FICTION / Occult & Supernatural. | GSAFD: Occult fiction.

Classification: LCC PS3604.U241 B49 2018 (print) | LCC PS3604.U241 (ebook) | DDC 813/.6--dc23.

To Christine and Ron

Fall

2001

The third path of initiation begins in the West,
the place of change and transition.

As the sunporch grew darker and chillier, I waited for a dead woman to tell me a story. What you believe to be real is real, I reminded myself, in part to keep me from running out of the room in fear for my sanity and in part because it was true. I believed Christine to be real, therefore she was.

BETWEEN
YESTERDAY AND
TOMORROW

Chapter One

IT WAS A TRICK of the light. It had to be. The house seemed to glow—the whiteness of its shingled surface blinding. I raised my hand to shield my eyes and stepped closer. Loamy earth sank beneath my feet. Twigs snapped. Crows cawed. It was a scene straight out of my dreams, the kind that had me burrowing deeper into the covers and wishing I'd never wake up.

I paused under a massive oak and tore my gaze from the three-storied Victorian long enough to look up and notice beards of Spanish moss dangling from the tree's crooked branches.

"This isn't quite what I expected," my sister said, halting by my side.

I didn't answer. I couldn't. During the short time Veronica and I had been wandering about, the house had cast a spell over me, as though I'd stumbled into another world, where time stood still and schedules and appointments, goals and ambitions no longer mattered. My limbs grew heavy. I wanted to curl up on a wicker chair in the sunporch that ran along the eastern portion of the house. Or better yet, explore the bell-domed turret that rose from its southeast corner.

Veronica poked me in the ribs. "Don't space out on me, Marjorie! We've got a car full of luggage to unload, and I'm hungry."

I nodded, her words only partly heard. The house and surrounding yard occupied over half a city block, its windows shaded to the outside world. It took another poke to my side from my sister to penetrate the fog in my head. I inhaled a gush of grass-scented air, intoxicating, as though my sense of smell had sharpened after months in outer space. "I can't believe Anne owns a house such as this. It's so massive, so—"

Veronica snorted. "It better have good heating and air, or I'm moving into one of those motels down the street." She turned and headed back to the Jeep, leaving a void, as if something important had been left unsaid.

Eager to fetch our bags and investigate what would be our home for the next few months, I hurried after my sister. We'd left the Jeep parked on the circular driveway surrounding a gazebo, birdbath, and low-growing junipers. Only the certainty that Veronica would have a fit if I made any sudden excursions kept me from running off and performing cartwheels in the park-like setting. We'd entered the property through a padlocked gate with a NO TRESPASSING sign—a bit intimidating as I'd fumbled with the keys to unlock it—so I wasn't prepared for the tranquil scene inside. Veronica, in contrast, appeared numb to it all, mumbling something about conspicuous consumption as she lifted the hatch of the Jeep and went straight for our food supplies. "Forget the suitcases for now," she said, tossing one of the plastic bags my way. "Let's see what we can whip up in the kitchen."

I caught the bag—the light one holding the cookies and chips—and nodded, though I wasn't in the least bit hungry. How could I eat with this house beckoning me? I could practically hear it whispering below the everyday sounds of bird chatter and street traffic.

Veronica paused from her grocery fervor long enough to give me a thorough look. "It's not like you to be so quiet, Sis. Hope you're not coming down with something."

"Yeah, me too," I said, before heading for the sunporch entry.

There was something wrong with me all right. One minute I wanted to curl up and take a nap, the next to frolic and play. I shrugged, not in the mood to analyze my unusual reaction to this place. It was upsetting enough that I'd been hearing a voice for the past six months, despite Dr. Mendez's assurances that I wasn't losing my mind.

"The voice may be part of your wake-up call," he'd said. "Otherwise known as 'The Dark Night of the Soul.' You would be surprised at how many people experience such a thing."

Dark Night of the Soul? Wake-up call? No, the subtle energy this

2

house transmitted was more than just about me. Something disturbing lay beneath its outward calm.

I set the grocery bag on the sunporch step. The keys—at least
ten of them in all shapes and sizes—jingled as I retrieved them from
the pocket of my jeans. Question was, which one fit the door? As I
sorted through them, Veronica suggested in a voice that sounded
almost whimsical, "Let's go in through the front instead. That way
we can get the full effect, kind of like entering the haunted mansion
at Disneyland, 'home to ghosts, ghouls, and supernatural surprises.'"

My sister was revealing a fanciful, quirky side I hadn't experienced before. I half expected her to follow up her haunted mansion
remark with a bad-ass-Disney-witch cackle.

"Not even close," I said. "No music, no Ghost Host, no hearse
parked outside."

"Crazy big though. Nice of Anne to lend it to us."

It was about time Veronica showed appreciation for Anne's kindness. I would never have guessed that my friend owned a house of
such humongous proportions. The Anne I knew was casual and un-
assuming. She slept in a yurt, for Pete's sake, wore long skirts and billowy blouses, walked in sandals. This house, let alone the property it
stood on, was easily worth a fortune. Yet, when Anne had discovered
that Veronica and I were headed for Pacific Grove to seek out our
inebriate father, she'd handed over the keys, no questions asked, as if
we were doing her a tremendous favor.

"Holy crap!" Veronica said as we rounded the building's west
corner. The words were crass, but the tone was right. I mean, any
words used to describe the front of this house deserved an exclama-
tion. The Victorian comprised three stories with too many windows
to count, all closed and shaded to the outside world. I glanced to the
left to see if I could spot the turret from where I stood but got a
blinding shaft of October sunlight instead. Too late, I closed my
eyes. Then all I saw was yellow dots.

"Check out the front door," Veronica said.

Blinking to clear the afterimage floating in the center of my vision, I edged forward. Only to hear another outburst from my sister. "Well, I'll be!"

At least she was impressed. It was hard to impress my twin. I focused on Veronica's back, identical to my own except for the clothes she wore—low-rise black jeans and a dinky red tee. Yes, even with the temperature in the low seventies.

Sight restored, I took in the house's entry. Panels of stained glass framed both sides of the front door and formed a half dome over the top, each patterned with monarch butterflies, wings set at all angles, suggesting movement and flight. No source of light illumined the glass from behind, yet shades of opalescent black, orange, and yellow layered over blue and white gave the panels a sense of depth and complexity. I gasped, having only seen glasswork this artfully crafted in windows of cathedrals and museums. "Can you imagine what those panels must look like at night with the interior lights on?"

Veronica gave a soft whistle. "Beats gargoyles."

I glanced at the keys in my hand, this time having no problem choosing which one fit the door. The big one with the scrolls shaped like a butterfly. I slipped it into the lock, gave it a twist, and turned the knob. "You first," I said, opening the door and stepping aside.

Veronica flashed me a look—a reminder that I was the younger twin—before she entered.

I closed my eyes and waited.

"You can come in now," Veronica said after a brief pause. Her voice sounded approving, even cheerful, suggesting her mood had lifted, which, of course, lifted mine. If that were possible. I was already flying higher than the crows inhabiting the property. For the first time in twenty-nine years, my sister and I would live together, if only for a short while.

When I stepped into the foyer, I heard a drawn breath as if by simply opening the front door, we'd provided the house with a much-needed dose of fresh air. The word *Welcome* came as a murmur whispered in my ear, but without the creaks and groans of devices hidden behind wallpapered walls. I half expected to see sliding panels and a smiling old woman holding a long-stemmed red rose. I shook my head to vanquish the haunted mansion scenario Veronica had planted in my mind. "Thank you."

"You talking to me?" Veronica asked from her position in front of a gilt mirror with leaf and shell moldings.

The air rippled and I felt dizzy as if we were experiencing an earth tremor common to California. I closed my eyes and took a deep breath. When I reopened them, all was still. I caught Veronica's reflection in the mirror. Our eyes met. "Ah," she said, "you're picking up on someone else's vibes again. Not Antonia's, though, or I'd be sensing them, too. Maybe it's the Ghost Host."

I shut the door behind me. Let her joke. She wasn't as receptive to the extrasensory as I was, though she had witnessed enough of the preternatural not to pass judgment. It had been a shock to learn that the voice I'd been hearing belonged to my mother, Antonia Flores, who'd died soon after giving birth to me. An equal shock, although more painful, was learning that I'd been adopted by Gerardo and Truus Veil (why hadn't they told me) and had an identical twin sister raised by our birth father, currently residing in Pacific Grove.

Anyway, dead people's voices no longer filled me with dread, least of all this one, which sounded kind, benevolent. It wasn't the voice drawing me forward, though, but the house itself. It greeted me with eager welcome as had its owner when I first met her during my stay in Big Sur. The dimly lit foyer was impressive, with its parquet floor, grand oak staircase, and crystal chandelier. I sniffed the air and caught a sweet sugary scent similar to that in my home in Menlo Park, thanks to the vanilla diffuser plugged into my entry outlet. "Anne gave no clue she lived in such opulence. I mean, in Big Sur she lived like a gypsy."

Veronica twirled in a slow circle, her gaze darting in all directions. "Yeah, makes one wonder why she'd give this up to go gallivanting in the woods."

"She mentioned something about inherited money not making her happy." I said, zeroing in on the crystal ball centered on the foyer table. "That happiness comes from helping others." I turned toward the stained-glass panels bordering the front door, wondering if they were the source of the ball's inner glow. But no, only faint light filtered through the rippled glass, deflecting like sunrays hitting water and bestowing the orange and black butterflies with dazzling aliveness.

"Inherited money," Veronica said in a voice so low I strained to hear it. "I know the feeling."

Of course, she did. Veronica grew up under the care of Bob, our father, and her stepmother, Elizabeth, in Maryland, money dangling like moss from the trees, while I was raised in California by middle-class parents, whom I'd believed to be my biological parents.

Searching for an anchor in this house of unusual charms, I refocused on Veronica's eyes in the mirror—blue like mine, yet so different. Twenty-nine years of living on opposite coasts under the influence of different parents had formed and shaped us in unique ways. Veronica had dyed her hair black. I'd left mine blonde. She'd developed into a powerful, forceful woman. I'd grown up more subdued, submissive.

"It smells good in here," Veronica said, "like someone's been baking. Wonder where the kitchen is." She passed through the heavy-framed archway into the dining room and headed for a door in its southwest corner.

The image of us sitting at a kitchen table huddled over freshly brewed coffee and baked treats urged me to follow, giving the dining room's furnishings only a cursory glance—burgundy drapes, mahogany table, upholstered chairs...

We entered a spacious kitchen facing a neglected backyard. Unlike the rest of the house, the windows here were unshaded, allowing sunlight to stream onto gleaming white cabinets, countertops, and a white dinette table in a breakfast nook. We'd found the home's center, its heart, but despite the warm scent of vanilla and melted butter, nothing recently baked awaited us there. Veronica plopped her bag of groceries onto the counter. "Could've sworn I smelled something yummy baking in the oven."

I set my grocery bag next to hers, feeling a mutual disappointment, though I should've known better. Who would be preparing something delectable to eat in this big empty house? I dug the scentless snickerdoodles out of my grocery bag and tried to sound cheerful. "Guess these'll have to do."

Veronica took the package from my hands, pried open the resealable cover, and helped herself to a cookie. "We'll need something to wash these down."

A coffee maker stood on the granite counter, and since we hadn't yet finished unloading our groceries, I headed for the pantry next to the refrigerator for something caffeinated to brew. After a short search through Anne's well-stocked food supply, I found a tin of Yuban rather than the organic variety she'd served at her campsite in Big Sur. She'd compared drinking the conventional brand to sipping pesticide.

"Maybe Anne has a housekeeper," Veronica said. "That would explain this place's immaculate appearance. And why it smells so damn good in here."

My hands shook as I filled the eight-cup machine with water and measured the "Rainforest Alliance Certified" grinds into the basket. At least Anne had chosen a brand that promoted environmental, social, and economic principles. While the coffee brewed, I leaned against the counter, more depleted than I'd realized.

Veronica, still busy ogling our surroundings, reached for another cookie. "Jeez," I said. "Save one for me."

She hesitated, cookie in midair, and blew out a long breath. "I work so hard at feeling full, yet my tank's always on empty."

I opened the glass-fronted cupboard for coffee mugs, praying her words weren't a sign of things to come.

No sooner had Veronica and I settled at the table than my eyelids started to droop. I took a sip of coffee, hoping the caffeine would revive me. Instead, my head grew heavy, my mind blank. "Veronica," I said, reaching out through the fog.

"Yeah."

"What were you thinking about just now?"

"Nothing."

"Same here. For a few minutes there, I forgot about the past, the future, even why we were here. I think I need a nap."

Veronica nodded. "Go ahead, while I finish unloading the car."

"I don't know what it is about this place, but I feel so—"

"It's okay," Veronica said. "I get it. Like you want to take a deep breath and slow down for a while."

I rubbed my eyes and yawned, as I'd done so many times as a child, when my adoptive father was still alive, when he tucked me in at night, when I'd felt safe and protected. I stood and headed for a door on the opposite side of the kitchen. It led into a hallway which I followed to another door as if guided by an invisible hand.

I entered the sunporch I'd observed from outdoors, and there, grouped around a braided rug and glass-topped table, stood a white wicker settee with a matching ottoman and chair cushioned in brown and white checkered fabric. I sank into the chair, dragged a quilt from the arm of the settee, and draped it over me. My last memory before falling asleep was lifting my feet onto the ottoman and releasing a heavy sigh.

❂❂❂

When I woke, the porch had turned dark and chilly. A soft *coooo OOOOO-woo-woo-woo* caught my attention, but I dismissed it in my sudden concern for Veronica. I'd left her alone in this humongous house. Where was she? What was she doing? I refolded the quilt over the arm of the settee and hurried back into the house in search of my sister.

I found her in the front parlor, nearly camouflaged by the velvet-flocked wallpaper, brocade valances, and silk-damask-upholstered furniture. She had turned on a lamp, started a fire in the hearth, and now sat in a plush armchair staring at the flames. "Sorry for conking out on you," I said, welcoming the warmth and scent of burning wood.

Veronica's stark expression indicated that our peaceful sojourn was over. I'd become sidetracked by the receptiveness of this house, its gift of serenity, its unspoken promise that all would be well.

"I put your suitcases in the turret room on the third floor," she said, staring at the play of the flames as if under the thrall of a living thing. "Seemed to suit you best."

"Thanks." I sank onto the overstuffed couch next to my sister, aware of the message her limp posture and jerky hand movements conveyed. Soon I'd be meeting my birth father for the first time. Part of me, the part that empathized with Veronica and protected my heart, wished we could put it off forever. The other part of me, the needy, greedy part, the part that ached to love and be loved, was all revved up to hurry. Just thinking about my father's close proximity made me want to cry in frustration. *What are we waiting for?*

Veronica had warned me that Bob was an alcoholic and destroyed the people he loved. Yet... Maybe I could help him. Maybe he could help me. Besides, Veronica and I had little choice in the matter, not with our birth mother coaching us from the grave. She'd shattered our sense of what was real and unreal and turned our worlds upside down before relaying that our father held a secret important to us both.

"Dad's renting a bungalow near here," Veronica said. "Tomorrow, I'll take you there." She closed her eyes and added, "Might as well get it over with."

My heart contracted as if I knew how Veronica felt, which I didn't.

She dragged her gaze from the fire, her eyes red and puffy. "The thought of seeing him again fills me with such despair... I find it hard to conjure up any hope."

For a few moments, I listened to the pop and crackle of the burning logs, trying to think of something comforting to say.

Veronica saved me the trouble by asking, "Are you okay with clam chowder out of a can tonight? I wasn't in the mood to fix anything from scratch."

"I'll slice the ciabatta bread and prepare a green salad and tea," I said. "Want to join me? Bet Anne has a bottle of wine stored somewhere."

Veronica stood with painstaking slowness, as though her bones had turned to mush and left her with no means of support. "It'll take more than a bottle of wine to help us now."

Chapter Two

THIS SHOULD HAVE BEEN one of the happiest days of my life. After all, I was meeting Bob, my birth father, for the first time. I'd worn a fitted navy jacket over a crisp white blouse along with my best pair of sandblasted jeans. I'd applied makeup, washed and styled my hair, and in final preparation—warnings be darned—I'd put Bob on a pedestal, along with Gerardo, my adoptive father. And why not? Antonia still loved him, didn't she? Even from the grave.

Instead, the sight of my father peering from the doorway of a small rented bungalow—likely the size of his maid's quarters back home—had me trembling. This man looked smaller, shabbier, more derelict than my mind had allowed. He squinted at Veronica and me, his jaw slack. We stood in silence, giving him—and ourselves—time to adjust. I, for one, was incapable of speaking, let alone coming up with anything appropriate to say.

Bob blinked and rubbed his eyes as though experiencing double vision due to too much alcohol. Had he forgotten that he'd fathered *two* daughters, that Veronica had a sister—me, his second born? Then it struck me. Maybe no one had told him my name. "Hello Father. I'm—"

"*Sunwalker?* Is that you?" He leaned forward, eyes narrowed for tighter focus. "Have you come to forgive me?"

His reaction should've pleased me, the contrition in his voice, the fact that he hadn't forgotten me, but... I hadn't considered forgiveness. In my fantasy, there had been no need to forgive. We'd be embracing by now, making up for lost time. And he smelled of alcohol. No, he reeked of it. Not only his breath, but his skin and clothes. Was he speaking from his heart? Or was booze doing the talking?

Bob turned to Veronica. She looked away. He would get no help from her. When he turned back to me, our gazes met and held. I'd longed for this moment, darn it. I'd longed to revel in our mutual love, father to daughter, blood to blood. But as I studied the thin, wasted man leaning against the doorframe of the bungalow with its orange tiled roof, soft beige walls, and tasteful green trim, I couldn't reach deep enough within me to find the love and compassion I knew to be there.

"This is ridiculous," Veronica said. And she was right. After all of her warnings, I'd allowed my reunion fantasy to blossom into a scene straight out of a romantic work of fiction. Instead, I stood, disconnected, dispassionate, looking into my father's watery eyes, trying to reach the core of him, my Papa's soul. For a moment, I allowed myself another fantasy: that he was overwhelmed with emotion at seeing me, his lost daughter, his little flower, his *Sunwalker*.

In reality, his eyes revealed nothing.

"I wanted you both," he said, darting a look at Veronica, who stood, shoulders hunched, as if she were bleeding inside, "but Antonia cried. So, I only took Veronica and left you. I tried to forget you, but..." He wiped his brow, hand trembling, jaw working up and down. At one time, he may have meant the words tumbling forth now, but to my ear, they sounded hollow, as if they'd been thought, spoken, or dreamed so many times, they'd lost all meaning. Maybe for him I'd been as much of a fantasy as he'd been for me. And maybe he, too, found the object of his fantasy lacking.

"Okay, that's it," Veronica said. "Quit gawking at Marjorie and invite us in, or we're leaving. I have better things to do."

"Yeah, sure," he said but made no move to step away from the door.

My father and I stood frozen; he stuck in a hell of his own making, I mired in the past, a past that was darkening my world. The present seemed unreal, little more than a blur, and the future promised more of the same. He smiled and opened his arms. "Home at last!"

I didn't step into his embrace, didn't feel the connection, the sympathy, the concern. "Not home," I said.

My reaction—or lack thereof—didn't seem to bother him. He dropped his arms, shrugged, and backed into the house, motioning for me to follow. "You're even more beautiful than your mother was."

Dear God. How could Antonia have loved this man?

The bungalow had no foyer, so I stepped directly into the small living room. Veronica followed, closing the door behind her. The space was dark and shadowy, the only light, fuzzy and unnatural, coming from a portable television perched on a rickety end table that looked like it had been through a lot over the years. Our father had been watching the news. The familiar drone of an anchorman shared all that was wrong with the world. It had only been twelve days since the 9/11 attacks on the World Trade Center by al-Qaeda and it was still a big story.

"The world's going to hell," Veronica said, glaring at the television as she'd glared at our father only moments before.

Shame burrowed through me. How could I expect peoples and nations to love and understand one another in the great in-between that binds instead of separates, when I couldn't even love and understand my own father? With all my education and so-called knowledge, I couldn't apply it to understanding in my life. It was far easier to demonize than to empathize.

The man who had sired me, stepped toward me, bringing his face close to mine. But all I could acknowledge was his red, cracked skin and the alcohol on his breath. "My sweet angel," he said. "Give your papa a hug."

I tried. Honestly, I did. I wanted desperately to show my love with a fond hug and a kiss. Instead, I backed off. Fathers weren't supposed to talk to their twenty-nine-year-old daughters like this, were they? A simple, "I love you," or, "I longed for this day," would've sufficed.

Veronica made a choking sound as she pulled away from the door she'd been leaning against and came to my aid. "Give her a break, Dad. She didn't even know you existed until six months ago."

For a moment, Bob's eyes dulled, as though he, too, sensed the weight of disappointment, but then as before, he shrugged; a quick recovery for a man who supposedly loved me.

I felt chilled in all the places where I should've felt warm, the voice of guilt a pulsing ache in my head. *What's wrong with you? This is your father. You may not get a second chance.*

Nothing. An emptiness I could drown in.

"Dad wasn't always like this," Veronica said. "He was—"

"Oh, quit whining," Bob said. "I'm doing just fine." He waved his hand over the coffee table cluttered with crumpled take-out bags and half eaten entrees from a myriad of fast-food restaurants, before pointing at an empty bottle of *Fat Bastard* chardonnay. "She wants me to quit drinking this stuff, but it's good for the blood." He toasted me with an imaginary glass, his smile defiant. "So, I'll be damned if I'll let her, or anyone else, take it from me."

If by "anyone else" he meant me, I was in trouble. I kept silent, too upset to speak, which was probably for the best. I doubt he would've been impressed with my opinion.

Veronica clapped her hands and whistled as if cheering at a football game. "Good going, Dad. Stand up for what you believe in, no matter whom it hurts. Stay on the course to destruction. When your liver deteriorates, you can start whining about your painful death."

My chest ached at the ferocity of Veronica's words. They spewed forth like shrapnel, wounding indiscriminately, its intent to mar, incapacitate.

"Of course, you'll expect your loving family to be at your beck and call during your time of need, right?" she said. "I mean, it's the least we can do after all you've done for us."

Sunlight couldn't penetrate the curtains that barricaded the windows. And the meager glow cast by the television seemed to close in on me as if burying me alive. Deep-seated emotions were erupting here, and if Veronica didn't let up soon, the damage would be irreversible.

My father's reaction should've, but didn't, surprise me. "Shut up, Veronica. You don't know the half of it. I've had it tough. No one understands me, even your stepmother. She turns a cold shoulder when she should be listening." He looked at his hands as if surprised they were shaking. "She's having an affair, you know."

"What goes around, comes around," Veronica said under her breath. "Elizabeth would have my blessing, if that were true."

"Don't look so shocked," Bob said as if he hadn't heard her. "I can prove it."

Veronica slapped her hand to her chest. "Give me a break. Nothing you say shocks me anymore. Even half sober, you make no sense. Too many dead brain cells."

"Don't talk to your father like that," Bob said, sounding old and weary. He turned away from my twin and sank onto the deep-seated couch, then pushed aside the stale sandwich on the coffee table to retrieve his remote. He clasped the control in his hand like a dear old friend and turned up the volume of the television just in time for us to hear about a methane gas explosion that killed thirteen miners in Alabama.

We stared at the screen, pausing from our own sorry plight long enough to acknowledge the misfortune of others. What these families had lost in the blink of an eye and through no fault of their own, Veronica and I were squandering. And there wasn't a darn thing I could do about it. At least not now. It was too soon. Too late.

Again, guilt spoke to me. *He's your birth father, the only one you'll ever have.*

Like father, like daughter came my silent response. Absorbed in pain and self-pity, we'd blundered our first and possibly most important meeting.

If only I had listened to Veronica. If only I had studied up on this terrible addiction before intruding on my father's life and passing judgment.

15

Veronica lurched for the television and turned it off. "Open a window, damn it. It smells like dirty socks in here." Hurt, anger, and fear seemed to ooze from her every pore. "You're as sick as your secrets," she flung at our father, a clue to her capacity for hate. "You need therapy."

Bob didn't bother to look her way. The blank television screen commanded his full attention. "Yeah. Yeah. Yeah."

"What are you ashamed of?" Veronica asked, her voice loud, a crescendo.

Bob turned to her, brows raised. "Me? Ashamed? Look who's missing the brain cells."

"Your pain and anger belong to you, not me," she said, as if trying to convince herself.

He sneered. "You owe me."

Veronica shrugged, then allowed her shoulders to droop as if blunting the impact of thrown stones. "You're not good for me," she said, her voice fading like someone experiencing the last moments before death.

They weren't listening to each other anymore if they'd been listening at all. *Man's cruelty to man.* The room and all it symbolized, its darkness, the malcontent circulating between its walls, the tales of destruction on the news, hit target. Bile rose in my throat, and I headed for the door, barely making it out in time.

❁❁❁

"That went well," Veronica said when she joined me several minutes later.

I was sitting on the sidewalk, head between my knees. "I didn't mean to judge him, only show him understanding and love."

Veronica didn't reply, but I sensed she knew how I felt.

"I meant to love him," I said, raising my head and spitting into the grass, "even after what he'd done to our mother. And now this. God…" I swallowed and winced at the nasty taste in my mouth. "Love can turn to hate so easily, can't it?"

Veronica nodded. "And hope to disappointment."

"How long has he been this way?"

"Since I was a kid. At first, he only drank socially. He didn't start first thing in the morning or have blackouts, and he didn't make promises he couldn't keep."

"But how long has he—"

"—been a drunk?" Veronica's hollow laugh held no humor. "How long has he been hiding booze all over the house while claiming he could quit any time? How long has he been disappearing for hours, even days, then not remembering where he'd been? How long has he been lying and cheating and tearing Elizabeth and me apart? Let me see now... Eight years, ten."

"He doesn't seem to care if he destroys himself or others," I said, rubbing my temples, which throbbed as if I, too, had over imbibed. "As though he has no feelings."

"Quite the contrary, sister dear. It's because he feels so strongly that he needs to numb the pain."

"Do you think he feels guilty?" I asked, all too familiar with guilt's persistent nagging.

"I'm sure of it," Veronica said. "But instead of just punishing himself, he's been taking it out on my stepmother and me, the ones he claims to love most."

Before I could comment, Veronica went on, "He's out of control, Marjorie. His main goal in life is to find and consume alcohol. And he's got the money to do it. I've tried, but there's nothing left to do, except stay away and take care of myself. If you have any ideas about stopping him, you'll be disappointed...the way I've been over and over."

It shocked me to see my sister come unhinged like this. As if our father was her kryptonite, robbing her of all strength. "But there must be something we can do."

Veronica looked at me with empty eyes. "Sorry, but I'm disillusioned by the whole scenario."

"Maybe if we work together," I said, though I understood what she was saying, that the situation was near hopeless, beyond anything she or I could say or do.

"Neither of us has that kind of power, Sis. In fact, one of his favorite pastimes, besides drinking, is to blame others for his problems. Maybe he can make you fall for it. Maybe he can convince you that it's your fault his life is a mess."

"Sounds like you've been to therapy," I said.

"I'm applying for the DEA, for God's sake. They do a character evaluation for disqualifying traits and pathologies, plus I have to pass a polygraph test. And from what I've heard, it isn't a pleasant experience. If a person is stressed out for any reason, it can skew the findings. Keeping our father out of my life has therefore become my number one priority."

"What about your anger?"

She smiled, but her eyes looked vacant. "Maybe our retreat in Anne's house will help in that department."

The look within place. "Maybe."

Veronica dropped back her head. "I was just getting my act together when Antonia started in with her crazy request."

What was Antonia's purpose in putting us through the pain of this meeting? What secret could our father hold that would make what we'd just experienced worthwhile? I wished Anne were here. She'd know what to do. She was a nurse, a witch, and an ex-nun. But she was using her holistic skills elsewhere, helping a friend and his son deal with another horrible disease—Alzheimer's. It could be months, even years, before she returned. "It's okay," I said, though it wasn't. We hadn't even come close to telling our father about Antonia or discovering their secret.

We would have to come back and try again.

Chapter Three

VERONICA AND I RETURNED to the Victorian in silence, and in silence we parted ways, two confused souls seeking rest, or, perhaps, temporary relief from the outside world. I sought out my room in the turret. Veronica mentioned something about checking out the basement.

The south-east wall of my bedroom suite formed the arch of the turret with six windows welcoming in a gentle light, the kind of light that filters through trees in a dense forest and through clouds after a pouring rain; the kind of light that soothes a bruised ego and nourishes the soul. I opened a window, inhaled the incoming stream of moist air, and focused on the gazebo below.

Though neglected and in need of a new coat of paint, the octagonal structure appealed to me. Its shingled roof provided shelter while its latticed walls opened to the cool fall breezes and panoramic view. Except for the chirping and cawing of birds and whisper of the wind, the gazebo stood in a shaded world of stillness, a perfect place to hang out for a while, alone with my thoughts.

The crows were loud and obtrusive, their persistent caws slicing the air like the peal of a telephone after midnight. The other birds, though, the brown and gray ones hiding in trees and bushes, trilled in sweet excitement, their voices as invisible as the wind. I sank into the Queen Anne chair in the windowed nook, noting how the green in the upholstery blended with the pattern of ivy creeping up the papered walls.

My vision blurred.

○○○

I woke with a start. Darn. I'd done it again, fallen asleep in the middle of the day, not the kind of company I'd envisioned for Veronica. By now, the sun had fallen, so I switched on the velvet-shaded lamp on the table next to my chair. The surrounding space filled with a warm rosy glow, leaving the rest of the room in shadow.

The wallpaper was almost invisible now, its green leaves and vine branches grayed to obscurity. My attention drifted to objects I'd missed before: a marble-topped washstand tucked into the small alcove next to the door, an oval mirror reflecting the glow of the lamp, an armoire, two nightstands in dark wood, and a four-poster bed.

I rose from the chair and eyed the deep queen mattress, tempted to remove its floral comforter and climb instead of heading downstairs to fix supper. However, choosing the land of nod in favor of the kitchen wasn't what brought my supper plans to a halt. It was the note from Veronica propped on the kitchen counter next to the keys to my Jeep.

Hi Sis! I've moved my stuff to the basement for a while. It's nice down there and fits my mood. I need a little down time, which means BEING ALONE. Please don't be offended. This has nothing to do with you. I'm a mess and need to recharge. I'll make it up to you later. Promise.

In case you're wondering, Anne, put me up to this. So, if you want to blame someone, blame her. Just before leaving for L.A., she told me to check out the basement. And all I can say is "Wow!" There's a microwave and refrigerator down there with plenty to eat, so don't worry, I won't starve. Love, Veronica

P.S. Have you noticed this house has no clocks or phones? Weird.

"Darn it, Veronica." I crumbled the note and shoved it into the pocket of my jeans. Her desertion hurt though part of me understood. She was trying to get her act together in preparation for her character evaluation with the DEA. Everyone needed time alone, as I had during my stay in Big Sur, the land of the Esselen, our birth mother's people. I'd gone there to make sense of Antonia's strange messages from the grave, but also to explore the second path of the Native American Medicine Wheel, the "Place of the South," where the process of finding one's true self begins.

While here in Pacific Grove, I would make it a priority to explore the third direction of the medicine wheel, the "Place of the West," the "Look Within Place," to determine what I needed to change to make progress in my life. Although I'd hoped to cram the twenty-nine years Veronica and I had missed being together into a matter of months and days, I would respect the necessity for both of us to stand back and face truths about our inner selves.

Dusk had turned the kitchen windows into dark mirrors, and as I stared at my shadowy reflection, I decided to do the next day what I'd been itching to do since we'd arrived: explore the gazebo and birdbath, maybe even turn some cartwheels.

And this time, Veronica wouldn't be there to stop me.

❁❁❁

Next morning, before the sun had crested the horizon, I settled onto one of the concrete benches in the gazebo. Insulated in a down jacket, sweats, thick cotton socks, and sneakers, I drew my legs to my chest and curled into a heat-preserving ball.

The caw of a crow pierced the wet veil of air like a gunshot, and a shiver sliced through me in rapid response, a shiver birthed in a part of me over which I had no control. I blew out a puff of air and allowed my mind to wander, an invitation for my subconscious to surface. It knew things my mind ignored.

Along with the sun and bird chatter came emerging texture and detail. The shelter turned out to be in decent shape, despite its neglect. It had plenty of supporting pillars, its security, its integrity, guaranteed, in case one of them failed.

Yesterday, one of my supporting pillars had failed, big time, with the discovery that my father wasn't the idealized parent I had imagined him to be. I'd expected a replication of the love, care, and admiration I'd received from my adoptive father. I'd expected wrong.

Anyway, my mission in coming to Pacific Grove wasn't just about me. It included the wants and needs of my birth mother, my sister, and, yes, even my father, the bearer of secrets.

Like the gazebo, I, too, had the support of extra pillars. Every step of my journey since leaving the security—and oppression—of my hometown had unveiled unique insights from which I had

21

learned. I'd encountered teachers and messengers, who, having walked the path before me, pointed out the ruts in the road. So, it took no genius on my part to conclude that a lesson also awaited me here, and that I would find the teachers to guide and support me.

A pulsating buzz invaded my ears as though a hundred crickets had taken up residence there. And despite the wet mist hanging in the air like damp laundry, the back of my neck grew warm. The scent of warm vanilla and melted butter entered the gazebo, faint at first, then growing stronger.

Was I sensing a teacher from the other side?

I much preferred the living kind, but in my experience messengers and teachers came and went at unexpected times and in unexpected ways. My job was to allow them access and the permission to help carry me forward.

"Did you often bake cookies while you were alive?" I asked.

A sigh moved through the air, sounding almost human.

I peered into the mist to find the source but saw nothing.

Besides hearing voices, I sometimes saw the dead, but I'd learned not to ask too many questions, just go with the flow.

"Was this once your house?" I asked.

Distant traffic. Bird calls. Rustling branches and trees.

I stood to leave. "Thanks for the company. Guess I'll go check out the bird bath now."

The buzz of cricket courtship in my ears ended.

The visit was over.

Spirits, I'd discovered, work at their own pace, their messages often confusing, even irritating.

But I always learned from them.

I found an old garden hose tangled between the bushes like a plate of spaghetti. I pulled out its kinks, connected it to a nearby spigot, and used it to dislodge the debris caked on the birdbath's pedestal base and detachable basin. Although it still needed a good scrubbing to bring back its original finish, I filled the stone bowl with water.

Satisfied with a job well done, I stepped back and looked into the restored basin.

"Jeez!" I screeched, dropping the hose as if it had shocked me. "What was that?"

I collapsed onto the straw-colored grass and drew my knees to my chin before chancing another look. Nothing special. Cast stone pitted with age. The bowl still needed additional elbow grease to remove the remaining algae and scum. And water tends to play tricks on the eye, the way it animates and highlights images captured within. What I'd seen was nothing more than a distortion.

Except...

The water's grey surface had projected my face in sharp color and detail. With a horrific scar.

I touched my right cheek. It felt normal enough. My imagination was playing tricks on me. No problem. I could handle this.

I got up and, with my breath running as fast as my heart, took another look into the birdbath. Nothing. Zilch. Just plain water.

When I'd approached Dr. Mendez about the weird things happening to me lately, he'd assured me that some events not currently understood by scientific knowledge have the potential of someday being explained scientifically with possibly a good natural explanation. He said non-ordinary experiences are no longer being dismissed as nonsense by quantum physicists and transpersonal psychologists.

I hoped to God this was true.

A quick survey of the grounds deemed the place in serious need of weeding. I took the back-porch entry for the rubber boots I'd seen standing next to the door. Perfect fit. Good.

As I passed through the kitchen for Anne's ring of keys, I noticed my hands were shaking. What would it take to clear my mind of the troubling image I'd seen in the birdbath?

I went out to the toolshed in back, certain I'd find what I needed for the job ahead. Sorting with hands that wouldn't cooperate, I located the key that fit the padlock on the door. Inside, I found a shovel, trowel, and rake, plus pruning shears and gloves hanging from hooks on the wall. I shook out the gloves before putting them on in case any critters had made a home there, then loaded the tools into a wheelbarrow and headed for the overgrown yard next to the kitchen.

The soil was soft and moist. Most of the weeds slid from the ground with minimum effort. For those refusing to release their grip, the shovel triggered a quick change of mind. Later, while whacking the overgrown bushes with pruning shears, my thoughts strayed to the peaceful hours I'd spent tending my backyard in Menlo Park. I missed my home. I missed Gabriel, the stray cat that often visited me there. But I couldn't go back. Not yet. Not until I'd finished my job here—a job that started six months ago, when Antonia first spoke to me.

Nothing, and no one, could've prepared me for such a thing. Ghosts and spirits, things that go bump in the night, belonged in fairy tales—or minds of the insane.

What would I have done without Dr. Mendez? I'd contacted him in a state of panic, ready to do just about anything to make the voice go away. And instead of pumping me full of pills and using up every free moment of my time and penny in my pocket for counseling, he'd assured me I wasn't losing my mind, only finding it. "Somehow and for some reason, you're hearing with the ears that too many ignore," he said before urging me to take a retreat, away from Menlo Park and away from Cliff and my mother. Thank God, I'd taken his advice. Because during that retreat, I'd discovered whose voice I'd been hearing—my birth mother's, contacting me from the other side, so desperate to get through that she'd ripped the veil that separated us and forced me to listen. Her nagging caused me to leave an unfulfilling job, a controlling fiancé, and my adoptive mother, who was imprisoning me with her love. And what I received in return still fills me with wonder.

Light comes out of darkness.

The voice again.

Not my mother's this time, but the one who'd welcomed me when Veronica and I had first entered Anne's house.

24

"Thanks," I said, feeling warmth flow into the hollow of my chest. Apparently, I had two dead people counseling me now. "What's your name?"

Silence.

"Okay," I said. "It's your party." With spirits, patience is the key. The wheelbarrow was full. I dumped the weeds and pruned branches in a compost bin behind the trellis in a far corner of the yard, then went back for more.

Time flew after that, back and forth, back and forth, disposing of weeds and trimmings until my back and thighs ached.

Just as I'd decided to quit or pay the price later, my shovel hit something hard, sending a jolt up my leg.

What was that?

Aching back and thighs be darned, I couldn't stop now.

I dropped to my knees and scraped away spidery fingers of Bermuda grass, twigs, and leaves until I'd uncovered part of what appeared to be a large concrete circle with strange markings. "Anne, my friend. What have you got hidden here?"

Chapter Four

NEXT MORNING, JUST ABOUT every muscle in my body ached as though I'd been stretched on a rack. Raising my arms was painful, which made getting up and getting dressed difficult, but did little to squelch my excitement. I loved a mystery, and the huge mazelike circle in Anne's backyard counted as a mystery in my book. Soreness my foot. I went back to work under dank clouds and rumbling thunder to clear the rest of the circle, one small section at a time.

With the sun breaking through the clouds overhead, I hosed down and swept the twenty-foot circle once trapped in a tangle of weeds. It looked medieval, like a spiritual tool similar to a Mandala. The interior was little more than a convoluted path with clockwise and counterclockwise turns leading to a rose-shaped center. Lunations edged the circle's circumference like teeth on a wheel.

I longed to share my new discovery with Veronica, but she'd made it clear that she didn't want to be bothered. I hobbled back into the house and paused at the door to the basement—*Darn it, Veronica; I miss you*—before climbing the stairs to my turret room for the belted pouch containing my mouse totem and medicine wheel marker stones. I'd worn the pouch just about every day for the past six months. Only since coming to Pacific Grove had I neglected to put it on. This house was having a strange effect on me. But if I'd learned anything since starting my journey in March, it was to follow my inner guide, which now urged me to re-unite with my spiritual tools.

With the resolve of someone determined not to get distracted—

difficult in this house of distractions—and despite throbbing muscles and stiff joints, I made it to my turret room and back into the chilly backyard within minutes. Following the soundless call of my soul, I unzipped my pouch and took out my colored markers, their jingle in the palm of my hand and the coolness of their touch evoking a sense of calm. Even so, I wondered about the rightfulness of what I was about to do—lay claim to someone else's sacred space.

Thunder rumbled in the distance like the hooves of bolting horses as I placed my marker stones along the perimeter of the circle—white in the north, yellow in the east, red in the south, black in the west, and green on the giant rose in the center.

The drizzling rain prevented me from smudging the surrounding space with smoke and burning sage, so I allowed the forces of nature to cleanse it for me. Muscles twitching, joints grinding, I pulled the hood of my jacket over my head and sat behind my black marker stone in the place of the West. Then I closed my eyes and took deep breaths, allowing my body to relax, one tired muscle at a time. My thoughts drifted like leaves caught in a stream to a place where time, like my spirit, was expansive and expandable.

The stream carried me to Carmel Valley where I'd awakened to a world I hadn't known existed. My plan had been to find a quiet place to deal with the voice in my head. Instead, peace and quiet had eluded me. At least in the way I had intended.

First, I'd chanced upon Morgan Van Dyke, whose intense interest in my welfare reminded me of Cliff, my ex-fiancé. That scored at least two strikes against him, which revealed a lot about Morgan's character, since he still managed to capture my heart. Just thinking about him now made me long for his voice, his touch, comforts I'd have to forgo for a while.

I'd also run into Veronica, my black-haired, hot-tempered, smart-mouthed twin, whom I hadn't even known existed. In response to her taunts and threats, I'd confronted Truus, my adoptive mother, and learned that the man and woman I'd believed to be my biological parents had, in fact, adopted me soon after my birth.

Then I met Ben *Gentle Bear* Mendoza, who'd introduced me to the Native American Medicine Wheel. He led me through the path of initiation, in the "Place of the East," the "Farsighted Place," where I learned to awaken to life and discover its joys.

A clap of thunder brought my thoughts back to the present. My hooded jacket protected my upper body from the drizzling rain, but my bottom was wet and the temperature of ice. I glanced at the black stone at my feet and thanked the Great Spirit in advance for whatever insights would be revealed to me here. My portable medicine wheel was more practical than this huge pavement circle, since I could construct it under cover on wet days like this. But someone had taken the time to construct the circle I'd uncovered, and I would return until I had uncovered its mysteries as well.

My stomach, rather than a watch or clock, signaled that it was past lunchtime. It wouldn't hurt to change out of my wet, grimy sweats and get something to eat before heading to town in search of a bookstore. I wanted to learn more about sacred circles and more about Anne than she'd been willing to share.

In the turret room, I sorted through my yet unpacked suitcase for a clean t-shirt and jeans, refusing to cave to the draw of the queen-sized bed. No time for that now. Instead, I headed for the bathroom attached to my suite.

❂❂❂

The walk to downtown Pacific Grove took longer than I'd expected. It was also a lot more fun. The clouds withheld their moisture while thunder continued to rumble in the distance. After six-blocks, to where Cedar Street crossed Lighthouse, my muscles stopped aching. I also started noticing things. The trees, for instance. They were wet and weepy, many dropping their leaves, and I couldn't identify even half of them. Sure, I knew the difference between a redwood and a eucalyptus, a cypress and a willow, but I had no clue as to the names of the smaller, leafy ones. I considered buying a pair of binoculars and a guidebook, then pictured myself in a floppy hat amid a group of senior citizens on a history tour scribbling into a notebook. Nah. Better start by paying attention.

Another six blocks down Lighthouse brought me to the post office.

It was fronted by a bronze statue titled "Butterfly Kids," which reminded me that Pacific Grove earned the nickname "Butterfly Town USA" for a reason. If I had my facts straight, thousands of Monarchs were currently headed this way from Alaska, Canada, and the Rocky Mountains. Any time now, they'd cluster in the pine, cypress, and eucalyptus trees all over town. And when the sun warmed their wings, they'd drift between the branches like mini shards of stained-glass. Beware the person who molested even one of them, though. According to Pacific Grove law, such an act warranted a $1,000 fine.

Down the street to my right, stood a sign advertising a bookstore/coffeehouse. Everyone has their take on wonderful. Mine happens to be browsing through shelves of books, the more the better. That reveals a lot about me, but as I've concluded long ago, I'm not, nor will ever be, the life of anyone's party.

I inquired at the register about sacred circles, and the woman behind the counter directed me to the metaphysical section. "We have several books on labyrinths there," she said, peering at me over thick black glasses. "They're actually growing in popularity these days."

"You mean mazes?" I asked.

The phone rang. Before she picked up, she said, "Oh, dear no. In a maze, you get lost. In a labyrinth, you find the way."

I pondered her words as I perused the shelves. If labyrinths were so popular, why hadn't I heard of them before, at least, outside of myths and fairytales? A short search rewarded me with a book titled *Walking a Sacred Path: Rediscovering the Labyrinth as a Spiritual Tool*, with a diagram of a sacred circle on its cover. Eager to start reading, I headed for the cashier, only to catch sight of a book about Monterey County propped on a stand next to the register. I checked its table of contents and found a chapter devoted to Pacific Grove. Jackpot! I handed both books to the cashier.

Purchases in hand, I followed the aroma of brewed coffee and baked pastries through the open archway to the shop next door. With two customers ahead of me having difficulty deciding between scones, cookies, and apple pie, I checked out my surroundings. Windows, interspersed with mirrors and stained glass, banked the north and west walls of the sitting area, creating a pleasant ambiance of shadow and light. Several students with laptops took up the green leather couch and loveseat that formed an L-shape around a dilapidated coffee table on the south end of the room. Wooden tables, chairs, bench seats, and bar stools filled the rest of the space, making for a busy, but cozy atmosphere.

No sooner had I purchased my hot white mocha and taken a seat at a table for two than someone paused by my side and cleared her throat. "Excuse me, but I overheard you asking about sacred circles."

"Yes," I said, part of me eager for her to move on so I could start my research, the other part recognizing that every person was a potential teacher. "Would you care to join me?"

The woman looked young, straight out of high school, with her long, straight hair and trendy denim jeans. She took the stool opposite mine and glanced at the bag still clutched in my hand. "Only for a minute. I'm expecting someone."

I took out the book on labyrinths. "Have you read it?"

She shook her head but zeroed in on the book as if expecting it to perform magic.

I extended my hand. "I'm Marjorie."

She covered it with her own. "Vanessa."

"Nice to meet you, Vanessa."

I'd barely had time to read the bold statement printed on her coral tank top, *Women who behave rarely make history*, before the bookstore clerk peered around the corner. "Nessa, dear, your customer's here."

Vanessa jerked to a stand. "Sorry. I shouldn't have bothered you..." She looked over her shoulder, then back at me. "I um...read palms...and..."

"*You're* the spiritual psychic?" I'd seen the ad—*Vanessa Steiner. Tarot and palm reader*—taped to a dividing wall in the bookstore but hadn't given it a second thought until now.

"I do readings and interpretations," she said, "and I read faces."

"Nessa!" It was the bookstore clerk again.

"Sorry for bothering you," she said. "Gotta go." She stepped away from her stool, then hesitated. "Maybe I can do a complimentary reading for you sometime."

"Sure," I said, wondering how she made a living offering her services for free.

This time, when Vanessa made to leave, she kept going.

Curiosity won over relief at her parting. Something told me that overhearing me ask about sacred circles wasn't the sole reason she'd sought me out. "I do readings and interpretations, and I read faces," she'd said. How was that for an intriguing introduction? One thing for sure, I wouldn't get much reading done with the distraction of Vanessa nearby. I'd paid big bucks for the white mocha still sitting on the table, but the price didn't include the stoneware mug it was served in. I'd have to leave my drink behind.

Still puzzling over my short acquaintance with Vanessa, the impact of exiting the warm coffee shop and entering the chilly outdoors didn't fully register. On a subconscious level, I must've been aware of the steady flow of car and foot traffic as I continued east along Lighthouse, but it wasn't until I caught a whiff of vanilla and melted butter that my attention snapped back to my surroundings.

The doors to the bakery across the street stood open, which prompted me to take the crosswalk and follow the sweet aroma to a display case full of delectable treats. "A chocolate chip cookie, please," I said to the woman behind the counter, "plus coffee, black."

I settled at a table next to a plate glass window facing the street.

Time to discover what I could about the mysterious circle in Anne's back yard.

Chapter Five

NEXT MORNING, OVER A breakfast of hot buttered toast, Gouda cheese, and black coffee, I stared at the labyrinth outside the kitchen window. Its swirling interior, still moist from the previous day's scrubbing and the dripping predawn fog, quivered under rays of the rising sun. According to what I'd read thus far, the labyrinth was a walking meditation, a meandering but purposeful path from edge to center and out again, with the purpose of quieting the mind and tapping into the resources within. Anne's labyrinth resembled the one lain into the floor of the Chartres Cathedral in France sometime between 1194 and 1220 A.D. and the ones lying inside and outside of the Grace Cathedral in San Francisco.

Labyrinths, according to my limited research, are universal patterns created in the realm of the collective unconscious and found in almost every religious tradition around the world. Could the labyrinth then, because of its all-inclusiveness, act as a bridge between different forms of spirituality?

I could've pondered this question for hours, but the best way to internalize the mystery of the labyrinth was to walk it. As I carried my dishes to the sink, I realized I was grateful for Veronica's temporary sojourn in the basement. I wanted to be alone when I first experienced the labyrinth.

Once outside, I was also grateful for my fleece-lined sweatshirt and the thick padding of my sneakers. My raggedy old jeans weren't as effective in the warmth department but would come in handy if I decided to clear more weeds after my walk. As I stepped onto the winding path of the labyrinth and followed it in a clockwise direction, I tried to relax and open to the experience as I had when I'd first encountered the Native American Medicine Wheel. I concentrated on the chirping birds, trying to distinguish one from the other. Impossible. Except for the crows. The crows were easy.

I pictured the sacred circle as a boat carrying me through swirling waters of change to the part of me I needed to reconnect with to face the challenges of my future. I took a 45-degree turn to the left, a U-turn to the right, then two more 45-degree turns left, edging ever closer to the center. "Row, row, row your boat," I whispered, a good mantra as any for keeping my judgments and expectations at bay. "Gently down the stream…" *Don't push the River. Release. Empty. Become quiet.* A U-turn to the left, another to the right, left turn, right turn, this time taking me away from the center. Right turn, left, right turn, left. From what I could see, the labyrinth like the medicine wheel was as a container where thoughts could emerge from the subconscious. The trick being to stop thinking long enough to allow it.

Reaching the center came as a surprise. The winding path had seemed so illogical that I didn't know I was there until I was there. I stared at the rose pattern beneath my feet. Was this the place where I'd receive what was there for me? My throat tightened. What if nothing happened?

I sat and the chill of the labyrinth's paved surface penetrated my jeans. I pulled my knees to my chest, slowed my breathing and closed my eyes. No rain. No thunder. Air warm and still, smelling of musk. Bird chatter fading into comforting static.

Who am I? What am I doing on this earth?

The intensity of bird chatter amplified. What had only a moment before been pleasant background noise rose to a crescendo. Whistles became shouts. Calls turned into screams. *PEEURR, KA-BRICK, KIT-KID-KIDDLKEDIT, CHIT-CHIT-CHIT-WEET-WEET.*

I opened my eyes.

At least seven black-billed, heavy-throated crows, with their glistening bodies and hard beady eyes, had clustered on a fence rail nearby. Backyard birds of varying colors and plumages rimmed the perimeter of the circle, their bodies churning like waves on a fitful ocean. It seemed the neighborhood bird population had gone crazy—and had me penned in the labyrinth's center.

My heart felt big and wild, squeezing and releasing, squeezing and releasing. My breaths came out shallow and quick. If the physical world was a printout of my consciousness as Dr. Mendez had suggested, I needed to change my thinking.

A voice sliced through the clamber. *Something long forgotten is being rediscovered.* Then silence. Like the silence at a crater on top of a volcanic island with the world's volume switched to mute.

Had the birds sensed the invisible presence before it spoke, thus their riotous chatter? If so, what did their sudden stillness convey?

And you are the cause, the voice said.

A crow swooped past my head, so close I felt friction in the air. It swooped again, causing my scalp to prickle. A third swoop had me ducking, hands over my head. I twisted around, looking for a stick, a rock, anything for protection.

Something dropped at my feet. A bird's nest.

The low-flying crow landed and tilted its head at me.

"What?" I asked.

The raven wannabe hopped closer and pecked at the nest with its long black bill, its large chunky body glossed purple in the mid-morning sun.

"Yeah, so?"

A rude caw as if I were too dense for words.

I'd heard a crow's vocal repertoire is complex, therefore hard to make sense of. Well, duh. I picked up the nest and balanced it in my right hand. "Satisfied?"

Another caw, lower in pitch and intensity this time, as if my new friend were impressed with my prowess.

Keeping an open mind has its merits, but this was reaching beyond where I felt my mind safe to go.

The bundle of twigs, string, and mud formed a circle as sacred as any. And by a stretch of the imagination, I could detect similarities to the labyrinth. Both comprised innumerable twists and folds that led to a vortex of safety and security for its occupants.

Closer inspection revealed the nest's Mandala-like configuration. A repeated pattern of jagged and wrinkled shapes made up its exterior. The interior, in contrast, appeared smooth and compressed, its center drawing me until I felt inspired to rephrase my earlier questions.

"Who the heck am I? What the hell am I doing on this earth?"

And lo-and-behold, I received an answer.

Not from the crow, but from the voice I'd heard twice since coming to Pacific Grove. So gentle, my throat tightened.

Reach within and recover the largeness your birth intended.

"What's my purpose?" I asked, craving the answer with such intensity that it felt like I was turning inside out.

Expand your mind and your heart.

Too simple—too hard.

I pulled the nest to me, almost crushing it in my longing to understand. It smelled damp and musty, like unwashed socks, which made me think of my father. I'd allowed no connection or unity between us. Instead, I'd judged him, found him lacking, and punished him in the only way I knew how. By closing my heart.

Rest child. Your soul is tired.

I looked at the Victorian—so white, so pure—once again captivated by its charm.

The crow flapped its wings and flew away with one last caw, energizing the flocked birds to do the same, their conspicuous voices and beating wings deafening.

The curtain of fleeing birds split to reveal the figure of a woman standing at the labyrinth entrance. Someone who looked just like me. Except for the raspberry-colored stain covering half her face.

35

"Jeez," I said, my heart going into squeeze-and-release mode again.

The birdbath vision hadn't been a distortion or figment of my imagination after all. Because there was no mistaking what I was seeing now.

I closed my eyes, willing woman to disappear.

Slow down heart. Someday this will all make sense.

When I reopened my eyes, she was gone, but I felt no relief. My mind wouldn't let go of what I'd seen.

Nessa. Nessa. Nessa. The name of the palm reader I'd met in the bookstore repeated in my head like a commercial jingle. Maybe she could make sense of this.

Chapter Six

THERE WERE NO DARK clouds obscuring the sun, no rolls of thunder, no mists of rain. Instead, the September morning was clear and breezy, perfect for my walk downtown. Yet, it felt like I was staggering through a storm. Nightmarish images of a face disfigured by a raspberry-colored stain filled my mind. I swallowed, determined to keep my breakfast down.

Nessa sat at a small table tucked into the metaphysical section of the bookstore, a cozy nook where the store's east and south walls converged. A quilted fabric in red, white, and blue covered the table which was lit by the incandescent glow of a floor lamp positioned nearby. I detected Nessa only because I was seeking her out. Otherwise, she would've been invisible to me, backed as she was by shelves of books, with their rich and colorful faces and spines arranged like poetic works of art. Two days before, I'd walked right past her, unaware that she'd be there.

I took a seat in the canvas director chair opposite Nessa and, without regard to her appointment schedule or need for a break, told her of my vision in the labyrinth and my suspicion that it was a premonition of things to come. Fear was making me rude.

"I don't predict the future," Nessa said, addressing my hands. "Nor do I heal people or tell them what to do."

A protest fluttered in the back of my mind— *Then what do you do?* —as she continued to discredit her psychic skills. "I read symbols and patterns in tarot cards, and I read palms, asking the universe for answers, but I don't read people's minds."

Who's asking you to?

"The best I can do is help a client with psychological understanding," she said, still staring at my hands. "If you're okay with that, we can begin."

With my attention so fully focused on Nessa and her denouncements, all else faded into the background. We were in a bubble of sorts, sealed from the outside world. I glanced at her tank top for a clue about the woman behind the verbal disclaimers. *Get over it* was the current catchphrase. Her attitude provoked rather than inspired. My first instinct was to remind her that only two days before, she had approached *me*, not the other way around, expressing an interest in sacred circles and, of all things, offering a complimentary reading as if she'd known I would need one. My guess was that she'd had a lot more on her mind than 'psychological understanding.'

She shifted in her chair, releasing the scent of violets. Odd. As far as I knew, perfume from violets was scarce. The seductive, sweeter-than-roses scent fit her, though, pervasive, even cloying, one moment, practically nonexistent the next. Violets, like Nessa, had a tendency to conceal themselves in their surroundings, which confused me. It was because of her unsolicited offer, that I'd come back, and now she was acting as if she were no more than an amateur therapist, who asked the universe for answers. Well, excuse me. Even I could do that.

I was tired of clues and riddles. My dead mother had bombarded me with enough brainteasers in the past six months to last a lifetime, brainteasers that never turned out to be what they seemed. Tarot cards and palm readings. No thanks. I preferred a crystal ball.

"If I remember correctly, your name is Marjorie," Nessa said. "What day were you born?"

"July eighth," I said, trying to curb my frustration.

"Ah, yes, I got a strong sense of the astrological sign of Cancer when we met. Loyal, dependable, adaptable…"

Clingy and oversensitive, I added silently.

"The sign of Cancer is mysterious," Nessa continued, "packed full of contradictions when it comes to independence. Cancers want security but seek adventure."

Darn, she wasn't telling me anything I couldn't pick up with a quick search on the Internet. "How much time do I get for the complimentary reading?"

"My basic reading takes about half an hour, but we could go deeper if you like."

"What's a basic reading?"

"I can either read your palm, which includes giving you a psychic mandala, or I can do a lifetime reading using tarot cards."

"Let's go with the tarot cards," I said.

Nessa gave me a probing look, and I looked back, sending out mental feelers to see if she would reveal anything useful. I sensed she was withholding something and wondered why. She blinked and gave a slight shake of her head, before picking up a deck of large cards—worn and tattered around the edges—and shuffling them. Unwieldy though they were, the cards shifted in her hands in such an assertive way I was impressed. She dropped the deck on the table. "Now put your hands on the cards and think of a question you'd like answered."

I put the pads of my fingers on the uppermost card. *Tell me about the scar on my face.*

A glance at Nessa confirmed that she was no longer with me, at least not on a mental plane. Her eyes were closed, her lips moving. After what seemed like no more than a minute, she reopened her eyes and eased the cards from under my hands. With a quick twist of the wrist, she dropped the bottom portion of the deck on the table and repositioned the displaced cards on top. Twice more, she repeated the process, all the while apparently 'asking the universe' to aid us in our reading. Finally, she leveled her gaze at me and instructed me to part the deck. After I'd done so, she took four cards off what had been the deck's center and placed them in front of me, face up.

I stared at the cards' vibrant colors and intricate details taken in by their beauty and, at the same time, jarred by their symbolic violence. The swords, the chariots, the wheel, and the skeleton, all appeared negative to me. I glanced up at Nessa. She was looking at the taro spread, eyes unfocused, face slack, as if blind to it.

While waiting for her to begin my reading, I focused on the sounds coming from the coffee shop next door, sounds I'd managed to block out until now. People chatting and laughing, the coffee machine gurgling and spurting. A clock attached to a nearby bookshelf struck out the quarter hour with the chirping of birds.

Nessa's sigh drew back my attention. She looked at me for what seemed like a long time, which had me shifting in my chair and eyeing the books above her head: *Circle of Stones; The Four Agreements; How We Die.* "Let's start with the Suit of Swords," she said. "It's one of the minor arcane, which reflects life's run-of-the-mill events and acts as a modifying factor on the major arcane."

I nodded, though I had no idea what she was talking about.

"The Suit of Swords reflects courage, strength, hope, and peace amid strife on your spiritual journey."

I tried not to show my disappointment. Was I about to get a generic reading that could be applied to just about anyone walking in off the street?

Nessa smiled, giving the impression that she could read minds after all. "Be patient. It gets better."

I looked at my hands. My nails had taken a beating during my stint in Anne's backyard—despite the gloves.

"When I turn this card," Nessa said, giving the Suit of Swords a half turn, "it predicts spiritual suffering, loneliness, sacrifice, loss, and defeat."

"Oh great," I said. "Just what I needed to hear."

She shook her head and smiled. "Pain and suffering are part of a successful journey."

"No pain, no gain," I quipped.

Nessa picked up another card. "The major arcane foretell important events and strong emotions. The Chariot here symbolizes struggle, but also triumph against the odds and unexpected news."

At this rate, I'd learn nothing about my disturbing vision. I covered her free hand with mine. "There's something you're not telling me, Nessa."

She looked at the card with the skeleton, then back at me. "I told you, I don't predict in that way."

"Do you see anything in my future about a facial scar?"

She leaned toward me. "You're a medium, too, aren't you?"

"No."

"I felt it two days ago, when we first meet. I feel it now."

"I hear voices and sometimes see and know things other people don't, but I'm not a medium."

Nessa turned her hand up in mine. "It's a burden, isn't it?"

Relief, anger, and confusion swirled in my chest like sludge. "My life has become uncomfortable and unfamiliar. I want to feel normal again."

"Have there been no benefits at all?" she asked.

I thought of my birth mother, who'd contacted me from the other side, forcing me to step out of a world of self-centeredness, material comforts, and limited receptivity into a larger world beyond ordinary life and perception. Were the extraordinary events she'd summoned into my life worth the resulting dissolution of the boundaries of my existence?

"Don't fight your abilities," Nessa said.

"You mean, like you do?"

"Only when I don't like what I see," she said.

The sludge in my chest turned to molten lava. "About me?"

"I see something that I don't understand, which makes me wary."

"About me?" I repeated.

She continued as if she hadn't heard me. "Often my visions have meanings that don't make themselves clear until later. I try not to jump to conclusions until I have enough information to see where they lead."

"Please," I said. "What do you see?"

Her forehead creased in what appeared to be concern. "Circles," she said. "At first, I thought they resembled the Suit of Pentacles, which symbolizes generosity, financial reward, and stability. But then I realized they had nothing to do with the symbols on tarot cards."

"I use the Native American Medicine Wheel as a tool for meditation and guidance," I said, grasping at straws. "And I've discovered a labyrinth behind the house where I'm staying."

Nessa sighed. "Anne Bolen's house."

"You know her?"

For some reason, Nessa looked relieved, as if the mention of Anne served was a balm somehow. "She's at peace with herself, which is more than I can say for her brother."

"Brother? I didn't know she had—"

"That's probably for the best," she said.

Part of me was curious to learn more about Anne's brother, but I wasn't yet ready to let the subject of circles go. "About the labyrinth..."

"The medicine wheel and labyrinth may be important elements of your spiritual journey," she said, "but I see another circle...and it is broken. Actually, it has a ragged tear."

"I've seen myself twice with..." I couldn't finish, the picture too disturbing.

Nessa massaged my trembling fingers, which brought almost instant relief. "Remember," she said. "Our visions are open to misinterpretation."

I eyed the remaining cards on the table. "What about the skeleton?"

Nessa gathered up the cards. "That's enough for today."

I eased the deck from her hand and placed the offending card on the table. The grotesque skeleton leaned gleefully over the large curved blade of a scythe. "Does it mean I'm going to die?"

"The card forecasts unwelcome change," Nessa said, her voice unsteady.

Her prediction was too vague, too generic. I wanted more control over the situation. I wanted to set things right, push the river. Letting go was too darn hard.

Nessa squeezed my hands until they hurt. "Just a small warning, from one psychic to another. Whatever you strongly imagine, you invite into your life."

Chapter Seven

LOOKING DOWN INTO THE basement from the top of the stairs, I felt like Alice in Wonderland about to fall into a rabbit hole. I gripped the stair rail, my senses skewed. My mind couldn't assimilate the message my eyes were transmitting. *Wow, Anne, this is strange, even for you.* The stairs and banister consisted of glass blocks resembling giant ice cubes stacked one on top of the other, which appeared wet and slippery as if melting under the brilliance of the fluorescent panels honeycombing the ceiling. The entire floor at the base of the stairs was covered with marble stone tile that shimmered like a massive sheet of ice. To add another odd twist to an already strange setting, where I'd expected to find shelves of dusty mason jars filled with fruits and jellies and stacks of cardboard boxes infested with spiders and rats, there arose floor to ceiling mirrors.

Last, I checked, basements were dark, cold, and musty and constructed of wall-to-wall concrete like underground caves. Then again, this was Anne's basement and nothing about her was ever what it seemed to be. I imagined her shaking her head. "Well, of course not, hon. The basement is a place where one goes within, to meditate and balance the soul. It's a place where a person can forget about time and get back to the Source. Why not convert it into a functional apartment?"

I took several steps down the translucent stairs, gripping the slick railing for support, before losing all sense of equilibrium. Below me lay a swirling vortex of light, reflection, and shine. No hewn stone or jewel-colored glass, nothing solid and heavy to hold on to. Instead, this space aspired to the hues, textures, and gravitation of heaven.

All that glass, marble, and mirror made the area at the bottom of the stairs appear distorted and out of focus. Maybe, by concentrating hard, I could make sense of this place. But no, the more I concentrated, the more disorienting my surroundings became. I allowed myself occasional peeks through half-closed lids to predict where my next step should be, the goal being to make it to the bottom of the stairs without breaking my neck. Only then would I confront the fear that drove me here. That something may have happened to my sister.

I reached the basement floor only to discover it looked as accessible as an ice rink to a novice skater. I released my stronghold on the banister and edged forward, my gaze darting all over the dizzying space. Eccentric, magical, beyond reason and ordinary, what was Anne's purpose in creating this carnival-like setting of shine and mirrors? And why had she directed Veronica here? Veronica had been up-ended when we parted three days ago. And now this?

With too much to take in at a cursory glance, I zeroed in on the left side of the basement. Camouflaged within the reflective space, was a small sitting area, with a white leather couch and loveseat, glass-topped tables, and crystal lamps. If it hadn't appeared so darn restful, I would've deemed it sterile and uninviting. As the fictional Alice would say, "Curiouser and curiouser."

The note Veronica had left propped on the kitchen counter had expressed her need for some down time, and I'd tried to respect her request, but maybe I should've checked on her sooner. She favored wearing black and red, so should stand out like a flashing billboard in this white chamber of reflection. So, where was she? A scarred face appeared in my mind's eye like a giant floater. I blinked. What if she had fallen and hurt herself? A wave of nausea hit me like a hangover. *Veronica!*

It wasn't until I got within five feet of the kitchen in this confusing and disorienting space that I recognized it for what it was. White cabinets, counters, and appliances blended with the white marble floor and mirrored walls to the point of obscurity. I focused on the area to the right of the kitchen, having difficulty distinguishing between truth and illusion.

A stereo unit. A set of speakers. And there, on a white mat the size of a beach blanket, lay my sister, flat on her back, eyes closed. "Veronica!" My sneakers screeched across the marble floor. *Dear God, what if she's dead?*

"Vonnie!" I dropped to my knees and pulled her to my chest. "Sis. Are you okay?" Her body was limp, but she was still warm and breathing. I garbled something in the way of thanks and was about to burst into tears of relief when she pushed me—yes, pushed me— before dropping back into a corpse-like pose. I gaped at her through blurred eyes.

"You scared the crap out of me," she said.

"Good," I said, nearly choking on my pride.

She opened her eyes and glared at me, reminding me of my friend the crow, with its dark, beady eyes. "I told you not to bother me."

Here I was half out of my mind with worry, and all she could do was tell me off. So, I did what I often do when upset, focused my attention on something else. In this case, the white camisole and low-rise sweats Veronica was wearing. Since when did my vampy-in-black-leather sister wear white? There was also something odd about the position of her legs. They were bent beneath her as if she'd been doing some kind of yoga pose. No wonder I'd thought she'd hurt herself. It hurt just looking at her.

A crooning sound came from behind me, followed by a voice giving instructions on stretch-and-balance exercises and a flute-like melody of air blowing across a single reed. "What's that?" I asked.

Veronica released a sigh suggesting impatience and annoyance before sitting up.

I felt a tinge of guilt, then shook it off. "For heaven's sake, Veronica. What's wrong with you?"

She yawned like a complacent cat, performed a slow, extended stretch, and then stood and turned off the CD player hidden under a white padded bench. "What's up?"

"You'd think it would be freezing down here," I said, "with all the marble, leather, and glass, but it's inviting, in a heavenly way."

"This place *is* heaven," Veronica said, "or as close to heaven as I'm likely to get. In case you didn't notice, I was worn out when we parted."

"Of course, I noticed. How insensitive do you—"

"I've discovered a few unexpected things down here."

"Like what?"

"Yoga."

Veronica and yoga? I had less trouble imagining oil blending with water. Though so many out-of-the-ordinary things had happened to me lately that, like the adventurous Alice, I was beginning to think few things impossible.

"There's all kinds of reference material down here to introduce me to *the path*."

"The path?"

"First on my bucket list is to sign up for a yoga class," she said. "I mean it, Marjorie," she added when she caught the frown on my face.

Good. That meant she'd be leaving the basement. "When do you plan to start?"

"Not me, Sis. We."

"We?"

"You of all people should champ at the bit to experience one of the master paths to enlightenment," Veronica said with an all-too-knowing smile. "Or have you forgotten why you're here instead of with Morgan and Joshua?"

Morgan and Joshua. Just the mention of their names made me happy, made me sad. What I wouldn't give to have them here with me now. But Morgan and I had an understanding. I needed time to discover who I was and what I could give. And for that I needed more time on my own. With Morgan around, I'd be tempted to allow him to take charge, as I had with Cliff. And that was no longer an option. If I didn't learn to say *no* to what hurt me, so I could say *yes* to love, our relationship didn't stand a chance.

"Understanding the nature of the world and my place in it is *one* reason I'm here," I said, "but I was thinking more along the line of ceremony, meditation, and prayer as paths to awakening my spiritual senses."

"The mind is only a small window through which to experience the spiritual," Veronica said, sounding like she'd memorized some of Anne's New Age reading material. She walked to the basement kitchen, and I followed, curious about what she'd been eating the past few days. She opened the refrigerator and stepped away for me to look inside. Bottled water. Nothing else.

Veronica loved to eat. I mean, this girl never stopped. Milkshakes, ice cream, steak, potatoes, you name it. Funny thing, she didn't look malnourished or hungry. "You must be starving."

Veronica opened one of the shiny white cabinet doors and took out two plastic bottles—one capped in red, one in green. "Check this out," she said with a lift in her voice suggesting enthusiasm, something she rarely displayed. "Whole-food-based nutrition from thirty different fruits, vegetables, grains and berries in convenient capsule form."

Food in capsules? "Sounds like what they feed astronauts."

Veronica waved another bottle with such enticing packaging that my mouth watered. "And these wafers are full of fruit powders to reduce hunger and increase fat metabolism and energy."

All this white, dizzying space must have frazzled her brain.

She set the bottles on the counter, opened another cabinet, and held out a canister the size of a medium coffee can. "This is an energy drink with carbohydrates, proteins, vegetables, and minerals." Her eyes sparkled like a true believer, not Veronica-like at all. "And Anne's got a stash of nuts and seeds, dried prunes and honey, wheat bran and..." She paused at the expression on my face, then shook her head and shrugged. "Oh Marge, don't be such a prude. I feel like I can tackle the world."

Marge? Prude? My sister was going weird on me.

I turned to explore a section of the basement I'd neglected before. A few inches from the mirrored wall, stood a circular bed covered with a white quilted spread. What would it feel like not knowing top from bottom, up from down? Probably like sleeping on a cloud.

"We'll start by signing up for a Hatha yoga class," Veronica said from behind me. "A yoga system for proper alignment and awareness of breath."

My body still ached from the hours spent clearing the labyrinth. More physical activity struck me as unappealing. "I don't want to take a yoga class."

"We need a live teacher, Marge. The experience will do us good."

Live teacher versus dead? Ha. But wasn't this what I'd been craving, quality time with my sister?

Veronica paced the floor. "We could also use the peer support."

"Will it be high impact?" I'd had enough high impact for a while, therefore more inclined to gentle and easy.

"Don't worry. I signed us up for the beginner's class. It's slow paced, just your style."

So, she'd used her cell phone, though we'd agreed not to during our stay in Pacific Grove. Rule breaker!

"Yoga will speed up your heart rate," Veronica said.

"My heart rate's just fine, thank you. When?"

"Tomorrow, but *now* we're going upstairs."

"Now?" Just as I was adjusting to this crazy, magical place. "How about we spend the night here and—"

"I've got to get out of here for a while before heading outdoors," Veronica said. "Otherwise, it'll be like coming up from the depths of the ocean. Come up too fast and you can blow your brains out."

Chapter Eight

ALTHOUGH THE STUDIO ENCOURAGED early arrival for their Saturday morning Hatha yoga class, we were late. Fortunately, Veronica had registered ahead. So, it was only a matter of checking in with the woman behind the desk and leaving our belongings in a red cubby next to the door before taking our place behind the other class members in the spacious and uncluttered room. While Veronica and I unrolled the yoga mats we'd carried in like giant scrolls, I noted our surroundings. The wood flooring was bamboo, the cream walls free of decor, the lighting dim. The room smelled of sandalwood and frankincense, reminding me of Anne, which calmed me. At least, until the yoga instructor started in. "Remember. Loose clothing and an open mind. No tight jeans. Too constricting. Nothing baggy. It gets in the way." Constricting jeans and a baggy sweatshirt. Great. Maybe the instructor should use me as an example of what *not* to wear. As far as having an open mind, only time would tell if I got that part right.

"I told you to wear leggings and a t-shirt," Veronica said.

Okay, so she'd read a few books on yoga and practiced with a half dozen CD's. That made her an expert all of a sudden? Anyway, I didn't own a pair of leggings. Or a t-shirt long enough to cover my behind.

"I need to see the contours of your body," the instructor said, "to access how you're holding your postures."

Since it was a female talking, I took no offense at her mentioning the contours of my body, but her next instruction meant I had blundered again. "No jewelry. No perfume."

Wristwatch. Hoop earrings. A misting of Anne's *Rich Hippie* organic perfume. *Too late.*

"So, let's get started with a warm up," the instructor said. "And remember, this isn't a competition, so go at your own pace."

While the instructor explained that the day's session would be an upper body workout, starting with the chanting of a mantra to help us ascend to a state of oneness with the universe, I studied the class members settled on their yoga mats. Fifteen were female, at least twenty-nine years or older. Good. I'd fit right in.

The mantra sounded like a sacred hymn sung in lullaby fashion. "HA-ree OHM. HA-ree OHM." My body still hurt from my workout in the garden, and we hadn't even gotten started yet. "Let's greet the morning, yoga-style, with some sun salutations," the instructor said. On cue, everyone stood. "Now lift your arms over your head and begin moving your spine."

Veronica swept up her arms, no warm-up required, so in sync with the rest of the class that she looked like she'd been part of it all along. She executed exaggerated cat-like movements with her spine, lifting one leg, then the other, and circling them around. I did my best to imitate her, but... Put it this way. I was glad the rest of the class was too preoccupied to notice my pathetic rendition of greeting the morning, yoga style.

"Now we'll open our chests and hearts with the Downward-Facing Dog Pose," our instructor said, pressing her palms to the mat and pushing up her hips. "It'll bring heat to your body and strengthen and stretch your spine."

Ignoring Veronica—she probably knew exactly what the Downward-Facing Dog Pose was—I imitated the woman in front of me.

"Now hold it for six full breaths," the instructor said. "Good job. Good job."

It was Saturday morning, so the fact that most of the participants had made it here by 8:45 said something about their determination and stamina. I'd rather have been in bed.

One of the four men in the class—the type who looked sophisticated even in a t-shirt and shorts—was doing the Downward-Facing Dog Pose next to me. With meditative slowness, he turned his head in my direction and glanced at me through half-closed eyes. Something about me must have pulled him out of the state of mental stillness, because he drew in a sharp breath, jerked to a stand, and stared at me with what appeared to be fear-widened eyes. This, of course, triggered my own brain's fear-central to where I probably looked as spooked as he did.

Veronica peered around me to see what had caught my attention, which nearly did the poor guy in. The corners of his lips pulled back and his nostrils flared.

"Shane," the instructor said from the front of the room, her tone disapproving. "These poses are meant to help you *withdraw* your senses from external objects."

External objects?

Shane continued to stare at us, though his enlarged-white-of-the-eye look had morphed into one of bewilderment. This was no pickup. In my experience, guys didn't look like they were about to have a coronary while in flirtation mode.

The class had come to a near halt, the participants looking around in confusion. However, Shane appeared unaware of the slowdown. One by one, heads turned his way, then back to the instructor. As if in a trance, Shane sat on his mat and shook his head. So much energy emanated from him that I could feel it from three feet away. Though Veronica and I often turned heads when we were together—identical twins hold a certain attraction, especially when they came in black and blonde—we'd never freaked anyone out before.

Shane's mouth opened and closed like a stranded fish, but he didn't seem able to get any words out.

"Hello," Veronica said, stepping around me to extend her hand. "I'm Veronica." After shaking his hand, she turned to me. "This is Marjorie. Anything we can do for you?"

He shook his head no.

"Okay, so now you've become acquainted with your neighbors, Shane, shall we resume our class?" the instructor asked in a voice that sounded far away.

No reaction from our new friend Shane. Or from me. All my attention was riveted on the man who appeared to have become incapacitated by anxiety or fear. The instructor shrugged and resumed the class without us, saying something about yoga not being about the pose, but refining the body.

"Nice to meet you Shane," Veronica said, cool, calm.

He nodded, his gaze darting back and forth between us. "I'm sorry. You're both so—"

"Treat the body as if it's a precious musical instrument," the instructor said.

"Want to step outside for a chat?" Veronica asked, motioning toward the door. "So, the class can carry on without further disruption."

My vote was to head home and never look back, but Shane had a counter suggestion. "There's a bakery half a block from here." He waved at the yoga instructor who was doing her best to keep the class on track.

Veronica looked at her yoga mat with what appeared to be regret before picking it up and rolling it back into a scroll. "Sure. Lead the way."

❂❂❂

We carried our drinks to the square bistro table under the awning outside the bakery and slid onto the sturdy wooden chairs. I wrapped my fingers around my coffee cup and looked into Shane's hazel eyes from across the table. Something besides his strange behavior put me off, though I couldn't pinpoint what it was. Veronica was drinking water out of a bottle. Healthy. Boring. She'd become a health freak overnight, and I hoped it wasn't contagious. I took a swallow of my full-strength black coffee just in case.

"I'm a plastic surgeon," Shane said.

The vision of a scarred face caused my coffee to go down the wrong pipe.

Veronica jumped up and slapped my back. "You okay?"

"A plastic surgeon?" I croaked. What an odd self-introduction.

"You have a problem with plastic surgeons?" Shane asked, gripping his Styrofoam coffee cup to the point of collapse.

I pictured him hovering over me with a scalpel about to peel off half my face.

"Plastic surgeons transform lives," Veronica said, sitting back down.

Shane eased the strangle hold on his cup. "But even God couldn't improve on the two of you."

"You don't look too good, Sis," Veronica said.

What kind of person, plastic surgeon or not, commented on someone's looks on such short acquaintance? This whole scene wasn't making sense.

Okay, so I was being judgmental again, one of the personality flaws I'd planned to work on during my stay in Pacific Grove. But something, call it a sixth sense, urged me to stand up and take my leave. "It was nice meeting you, Dr..."

"Donovan," he said. "Dr. Shane Donovan."

"So, you think even God couldn't improve on the two of us," Veronica said as she rose from her chair. Her smile was lit with a sadness that seemed to emerge from the core of her for reasons I could only guess at on our short acquaintance, a sadness I wished it was within my power to erase. "I'd say you've got that wrong."

Chapter Nine

VERONICA DIDN'T SEEM TO be listening to my abbreviated version of Monday's labyrinth discovery. It had been six days since my surprising find, but this was my first opportunity to share it with her. She'd taken no notice of the cleared circle when we passed it on our way to yoga class. Now, here we were back in the basement, she sitting cross-legged on her yoga mat, eyes closed, and me pacing the marble-tiled floor. She placed her arms behind her back, clasped her hands, and lowered her head to her knees.

"You never would've known it was there," I said, feeling as though I were talking to myself. "The yard was so overgrown, I did some clearing, and—"

"The labyrinth was completely covered?" Veronica asked, face to the floor.

"Yes. I bought this book and…"

Veronica returned to an upright position. "Grab me a bottle of water, will you?"

Why was she behaving like this? Was she that uncaring? The thought filled me with an emptiness more painful than her neglect. No, I wouldn't believe that of my sister. Her actions reflected where she was on her spiritual journey. She was seeking relief within the confines of herself—a religion of one, which didn't include me.

After retrieving water from the refrigerator, I turned and watched Veronica go through a yoga pose I recognized as the Downward-Facing Dog: Bring the body into shape of an "A". Lift through pelvis, sit bones up toward ceiling. Press down through heels and palms of hands. Our bodies were duplicates, but I found even this basic pose a challenge. Veronica would say that what you dislike most, you need most, but I preferred to let her reap the benefits of this stress-relieving pose for now.

It was quiet down here, the only sounds being Veronica's deep breathing and the steady hum of the refrigerator. After placing the water next to my sister, I stretched out on my back and extended my arms, imagining myself floating on a lake of cool water. The ceiling lights were off, the only illumination coming from the cove lighting along the floor. Mirrors reflected the soft, golden light back into the room, giving it a warm, dreamy feel. "How do you know what time of day it is down here?" I asked.

Veronica took a gulp of water, recapped the bottle, and set it back down. "I don't."

At that point, I let her have it, couldn't hold it back.

I told her I wanted to spend more time with her, that soon it would be too late, and that time was precious and shouldn't be wasted. I went on about how we still had to meet with our father, how he needed us and we needed him, and that this wasn't the way things were supposed to be.

When I ran out of words, Veronica said, "Sorry can't do."

"But Antonia asked us both to—"

"I'm not ready."

Her words came out in a whisper, which caused me to pause before continuing, my tone less angry. "But you're the one good at gathering evidence and at negotiation, the one who can't be led by the nose."

"Exactly," she said. "Not by our father, not by our dead mother, and not by you."

I sat up and rose to my feet, wishing the basement weren't so comfortable. No wonder Veronica didn't want to leave. "When you're done hibernating look me up," I said, "because I'm not coming back down."

"Is that a promise?"

I shrugged and headed for the stairs. For the first time I understood how Morgan must have felt when I insisted on us remaining separate until I got my act together. It was time to cut Veronica some slack, as Morgan had done for me. The space Veronica couldn't fill, I'd have to fill myself, possibly even make room for someone else.

❀❀❀

My mind in neutral, my feet on overdrive, I followed Lighthouse Avenue past the post office, then turned left and forged on until I came to Center. From there, I took a right and continued past Jewell Park, the Pacific Grove Museum of Natural History, and the library. I wasn't in the mood to rest or dawdle. I wasn't in the mood to do much of anything but walk, one foot in front of the other, one step at a time.

Near 12th Street, stood a Gothic-style building, which encouraged me to slow and come to a halt. St. Mary's by-the-Sea Episcopal Church, constructed of redwood beams and siding, exuded a warmth that appealed to me. The door to the church's entry stood open. Music came from within, an invitation to enter, which I accepted.

I was penetrating the sacred space of another faith, drawn not only by curiosity, but by the promptings of my spirit. Ignoring sirens of discomfort and misunderstanding, I stumbled into the commencement of St. Mary's 10 a.m. service. The organist was playing an Irish hymn, the piped air imitating bagpipes, a keening sound that caused goose flesh to rise on my skin and my chest to swell to accommodate the new rhythm. The faithful stood as the priest approached the altar. The pew below the Sixth Station of the Cross—*Jesus and Veronica*—stood empty, so I genuflected and slipped in. The dark wooden walls and ceiling resembled the hull of an overturned ship, and I felt safe and protected within its hold. The beautifully crafted, stained glass windows and vibrating music encouraged me to give up my melancholy mood and give in to a sense of peace, gratitude, and joy.

However, nothing prepared me for the alto in the choir.

I've long admired the voice of the soprano because of its ability to reach such high notes and put enough tension in the air to lift one off one's seat, but the voice of the alto, especially if female, can fill the air with waves of comfort that cradles like the arms of a mother.

57

The alto singing now did that and more.

You shall cross the barren desert, but you shall not die of thirst.

You will wander far in safety, though you do not know the way.

I craned my neck to see where the voice originated from, but though the choir faced the congregation from the chancel rail, the singer evaded my view.

Be not afraid. I go before you always.

Come follow me, and I will give you rest.

Later, while the lectors read from the Old Testament and the priest read from one of the Gospels—something about Lazarus being an "invisible" person in the rich man's line of vision—I still savored the captivating voice I had heard.

The priest talked about the sin of ignoring the needs of others and not sharing one's wealth to alleviate their pain. He talked about the people in the world who were hungry, lost, lonely, sick, and dying and asked, "Do we turn away from their needs? Do we pretend they do not exist?" And all the while, I thought of the invisible alto that had sung her way into my heart.

The priest invited all baptized Christians, regardless of denomination, to receive communion with the rest of the congregation. I, a Roman Catholic, being invited by the Episcopalians to join in their Eucharistic meal? Another invitation I accepted. While the choir sang, *Here the hungry find plenty, here the thirsty shall drink*, I received the bread and wine and headed back to my pew, where I knelt and prayed in thanksgiving for the gift of this little red church—home away from home, as God intended His house to be.

When the worshipers left their pews and headed for the door, I stayed behind, head bowed, listening to the choir and alto angel sing the closing hymn: *Go and share.*

I recalled the priest's words about the sin of ignoring the needs of others and thought of my father, a man who on first sight had filled me with revulsion and later with guilt and regret. He was in pain, even if self-inflicted as Veronica had suggested. But I was afraid. I'd heard about alcoholism and how it destroyed people's lives. And I now understood Veronica's warnings about our father's ability to take people down. Even those he professed to love.

How could I help him without destroying myself?

Chapter Ten

SOMEONE WAS FOLLOWING ME.
   I saw nothing out of the ordinary, not a blur out of the corner of my eye, not a stranger peering from behind an unfurled newspaper or the shelter of a building, not a pedestrian trailing a mite too close. Neither did I hear footsteps, nor the rustle of clothing rubbing together. It was just a feeling, the hair-standing-on-end kind of feeling, a shiver passing through me like a low-voltage shock, guidance from the gut. *Someone is following you.*

My first impulse was to stop and search my surroundings. As if that would do any good. For one thing, it was foggy, and fog tends to mess with the imagination. Look too closely into the misty veil and be prepared to see any number of eerie pursuers. For another, I was relying on a sixth sense, nothing I could see, hear, or smell, which told me I had no one to fear. So, instead of peering over my shoulder and alerting my stalker that I knew I was being followed, I pretended to be on a carefree stroll.

Something I wasn't about to do, though, was lead whomever it was to where Veronica and I lived. I pivoted left onto 17-Mile Drive, then, after some brisk footwork, took a right on Short Street and another on Ridge Road. There was a monarch sanctuary out here somewhere; I'd seen the signs. I increased my pace, eager to make it to the butterfly haven, hunker down between the trees, and wait for whoever was tailing me.

By the time I reached the grove of eucalyptus and pine, I was shaking, a nervous kind of shake rather than one of fear, the kind one experiences when about to speak in front of a large and unfamiliar crowd. I sat beneath a eucalyptus tree on a litter of rooster-tail leaves and cinnamon-stick tubes of bark. The strong scent of menthol gave the suggestion of warmth and comfort where I knew there was none.

I'd only met three people since coming to Pacific Grove—Nessa, Dr. Shane Donovan, and my father—and could think of no reason for any of them to be following me. Sure, Nessa had expressed interest in labyrinths, but she had no need to shadow me to find one. She knew of the labyrinth in Anne's backyard. Plus, she was a palm reader, and, though she denied it, my guess was she could read my mind. Stalking me would be a complete waste of her time. And although Dr. Donovan struck me as rather odd—okay, really odd—I couldn't picture him playing spy either. Being the type of person people noticed, he couldn't trail me on foot for miles without standing out like a sore thumb—despite the fog. Which left my father. Veronica mentioned during our stay in Big Sur that he often tracked her down. That he had nothing better to do. Too much money, too much liquor, too much time. I shivered. *Please don't let it be him.*

Regret for my hasty decision in coming here settled into my bones. What if my intuition had been wrong? What if my pursuer *did* mean me harm? I had no means of defending myself. I picked up a floppy eucalyptus branch and weighed it in my hand. A strike across the face would do the trick, or maybe a quick jab to the eyes.

Halfhearted sunlight trickled through the branches above. For a site known worldwide to observe clusters of monarchs hanging from trees like stained glass ornaments, the grove felt lonely and drab. I strained to hear or see movement, some sign of my stalker. "Come out, come out, wherever you are," I whispered, seized by the sense of being watched. From my vantage point between the eucalyptus, pine, and fog, I glimpsed a flash of color, something nonexistent before, something moving and rearranging itself. My face and neck broke out in a sweat. "Showtime," I whispered, ignoring the whine of fear. *Stay calm. Trust your gut.*

Someone stepped from between the trees and into my line of vision. I dropped the branch I was holding and pressed my hand over my mouth, but not in time to suppress the cry that escaped from a part of me I hadn't known existed.

A woman had materialized out of the swirling mist as if from behind a hidden door and stood motionless in this sanctuary for the delicate and travel-weary butterfly, a wax figure, so realistic, yet so uncannily still. Would her image disappear as it had the other two times I'd seen her? I'd believed then that I was seeing myself, a premonition of things to come. But it hadn't been me at all. Only someone who looked like me.

She smiled, causing the disfigured side of her face to pucker and turn a deeper shade of red. I smiled back, experiencing a softening around my heart, as though the sun had penetrated the fog and melted my skin, my muscles, my bones. I eased my hand from my mouth and, with a knot in my throat that felt like it might choke me, I rose to a stand.

She stepped forward. I did the same.

The words Antonia had cried out in Big Sur made sense now. *Fallen Light,* the missing piece of the circle ripped apart after our birth. Veronica and I weren't twins. We were triplets.

"Welcome," I said as we stepped into each other's arms.

My sister's body trembled, as did mine.

"Who are you?" she asked.

I'd found a part of myself I hadn't known I'd lost. "Your sister."

She drew back. "Sister?"

I looked into her eyes, so blue they appeared violet. *Are we alike inside, too?*

"I try not to do that anymore," she said, her smile slipping. "Long ago, I decided other people's thoughts were none of my business. But I couldn't ignore the dreams. I've seen you in my dreams."

For twenty-nine years, I'd had another sister without knowing her hopes and dreams, her fears, her joys. Why hadn't I sensed something was wrong, that another huge chunk of my life had been missing? If it hadn't been for Antonia, nagging me from the grave, I would never have known about Maya.

Fallen Light allowed me to cry, in no apparent hurry to suppress the part of me giving in to a deep sense of loss. She became still as the pine, cypress, and eucalyptus that surrounded us, a pillar, a silent witness. Finally, her calmness got through to me. I peered at her through blurry eyes. When she smiled, her deformity appeared more of a boon than an impediment, a valuable prize, an important part of whom she was.

"There's another one of us, isn't there?" she asked. "With black hair."

"Yes," I said. "Veronica."

"And you are?"

"Marjorie."

She sighed.

"What's your name other than *Fallen Light*?" I asked.

Her brows rose, but she didn't ask how I knew her Native American name. "Maya."

"So, you knew about us before now?" My throat almost closed around the words. "You knew you had two sisters?"

"No."

"Then how—"

"I had a vision seven months ago, on Ash Wednesday, while the priest was putting blessed ashes on my forehead as a sign of penitence and a reminder of my mortality. You and Veronica were standing on both sides of me facing the altar. I thought you were my guardian angels, perfect in every way. I didn't know you were my sisters. I didn't think you were real."

I squeezed her hands. "But—"

"It was a shock seeing you in church today, and it took me a while to recover. I was afraid to approach you, afraid you'd disappear as you always do in my dreams. So, instead I followed you."

How odd that our mother hadn't contacted Maya as she'd contacted Veronica and me, that she hadn't scared her half to death, that Maya had been spared.

She raised her hand to her face, then ran her fingers over the raspberry stain covering her right cheek. "I was brought up by our mother's people, but they never told me about having two sisters. Am I the only one with the mark?"

The mark? I stared at the stained and distorted skin that covered nearly half her face. Was that what she called her deformity? As if it were no more than a bruise or a scratch?

Her fingers trembled. "The mark of the Great Spirit."

Dear God, she was proud of her flaw. Whereas I would've been horrified.

"Without it, I..." She took my hand and placed it over the vivid red mark. "Close your eyes and tell me what you feel."

My fingers tingled and something warm traveled up my arms and spread through my chest as if her blood was transfusing into mine. The fog appeared to lift, the atmosphere to brighten. How tall the eucalyptus trees were, 100 feet or more, with thick, smooth trunks and brown, stringy bark. Their menthol scent became stronger as a breeze swooshed through the canopy of their branches and made their leathery leaves rattle.

It was early October, too soon to expect the monarchs to have completed their laborious journey to Pacific Grove from as far north as Canada. I felt a deep love for the monarchs. The way they transformed from earthbound caterpillars into glorious flying insects. The transfiguration seemed impossible, which made it credible to believe in other miraculous conversions as well.

I looked at my sister, my mind numb with wonder. "Do you always feel like this?"

"Yes," she said.

I stared at the mark on her face and saw it through a different lens of perception. It looked beautiful. Maya looked beautiful.

"I'd share it if I could," she said.

She would share her most precious gift with me, a woman she'd just met. I hugged her, feeling the beat of her heart and heat of her body. "You just did."

She smiled.

"Veronica..." I paused, not sure how to proceed. I was excited about introducing Maya to her, but...

Maya put her hand on my shoulder. "She isn't ready. Give her time. She needs to go within herself to seek answers."

I didn't ask how she knew. Instead, I looked at the closed canopy of Monterey pine and eucalyptus, disappointed at how drab they appeared, when only moments before, they'd radiated magnificence and otherworldliness.

Maya picked up several of the lance-shaped eucalyptus leaves clustered at our feet, then inhaled their fragrance and smiled. "Every day is full of gifts, but meeting you... Nothing can compare." She released the leaves, and they resettled onto the loamy earth. "When I receive a gift, I accept it greedily."

"Our father is staying in a rented cottage nearby," I said.

She looked toward Lighthouse Avenue as though she already knew of his existence and whereabouts.

"Have you dreamt about him, too?" I asked.

She took my hand and again placed it on her scarred cheek. I felt an inexplicable rush of gratitude and joy. Wow. To always feel this way. What an awesome gift. My view expanded to include every blade of grass, every leaf on the trees, the birds, my sister—life. My skin no longer blocked the outside world from the world within. I wanted to float in this state forever.

"Maybe you have a mark, too, somewhere," Maya said.

"No. And, as far as I know, neither does Veronica."

"What's your last name?"

"Veil," I said.

"And Veronica's?"

"Mask."

"Veil and Mask. You didn't just make that up. No, of course not. This is too cool."

"Yeah, beyond coincidence," I said, shaking my head. Veronica and I, with no visible scars, bore last names that symbolized covering up and separation.

"I carry our mother's last name," Maya said. "Flores, which means flowers."

How she differed from Veronica, whose attitude toward life was a mask of sarcasm. To understand Veronica, one had to read between her words for their meaning. She exuded power. She did her own thing. Then there was me. I spoke my mind, which set me up for pain and embarrassment—and new discoveries. While following my life path, I often overlooked or misunderstood the clues given by my mother, the earth, and the Great Spirit, as if a veil existed between us. Maya was the flower, the most aware of the three of us. No wonder Antonia hadn't spoken to her.

Maya already knew.

Chapter Eleven

THE REST OF THE week was torture for me. Knowing I had two sisters living within easy reach, yet so far away, just about drove me nuts. I respected Veronica's need to be alone to face her inner demons and Maya's hesitation to immediately absorb me into her life, but that didn't make it any easier to exist in a vacuum. I considered visiting my father, but feared merging our current black holes might produce destructive gravitational waves that would throw us even more off kilter.

Saturday morning, I walked into the kitchen still thinking about Maya, how I hadn't known she existed until now, yet felt I knew her intimately, as though she'd been shadowing me since the day of our birth. I smelled coffee, which gave me pause, until I caught sight of Veronica at the dinette table, chanting a stretched out "aaawe" that rolled into an "ooo" and ended with a prolonged "mmmm."

In the quiet that followed, I recalled a detail stored somewhere in my trivia bank about *Om* being the basic sound of the universe and chanting the sound was a way of acknowledging, tuning into, and connecting with all living things. During Veronica's next round of intonations, I found myself silently chanting along.

The filmy gray light filtering through the windows of the nook caused Veronica's image to shimmer and blur like a mirage. Though her back was to me, the slight stiffening of her shoulders indicated she knew I was there. "Yoga can accomplish many of the same things we pay chiropractors for," she said by way of morning greeting.

Here we go again. "I wouldn't know, since I've never been to a chiropractor."

Veronica picked up a glass of something thick and chalky and held it up to the dim morning light as if toasting the day. "Our bodies are out of whack, Sis. We're just not aware of it."

"If you say so."

She turned and waved the glass at me. "But even if you're in top physical condition, yoga can help sharpen your mind."

"Okaaaay."

"It's a key to freedom and liberation," Veronica continued in what sounded like another passage from Anne's wellness and fitness library. "It clarifies the spirit and helps you feel one with the universe."

I'd worked my way toward freedom and liberation and clarifying the spirit for months now via the Native American Medicine Wheel, and Maya seemed to have reached these states without the benefits of yoga, but if this spiritual tradition got my sister out of the doldrums and out of the basement, I was all for it.

I headed for the coffee pot, surprised anew at how all the glossy white surfaces and polished glass and steel could exude such warmth and coziness. Then again, Heaven was professed to be dazzling white while at the same time comforting and welcoming. Why not Anne's kitchen?

"Are we going to yoga class today?" I asked.

"Did I tell you that this meal replacer contains seventeen different fruits, vegetables, and grains, plus vitamins, minerals, carbohydrates, and proteins?"

I poured myself a mug of coffee and sniffed it, eyes closed. The thought of beginning a day without caffeine made me cringe. "Yeah, you already mentioned that."

"You can't abuse your body forever, Marge."

I scanned the counter for something sweet to go with the coffee. "I can't believe it's you talking, Miss I-can-eat-anything-because-my-body's-genetically superior. Anyway, I don't smoke, over indulge on booze, or take drugs. *That* would be abusing my body."

She toasted me with her empty glass, now lined with a foamy white residue.

"Have you seen the cranberry scones?" I asked.

Veronica drove the Jeep to yoga class—the long way this time, taking Forest and Central past the Pacific Grove Museum and Jewell Park, then Grand past Holman's department store (now an antique mall) where Steinbeck purchased writing supplies, back to Lighthouse past the Scotch Bakery, on to Fountain to the corner of Ricketts Row, then 11ᵗʰ and Eardley past Steinbeck's Cottage, the spiritual home he returned to when he needed to rediscover himself. The wind breezed through the window on Veronica's side of the car, causing her hair to fly in all directions like a flock of black crows, while she touted the advantages of yoga over other forms of therapy, how it was more conducive to renewal and self-understanding than hours on a therapist's couch. "Motion instead of talk," she said. "I don't like spilling my guts to a stranger, spinning in circles, getting buried deeper and deeper. Ever wonder why they call psychotherapists shrinks?"

I thought of my sessions with Dr. Tony Mendez, the comforting sound of his voice, how he'd helped prevent my descent into the deep hole of insanity. He'd urged me to get out of town, away from all that was familiar, a journey I was still on today. "That's not how *transpersonal* psychology works," I said. "It's about emergence not reduction. It expands rather than shrinks."

Veronica parked in a lot behind the small building where the yoga classes were held, then looked in the mirror and grimaced at the state of her hair before easing up the window and turning off the ignition. "Instead of bombarding me with evidence to support psychotherapy, how about squeezing a little yoga into your world? Use it or lose it."

The clouds parted and sunlight flooded over us like an outpouring of love. I could practically hear it "Om" as it touched my cheeks and shoulders with its warmth.

"I enjoy… No, I *love* your company," I said. "But our paths to self-understanding may run out of sync for a while, even in opposite directions. Since you prefer yoga, you'll work harder at it and might make some profound discoveries. I, on the other hand, don't want to divert my attention with yet another empowering tool. Yoga makes me nervous, especially with Dr. Donovan around. My energy supports circles, outdoors, where the world is alive and where I feel like a full participant instead of a detached observer, which makes the medicine wheel and labyrinth my avenues of choice right now."

"Come on, Marjorie, give it another try."

"That's why I'm here, though my heart's not in it."

❂❂❂

"Grab your mats and turf it!" our instructor said as we walked through the door. The room smelled of incense and sweat. "On the floor." Dr. Donovan motioned for us to take the empty spaces on either side of him. I hurried forward, not wanting to draw attention to our tardiness. Veronica followed at a slower pace, apparently unconcerned about disrupting the class a second time She waved at the instructor, who nodded and smiled.

"For the sake of our newest yoga students," she said, "my name is Sandra. As for the rest of the class, the black-haired woman who just entered is Veronica and the blonde, her sister, Marjorie."

You'd think I'd be used to people's stares by now at seeing Veronica and me together. What, I wondered, would their reaction be if we added a third look alike to the mix?

Veronica spread her mat to the left of Dr. Donovan. I settled on his right.

"Today we'll start with one of our calming poses to quiet the mind and body," Sandra said. She brought the soles of her feet together and drew them toward her body. "It's called the Baddha Konasana or Butterfly Pose and imitates a butterfly resting its wings on a lotus blossom."

The class imitated the instructor with varying degrees of success.

Not even a wince from Veronica as she pulled her feet forward, a dead giveaway that she'd been practicing down in the basement.

"Now press your knees to the ground as far as you can," Sandra said, singling me out with a hard stare from the front of the room. "Come on, you can do it."

Sure thing. I tried to keep a straight face while I pressed my knees down. *Ow!*

"Bow forward," Sandra said, eyes still trained on me.

70

Hey? Did I look that bad?

"Some people find the Butterfly Pose easy," she said. "Those less flexible in the hips, have more difficulty."

Veronica snickered. "That would be you, Marge. Need pillows for under your knees?"

Smart aleck. Just because she'd been at it for a week or two, while I was—and would continue to be—a yoga novice. I visualized touching Maya's birthmark with the tips of my fingers, and my discomfort and irritation eased.

"Hold on to your thighs if you can't reach your feet," Sandra said. "Think about the butterfly and its delicate beauty as you fold yourself down over your knees."

A quick glance at Veronica confirmed what I'd suspected. Her face came close to touching the mat between her knees. I glanced at Sandra. She smiled. "This isn't a competition," she said. "Don't strain yourself or pull any muscles. You'll get there in time."

I smiled back and mouthed a thank you.

She led us through two more calming poses, the Dandasana, otherwise known as Staff Pose and the Gomukhasana or Cow Face Pose, followed by a stream of poses called Easy Pose, Kneeling Pose, Lotus Pose, and Bound Lotus Pose, meant to arrange the body in a way ideal for meditation. Despite moments of discomfort, I felt relaxed by the time we were through. I even managed to get up off the floor.

Not having read up on yoga as Veronica had, and not having started this class on day one, I felt satisfied with my progress. As was Sandra. "Good job Marjorie. You'll catch on in no time. Next week, I'll teach you more about using your breath optimally."

Next week? I don't think so.

It wasn't until Veronica and I had rolled up our mats and propped them under our arms for our departure that Dr. Donovan made a request. "How about joining me for lunch?"

"Sure," Veronica said before I could object. "As long as you know a place that serves Sattvic food."

"Sattvic food?" I asked.

"Nothing canned or processed," Veronica said. "Or prepared with chemical fertilizers or sprays. In other words, foods rich in Prana life force."

Was my sister's new diet a sign of vigilance and dedication or taking healthy eating to an extreme? "Which leaves what?"

"Organic fruits and veggies, nuts, seeds, and honey."

"Jeez," I said, suddenly craving a burger and fries. "Hope there's a place that serves hearty food as well?"

Dr. Donovan laughed. "Just leave it to me."

"Will do," Veronica said. "We'll even let your drive."

Chapter Twelve

SHANE, AKA DR. SHANE Donovan aka Dr. Donovan, drove a Mercedes, as had Cliff, the man I was engaged to back home in Menlo Park. Unlike Cliff, though, the doctor treated his car as a mode of transportation rather than a favorite toy. Veronica sat in front, I in back, positioned so not to be visible in the rear-view mirror. I closed my eyes, needing time to think. Something told me that Dr. Donovan knew Maya, and knew her well, which would explain his odd reaction on first meeting Veronica and me and the resulting comments on our appearance. I also suspected this lunch date had something to do with Maya. What I couldn't figure out was how to act during the upcoming ordeal. Good thing Veronica couldn't see my face, because I was sure my secret was as conspicuous as a flashing neon sign. *I know something you don't know.* How would Veronica react when she discovered I'd withheld the news of our sister's existence?

That we were triplets instead of twins.

As we veered off Lighthouse onto Forest, then Ocean View, Veronica and Dr. Donovan discussed the attributes of Pacific Grove, which proved to be many for those in the right frame of mind. The coastal city with its glut of historical homes, they decided, was the place to be for those seeking rest and tranquility. However, for the tourist bent on visiting art galleries and a fish aquarium, shopping for souvenirs, and eating in a vast array of restaurants, Monterey and Carmel won the draw.

Heck, they made Pacific Grove sound as attractive as a cemetery.

After street parking on Ocean View, our self-appointed guide led us into the Tinnery Restaurant with its panoramic view of Lovers

Point Beach. "This place serves good yogi food," he said, "and the best burgers and fries in town."

Good. Organic fruits and veggies had their place in a balanced diet, but so did beef and fried potatoes.

No sooner had the waitress taken our orders and brought tall glasses of water than Dr. Donovan announced, "I'm in love with your sister."

Veronica choked on her drink. And so many stress hormones bombarded my system at once that my stomach twisted into a tight knot. In love with Maya? Darn. This was serious. And he was about to ruin our meal by telling us about it.

"Just so you know," Veronica said after recovering from a bout of coughing. "Marjorie's not your type."

My silence alerted her that something was off. She punched my shoulder. "Okay, out with it. What's going on?"

High on a cliff to the north of us, above the churning gray ocean, I caught a beam of light before it disappeared.

"What have you been up to while I've been hibernating in the basement?" Veronica asked.

I pulled my gaze from the turbulent view to meet her narrowed blue eyes. "Not what you're thinking."

The waitress approached with a serving tray balanced on her open palm as though it were an extension of her body. With her free hand, she pulled a fold-out stand from a cubby next to our table and set the serving tray on top before distributing our meals like a pro.

Bet she hadn't learned that in yoga class.

Only Dr. Donovan seemed to have kept his appetite. He dug into his calamari and noodles as if we'd been discussing the weather. Maybe he expected me to clue Veronica in about Maya. But how could I inform her, out of the blue, about a sister I'd met a week ago and kept secret from her? I longed for more time to prepare and for some place private to share what I knew without Dr. Shane Donovan listening in. Veronica looked at me as though she'd just caught

74

me shoplifting or cheating at cards. "You're dumping Morgan for Shane?"

"Hell no. I wouldn't dump Morgan for any man, let alone someone I just met."

Veronica blew out her breath and turned to Dr. Donovan, brows raised.

I gave the doctor a look I reserved for the totally clueless, such as my ex-fiancé, but he was too busy feeding his face to notice. If he was truly Maya's friend and confidant, he'd know Veronica hadn't yet met her. Did he relish the element of surprise, or was he just being cruel?

"Veronica—" I began.

"You mean, you don't know?" Dr. Donovan asked.

I prayed that Veronica's sarcastic sense of humor, even her anger, would rise to the occasion, because the good doctor was itching to give her the shock of her life.

And I didn't know how to spare her.

"Remember our father's secret?" I asked. Maybe, Dr. Donovan would resume eating and keep his mouth shut.

Veronica didn't answer, just presented that what-do-you-take-me-for? look she'd perfected since our first meeting.

"I think I may know what it is."

No response, except for a tightening of her jaw.

God this was hard. "If you hadn't been hiding out in the basement, you'd know too," I said in my defense. Because a defense I would need, for keeping the news of Maya's existence from Veronica. Even though Maya asked me to. "I planned to tell you, when the time was right, so don't be mad." I turned to Dr. Donovan, jabbed my finger at him. "It's your buddy here who's being the asshole."

The doctor's eyes widened. Good. Hope I shocked him. Did he think I was such a pushover that I'd sit by while he dropped his emotional time bomb and put a wedge between Veronica and me? She shouldn't be hit with the news of Maya's existence in this way. What could I do to soften the blow? "Veronica..."

"Out with it, Sis. You're driving me nuts with suspense."

"We have a sister."

Veronica stared at me blank-faced.

I took her hand, forcing myself to finish before the doctor could intervene. "We're triplets, not twins."

No reaction. Nothing. Where was her spunk, her sarcasm, her anger? "For some reason, our parents kept it from us," I said.

Veronica shuddered and took in a ragged breath. "A sister? What the hell?"

Finally, a reaction. I let go of her hand and folded my arms across my chest to prevent the onset of shaking. "Antonia must've changed her mind, which explains her request for us to meet with our father."

"I think I'm going to be sick," Veronica said, her plate of "Sattvic food" untouched.

"What I can't believe is that after all these years, Bob hasn't told you about this, and that Antonia has waited until now to—"

"Oh, please," Veronica said. "Antonia probably couldn't get through the pearly gates without making amends. As for our father… I think he's paying a heavy price for his reticence about many things. But a sister. That plain takes the cake."

"Twenty-nine years is a long time for Antonia to spend in purgatory," I said.

"Or in hell like Pop," Veronica replied.

Dr. Donovan set down his fork and cleared his throat. "If your mother's dead, how do you know she changed her mind about anything?"

"She talks to us," I said before continuing my discussion with Veronica. "I didn't tell you about Maya because she asked me not to. She said you needed time—"

"Maya?"

"That's our sister's name."

"What did you tell her about me?"

"Not much."

"Then how did she know I—"

"She dreams."

"This is crazy."

"I know."

Veronica dropped her napkin onto her untouched Cobb salad. "It's time we talk to our father. I mean, really talk."

"I agree." But this time I wouldn't be sidetracked by disappointment and fear. This time it wouldn't be about me.

"Your sister was born with a condition called capillary hemangiomata," Dr. Donovan said. "It's congenital, but not necessarily hereditary, that's why the two of you—"

"What the hell's he talking about?" Veronica asked, looking at me as if I were suddenly his interpreter.

"The capillaries underneath the surface of her right cheek, nose, and brow are dilated," the doctor said, "causing them to be covered with a wine-colored stain. There are also bulb-like growths disfiguring her nose and chin."

A moment passed before Veronica said, "Shit."

"She doesn't seem to mind," I added.

Dr. Donovan continued as if he hadn't heard me or, worse, as if Maya's feelings about her condition didn't count. "In most cases, infantile hemangiomas resolve completely by age seven, and intervention isn't required. But in Maya's case, the malformation didn't go away and has become unsightly."

"If she looks that bad, how come—" Veronica began.

"I can fix it," the doctor said.

"So, what's holding you back?" Veronica asked.

"Maya is."

It was obvious the doctor wasn't planning to share Maya's side of the story. "Let me get this straight," I said, aiming for diplomacy. "Maya's birthmark is cosmetically disturbing, but she won't let you 'fix it.'"

"That's right."

Veronica signaled the waiter for more water. "Maybe it's a matter of cost."

She assumed, of course, that Maya was ashamed of her birthmark. No surprise there. I'd assumed the same until Maya convinced me otherwise. Which brought up another question. "Have you touched Maya's mark, Dr. Donovan? I mean, really touched it?"

"No, but I want to, believe me."

With a scalpel! I thought of puppy love and pedestals and unattainable expectations. "Remove it, not experience it?"

He glared at me with an intensity that at one time would've frightened me. Now, it just made me mad. "Be serious," he said. "We have the technology to make her beautiful. As she was meant to be."

"She sees the birthmark as a gift, not a deformity," I said.

Veronica sucked in her breath. "You've got to be kidding."

Dr. Donovan leaned across the table, got close to my face. "People stare at her and make fun of her. You have no idea."

"And what does Maya think and say about that?" I asked.

"She claims not to notice, but I know better."

I closed my eyes and took a deep breath. Cliff had also insisted he knew what was best for me, overriding my wishes until I'd forgotten I had a voice. I'd allowed him to take over my life rather than taking responsibility for and facing it on my own. "If you love Maya, you'll accept her as she is."

"You're her sister," he said. "You're supposed to help her."

"And that's what I plan to do."

I slid out of the booth and dropped two twenties on the table, covering a tip for the waitress who'd made a difficult job look easy. "You're the one with experience in law enforcement, Veronica. Deal with him."

"Law enforcement?" the doctor asked as I headed for the door.

Chapter Thirteen

"YOU WERE PRETTY RUDE to Shane," Veronica said the following morning. She'd done it again, beat me to the kitchen and brewed a pot of coffee, though she wasn't having any.

My stomach felt queasy at the very mention of Dr. Shane Donovan. I poured myself a cup of coffee anyway. Why was Veronica defending the doctor when Maya should be foremost in her mind? "So, you have a monopoly on rudeness?"

Veronica's eyes flickered with what appeared to be approval for my ability to give as well as take a stinging comeback. "Good heavens. My little sister has teeth after all."

"He's Cliff all over again," I said. "Selfish and domineering and thinks he knows better than Maya how to live her own life. Why do we attract men like that?"

"Not we."

"Okay, so you at least agree he's overbearing."

Veronica stared out the window, which might as well have been shuttered given her gaze didn't seem to settle on the tranquil scene outside. "It's hard to believe Maya isn't bothered by her deformity."

"Then you're in for a big surprise, because it's true."

"It's a birthmark, not a beauty mark."

"Tell that to Maya."

"Can't do, unless I meet her, so let's cut the crap about me not being ready."

I settled into the chair next to hers, slumped over the table, and rested my chin in my hands. "I don't know how to contact her."

"You let her go without asking where she lives?"

"She wasn't exactly handing out business cards. And don't suggest asking Dr. Donovan, because, in case you haven't noticed, I can't stand the guy. Anyway, I have a plan."

"Oh boy, here we go."

"Maya followed me to the butterfly sanctuary from St. Mary's by-the-Sea Church last Sunday, so I figured if I attended the service again today, we might reengage."

Veronica got up and rinsed the white foam from her glass. "I haven't been to church in ages, except last Easter to celebrate our rescue from the cave. What time's the service?"

"Ten."

"Catholic?"

"Episcopalian."

She scanned the pristine kitchen walls as if searching for cobwebs. "Not having a clock around is great until you actually need one." She glanced at the control pads on the electric range and microwave, which should've displayed the minute and hour in bright green digits. Instead, they were dark. "Even the appliances don't know the time."

I checked my watch. "It's nine thirty-five, and it takes about ten minutes to get to St. Mary's by car. Another five to find a place to park."

"Yikes." Veronica grabbed a sweater off the back of her chair, one I hadn't seen before. In fact, her entire outfit looked new: denim skirt, lilac shoes, kiwi sweater, not Veronica-like at all. It occurred to me that she was helping herself to Anne's clothes, as well as her nutritional supplies. Anne would be thrilled.

"We better get moving," Veronica said.

Having already planned to attend Mass today, I was set to go. I finished my coffee, grabbed my purse, and followed Veronica out the door.

❸❸❸

We parked on 12th Street next to Greenwood Park, a full block of natural landscape studded with eucalyptus trees. "I didn't realize this many people still attended Mass these days," Veronica said, gesturing toward the cars parked nose to rear along the residential streets surrounding the church. The organ was playing and the congregation standing when we entered through the porch entrance. Memories of all the Sundays I'd spent in church during my youth came flooding back, carrying a sense of sadness at what I'd since missed and joy at my return. While we waited for the worshipers to sit, the alto I remembered from my previous visit broke into a hymn I hadn't heard before. And though rows of people blocked my view, they couldn't block the effect the singer had on my soul.

The Lord stands knocking at the door to your heart,
A door that opens from within. Let him in.

Veronica nudged me, which was a good thing. Otherwise, I would've remained locked in a daze, unaware of the passage of time. "There's room in the pew up ahead," she said.

The service was a blur after that. The alto who had affected me so deeply left little space in my mind and heart for inspiration from the priest or the liturgy of the Mass.

Veronica sat, stood, and knelt at the appropriate times during the service, but appeared to have settled into a world of her own. It wasn't until most of the worshipers had left the church and our pew had emptied that she opened her eyes and said, "I like this place."

I made the sign of the cross. "Me too."

"Beautiful music."

"Yes."

"Do you think she's here?"

"Don't know."

After a short silence, I realized Veronica was staring at me. "You okay?" she asked.

"A little groggy. You?"

"Like I've had too much wine. Let's go."

❂❂❂

The sun pierced the billowy October clouds and highlighted the park-like setting on the opposite side of the street. Small groups of parishioners clustered around the church entrance as though reluctant to return to their ordinary lives.

"How about we go for a walk," I said. "Maybe Maya will follow."

Veronica waved at an older couple dressed in their Sunday best. They waved back and called out, "Hello."

"Any sightseeing suggestions for a couple of out-of-towners?" Veronica asked.

"The Point Pinos Lighthouse," the woman said. "It opens at one." The man shook his head. "Nothing beats a walk along Ocean View Boulevard to Lovers Point."

We waved our thanks and headed down Central Avenue.

The sky darkened as clouds drifted back over the sun. I zipped my coral jacket, glad I wore a cardigan underneath. Veronica looked chic, even in denim and clogs. Kiwi and lilac; who would've guessed, when she favored black and red? "I've never seen you in green or lilac before," I ventured.

She executed a model pose before revealing a hidden zipper in the fold of her ankle-length skirt. She unzipped the bottom portion of the skirt, stepped out of it, and twirled it over her head like a stripper. "Maxi to mini. Perfect for a Sunday stroll." She folded the denim tube and slipped it into her hobo bag.

"I should've known," I said.

"What?"

"Never mind."

Veronica laughed. "Casual chic isn't my thing. But I get the feeling you like it that way. My questionable taste in fashion adds a little flair to your otherwise dull existence."

Dull existence? Ha! "Compared to six months ago, working fifty hours a week for a venture capital firm and dealing with an overprotective mother and manipulative fiancé, I'd say I'm living a life of incredible excitement."

"If you call our current setup exciting," Veronica said, "you've forgotten our adventure in Tassajara."

"Excitement like that can get you killed."

The look on my face must've hit her funny bone, because Veronica laughed until I thought she might drop to the ground. "You're so—" She couldn't finish, instead, gave in to another bout of laughter.

Despite my determination not to, I smiled. It felt good yukking it up with my sister. A Bible verse popped out of my memory bank as though planted and saved there by someone other than me. *And Sarah said, God hath made me to laugh, so that all that hear will laugh with me.* Then I, too, stated to laugh, and each time our merriment subsided, we'd look at each other and start back in again. I pressed my hands to my stomach. "Stop, please."

"You first," Veronica said.

Maybe if I didn't look at her, I'd get myself under control. I spun around to face the church and my gaze locked onto Maya, who stood several feet away, wiping her eyes with the back of her hand. "Veronica," I said, suddenly sober. "We've got company."

No response.

I turned and caught my tough, smart-aleck sister, with her mouth hanging open.

"I like your hair," Maya said to Veronica. "I thought about dyeing mine red, but chickened out. And your skirt... Have you ever considered modeling?"

What was it with the trivial chitchat? Was this Maya's way of putting Veronica at ease? If so, it didn't seem to be working. Veronica gave Maya a tight smile, as if greeting a complete stranger, which to be fair, wasn't far off. To know about Maya's existence was one thing, meeting her for the first time was quite another. Maya's birthmark took getting used to. What was it costing Veronica not to cry out as I had when I'd first seen her red puckered skin?

Veronica's smile relaxed, and just like that, she appeared composed and unruffled, as if she'd retreated some place inside where it was possible to block out all emotion. She was good at that, so very good. She checked out Maya's brown cargo pants and jacket. "I'm surprised they allowed you into church dressed like that."

"Ditto," Maya said, giving Veronica a head-to-toe once-over. She tipped back the rounded bill of her baseball cap. "The pants and jacket express my rebellious side, and the hat is for comfort. Anyway, I stand in back of the choir. Less distracting that way."

"You sing in the choir?" Why was I surprised? I'd heard Veronica sing around the campfire in a strong, clear alto during our guided tour through Tassajara. Something clicked in my mind. "You're the one who sang solo at the start of Mass." My voice sounded distant, accompanied by a rushing sound, as if I had seashells pressed to my ears.

"Any choir member, willing and able, gets to sing solo now and then," Maya said.

"What a gift to the parishioners," I said. "Your singing gave me goose bumps." I turned to Veronica. "Wasn't she wonderful?"

"At first, I thought someone had recorded my voice," Veronica said, straight-faced. "But then I realized I'd never sung that song before. Spiritual music isn't my thing."

"Sometimes a good voice just needs to team up with the right song to make it beautiful," I said.

"My voice is more than *good,* thank you," Veronica said. "As would be yours, if you used it now and then. Like maybe once a year."

Maya touched the mark on her face in a way similar to the way I touched my mouse totem when seeking comfort. "So much about life seems impossible," she said. "Like meeting the two of you. For so long I've felt your presence in my heart, and you're both just as I'd imagined. One sweet, one sassy."

"I'm the sweet one, right?" Veronica said.

Maya laughed.

"How about you?" Veronica asked. "Sweet? Sassy? A bit of both?"

I listened to the exchange with a burning sensation in my chest. How much happiness could one absorb? How much happiness could one endure?

"Sweet and sassy are both taken," Maya said, "so, how about smart?"

Veronica humphed. "You'll have a hard time living up to that one with two brilliant sisters around."

"We're just talking labels here, not living up to them." Maya touched her face and grinned. "Anyway, I have extra artillery you two were born without."

Wow, she'd brought up the subject we'd been avoiding via small talk. I eyed Veronica. Would she pick up the ball and run with it?

"Sweetie," she said. "Let me give you a hug. Then we need to talk. Would the park across the street work out okay?"

Chapter Fourteen

"I HAVE A BETTER idea," Maya said, which made me smile. People rarely had the gumption to come up with alternate plans to Veronica's; at least ones they'd own up to. Me included. "Let's go to the Point Pinos Lighthouse."

Veronica looked down at her bare legs and frowned, then pulled the folded tube of denim out of her hobo bag with the theatrics of a magician pulling a rabbit out of a hat and zipped it back in place.

Maya whistled. "You and Emily Fish may have a lot in common."

"Fish?" Veronica said. "Tell me you're not serious."

"Emily Fish. The Point Pinos Lighthouse keeper. She's been dead for 70 years. But I often feel her presence there."

Veronica rolled her eyes, and I imagined her thinking, *Help. Hypomania is genetic.*

"So, it's a go," Maya said. It was not a question.

"Sure, why not? Right up Marjorie's alley."

"I love lighthouses," I said to seal the deal, but also out of curiosity. Would I, too, feel Emily Fish's presence? Part of me thrilled at the idea, the other part, not so. Fear of my drifts into the spiritual realm had faded thanks to Dr. Mendez, but absorbing and comprehending the possibility of connecting with a world beyond the earthly didn't jibe with my twenty-nine-year conditioning about what constituted reality.

During the drive to the lighthouse with me at the wheel, Maya's stories about Emily Fish prevented any mention of her disfigurement. Veronica would get to it in time though. She'd wait until just the right moment.

"Emily served as lighthouse keeper for twenty-one years," Maya said, "an occupation usually reserved for men. I often wonder how she lorded it over all those men who stood watch and maintained the grounds, when I can't even handle one."

If she was referring to Dr. Donovan, we both had our albatross. Cliff Smotherman happened to be mine. Unlike Dr. Donovan, though, Cliff was old news. Hopefully, like old news, he'd soon fade to the recesses of my mind as a distant memory.

Maya directed me into the lighthouse parking lot and said, "Emily even kept her cool during the earthquake of 1906. Can you imagine, with the lighthouse shaking, shifting, and cracking?"

Strong, just like Veronica, at least so she'd appeared to the outside world. Was Emily ever lonely? Did she cry when she thought she was alone? Who was *her* albatross?

"Her funeral service was held at St. Mary's by-the-Sea Episcopal Church on June 24, 1931," Maya said.

It was only a short walk from the parking lot to the lighthouse, but the wind was brisk and chilly and whistled as it swooshed through dense sprays of flat-topped cypress. Gray clouds swelled overhead, promising rain. We bent forward, fighting the force of the wind as the ocean roared its greeting. The flag on the flagpole snapped as if someone were using it as a whip.

"Let's go inside," Maya said, her drab outfit more practical as insulation from the piercing wind than our more stylish ones.

We hurried up five steps and entered the well-maintained Cape Cod bungalow through a small front porch. No other visitors were in attendance, so after putting our contributions into the donation box, we opted for a self-guided tour. Maya led us into a small parlor which, with its rocking chair, flowered area rug, and unlit fireplace, provided a cozy retreat for a cold winter's day. We took the spiral staircase to Emily's bedroom, which also featured a rocking chair and fireplace, along with a Victorian-style twin bed and a desk and a dresser. My favorite area, though, turned out to be the lookout room. A wall of windows faced the ocean with sunlight streaming through, eliciting a sense of awe and a longing for self-reflection. I imagined myself sitting here hour after hour, day after day, filling a logbook with my observations.

"If you stand here long enough and allow it to happen, you can sense her," Maya said as she eased into the narrow space at my side. The warmth of Maya's presence made me wonder about the long hours Emily Fish must've stood at this very spot, alone. What a strong, self-possessed woman she must've been.

We gazed at the churning ocean in quiet contemplation until Veronica broke in, "I'd say, with Emily's grit and fortitude to inspire us, this would be a good time to have a little talk." She sat in Emily's chair, probably against tour rules, but fitting. Veronica, too, could have handled a thirty-man crew and an earthquake.

She turned the chair to face Maya. "You wouldn't guess by looking at me now, but wearing black boosts my mood and self-image, especially if it's black leather. Red comes in a close second, leather or not." She eyed her denim ensemble and frowned, then focused on me. "Marjorie garners comfort and strength from the mouse totem she carries around, usually in a fanny pack, today probably in one of her jacket pockets."

I knew what was coming, but if Maya had a clue, she didn't let on. In fact, she looked interested in what Veronica was about to say. And Veronica didn't disappoint. "What is it, dear sister, that gives you that extra sense of comfort and strength?"

Maya's hand went to her face, as I knew it would, and what happened next was also predictable, though it didn't prevent me from holding my breath. She took Veronica's hand and placed it over her birthmark, a deformity that marked her as different from her otherwise identical sisters, a deformity that made her whom she was.

At first, Veronica offered a tolerant smile, the look of someone willing to bend for the sake of a cause. But her smile soon faded into a frown, tolerance into confusion, then understanding. "Beats black leather to hell," she said, her eyes welling with tears.

I knew what she was experiencing, a sudden realization that something as unsightly as the birthmark on Maya's face could be something of value. Would anyone choose beauty over such incredible contentment? Maybe. But just as many would pay a fortune to perceive what Maya perceived on a daily basis.

"I wish I could bottle how it makes me feel and share it with the world," Maya said, "but I gave up on that idea a long time ago. All I can do is share my gift in other ways, by striving to brighten other people's lives through service. If I kept all this happiness pent up inside, I'd burst."

"What about Dr. Donovan?" I asked. "We met him at yoga class. He said he wants to remove your mark."

She smiled, but I glimpsed a touch of sadness in her eyes, not sadness that rose from the core of her as I'd sensed in Veronica, but sadness for the pain of others, which was her life mission to help ease, if not erase. "Shane's vocation requires intelligence, courage, and creativity, not necessarily an open and understanding heart. What he sees as broken is what I most prize."

"Have you told him how you feel?" I asked, already presuming the answer.

"Many times. But he's absorbed with the idea of 'fixing' me rather than grasping the selfless union that true love inspires."

Veronica shot out of her chair. "Then just say no."

"Let's head outdoors," Maya said, "where it'll be easier for me to explain my relationship with Shane."

Once outside, Maya removed her baseball cap and shook her hair free. She braced her legs and leaned forward, arms spread wide. The wind buffeted her, but she held firm. "Do you feel the wind's force, how hard it is to stand up to it and not bend to its will?"

"Well, yeah," Veronica said, dropping back her head and closing her eyes.

I silently sang the lyrics to "Blowing in the Wind." *The answer, my friend, is...*

"When you sense the power of the ocean as it slams against the rocks," Maya continued, "does it fill you with excitement and at the same time fear?" We both nodded, but she didn't appear to notice. "That's how it is when I'm around Shane. He thrills me. Yet I know if I allow it, he will crush me."

The three of us joined hands, an unspoken gesture of unity and defiance against the ocean, the wind, maybe even Dr. Shane Donovan. Our clothes snapped. Our bodies swayed. But we pressed our weight forward and stretched to our full height. "We're with you on this one," I said, thinking about Cliff and how he'd tried to control me in the name of love.

Maya stood between Veronica and me, and I wondered if she had unconsciously taken her place as the middle sister. Was she born second and I third, or the other way around? Maybe soon our father would provide the answer.

"Thank you," Maya said. She let go of our hands and turned toward the road behind us—something I'll always remember, her letting go, her turning away. "El Carmelo Cemetery is across the road from where we're parked. I'd like to take you there."

I glanced at Veronica. Her response, a shudder.

"Come on," Maya called over her shoulder as she sprinted down the paved lane leading to the parking lot.

Veronica and I followed at a slower pace.

"What's gotten into her?" Veronica asked.

"Don't know," I said.

Maya crossed Asilomar Avenue, but instead of swerving toward the cemetery, she made a sharp left and halted in front of a nondescript building standing close to the road. "It's called the Little Chapel by the Sea," she said when we caught up to her. "Such a peaceful place to rest."

I glanced at Veronica, wondering if she, too, sensed something wrong, but expression gave nothing away.

We followed Maya to the cemetery, only a short jaunt south of the chapel. Okay, so the maintained grounds exemplified a peaceful place of repose, the purpose of cemeteries after all, but Maya was only twenty-nine, too young to favor the resting place of the dead.

"Are we visiting someone's grave?" I asked.

"No grave in particular," she said, "though many of the people here feel like close acquaintances. I visit them often enough." She twirled, arms raised, bringing to mind visions of my childhood when I did the same, though not in cemeteries.

"Isn't this kind of morbid," Veronica asked, pinning Maya with her gaze, "even for someone as well-adjusted and contented as you?"

"Heavens no," Maya said, still twirling amid the gravestones. Next, she'd be turning cartwheels. "Death is a transition, not the end of our conscious experience. These people's souls are free from the shackles of their physical bodies and have transcended to the heavenly realm, where the body is no longer needed."

"Heaven for all?" Veronica asked, as if catching her in a lie or gross overstatement. "What about hell?"

Maya shrugged. "People experience hell on earth, not in the hereafter."

A quote attributed to Native American author Vine Deloria Jr. sprang from my ever-expanding memory. "Religious people believe in hell. Spiritual people have been there."

Turning in a slow circle, arms raised to encompass all the graves, I asked, "You believe all these people are happy?"

"Yes," Maya said, "as we will be someday."

"No matter what wrongs they committed while here on earth?"

"They suffered enough for their wrongs before they died."

"Tell you what," I said. "Veronica and I are staying at a place that is close to heaven. I'd like to take you there."

Chapter Fifteen

MAYA HAD PROMISED THAT if we met her at St. Mary's the following Sunday, she'd visit us at Anne's house. That left a week for Veronica and me to entertain ourselves. Veronica disappeared into the basement again, with occasional trips upstairs for a meal. These trips came without warning, though, so I didn't have enough food prepared for both of us. No problem. According to Veronica, she could survive on the nutritional supplements she'd discovered in the basement.

My particular form of entertainment was walking. During the week, I explored Lighthouse Avenue from one end of Pacific Grove to the other, roamed large sections of Ocean View Boulevard, and, at dusk on Friday, ended up back at the Point Pinos Lighthouse. I love lighthouses in general, but this one was particularly accessible. Instead of confining myself inside, though, I sat on a bench below a windswept cypress facing the ocean.

I can't say how long I listened to the crashing waves and screeching seagulls before I felt a presence as palpable as if a real person were sitting next to me. At first, I thought it might be Emily Fish, since Maya had mentioned feeling her presence here. I eliminated that possibility though. This being, this consciousness, didn't come across as forceful enough, not the type who could manage a lighthouse and a crew of thirty on a lonely peninsula during an earthquake.

I then thought perhaps it was my ancestor, Margarita, but as time passed and the presence revealed no more of itself, I also eliminated that possibility. Though Margarita had never spoken to me directly, I would've been able to follow her thoughts like impressions on the surrounding landscape.

Antonia, too, would've made herself known by now, probing, prodding, plotting.

I continued to sit, unperturbed by my silent companion. In fact, I felt a familiar intimacy with whomever it was, a deep understanding.

Marjorie? It's Maya.

"Hold it," I said. "You're alive. I only hear the—"

Alive and have the whole St. Mary's choir as a witness.

"Please tell me they aren't listening to you right now."

Nah. I have my eyes closed. They think I'm praying.

"Can you see me?"

Of course. I'm sitting right next to you.

Until now, my only telepathic communication had been with the dead. Not that they ever listened. It was more of a one-sided conversation, with them doing the talking and me doing the listening. Apparently, I was a better receiver than transmitter. "No, you're not."

Something brushed against my cheek, followed by a charge running through me as if I'd rubbed against something wooly and experienced the resulting static.

"Okay, okay I believe you."

As far as I knew, there was no scientific evidence to support telepathy in twins or triplets. Sure, multiples had deep emotional connections, but nothing out of the ordinary. Veronica, Maya, and I didn't dress alike; we had different occupations, different temperaments. What was going on here?

We're one, Marjorie, a connection that can't be severed.

"You mean united until death."

Even at death, especially then. We'll always be together.

I stood and faced the ocean on unsteady legs. The sun would set soon, which meant another miraculous watercolor display, but the only miracle that concerned me now was that Maya was communicating with me from miles away without the use of a cell phone or CB. Brain power, instead of towers or satellites. Impossible. Yet, I couldn't deny what I'd heard.

What was the purpose of Maya's little experiment, besides playing with fire? I'd seen on the Discovery Channel once that priests had to exorcize a young man who'd brought evil spirits into his life simply by messing with a Quija Board.

The first time Antonia spoke to me, she'd scared me half to death, calling me "Sunwalker" and telling me there was something I must know. Until then my life had been normal, predictable. I'd believed dead people stayed dead and that their spirits resided in heaven or hell or someplace in-between. I'd never dreamt that only a thin veil separated the dead from the living and that the reason we couldn't hear the deceased was because we weren't listening. At least not with the appropriate ears.

My stomach ached, a familiar case of spiritual indigestion. How did this mind-to-mind communication work? Was it a God-given gift, a sixth sense meant to be used, or more like partaking of a forbidden fruit? Would God kick me out of Eden for using it?

Maya came as close to an angel as anyone in my experience, and she'd just used her telepathic powers on me. Was this anymore evil than picking up a cell phone, punching in a few numbers, and hitting send?

"What do you want?" I blurted, not meaning to be rude.

To lead the part of you that's not constrained by your physical body to the place you visit in your dreams. Veronica's next.

"No," I said. "If Veronica gets wind of what you're trying to do, she'll block you out for sure."

Okay then, forget about Veronica for now. Close your eyes and concentrate on the ocean waves.

"Not before I have a little chit chat with our Creator," I said, feeling the need for some godly support.

No comment from Maya.

"If what I'm about to do is wrong, God, please send me a sign, and I promise not to do it again."

Now sit back down and breathe deeply. Maya said.

"What if someone attacks me while I'm gone?"

I'll be there to protect you.

As Veronica would say, "Oh shit."

I sat back down, per Maya's instructions, and took several deep breaths.

Concentrate on the waves.

"Got it, close my eyes and concentrate on the ocean waves." Wild waves, advancing and receding, advancing and receding.

Now give me your hand.

I felt Maya's icy touch and shivered. "You're pushing me to places I don't want to go."

Just leading you to your center where you'll find your true self.

"I doubt it."

Maya's invisible presence was added proof to what I'd experienced with Margarita and Antonia, that consciousness could exist beyond the confines of the physical body. Either that, or I was having a disturbingly lucid hallucination. "Do I need to lie down for this?"

Sitting is fine.

After another bout of deep breathing, I experienced a wavering sense of instability. Strong vibrations erupted from the pit of me, accompanied by what sounded like an orchestra of field crickets rubbing their leathery front wings together. Maya was no longer holding my hand, at least not the hand now suspended above my physical one, a hand I saw even with my eyes closed, as though one part of me had separated from, and was floating above, the other.

Waves of pulsating colors, skin electric. boundaries expanding, relax, relax. I'm running across the grassy stretch behind the lighthouse. The earth feels soft and supple, yielding to the impressions of my feet. I take a giant leap, my translucent arms stretched to the sky. No words can express the lightness, the freedom of release from my earthly burden. I land softly, take another leap. Oh Lord, I'm floating. Higher and higher. No salty smell of iodine in the air, no resistance of wind against my skin, no separation between past and present, present and future. This has to be an illusion. The mind can't travel beyond the confines of the body or see the earth or hear the ocean below without physical eyes and ears. I'm floating over El Carmelo Cemetery, past a car and a pedestrian, then swerve left.

Anne's house is below. Round-roofed turret, circular driveway, gazebo, bird-bath—front door. It's locked. No problem. I ease right through it. A reflection in the crystal ball, then the mirror. Don't look. Don't want to wake from the dream. Down the basement stairs with no fear of falling. Flying like an angel. Veronica is lying on the round bed. Crying. Not real. Veronica never cries. She's too strong.

"Hey, Sis," I say.

Veronica jerks up, pulls something from under her pillow. "Who's there?"

I've never had a pistol pointed at me before. Can't hurt me, though. This isn't real. "It's me, Marjorie."

Veronica lowers her handgun. "Where are you?"

"Sitting on a bench behind the Point Pinos Lighthouse."

"Yeah, and I'm the tooth fairy."

"I don't quite believe it myself. Why don't you take the Jeep and meet me there?"

Veronica slides off the bed, tucks the pistol back under her pillow. If nothing else, she's no longer crying. "This is nuts. I'm nuts. No chance of getting into the DEA now."

Back to the lighthouse. Hurry. Have to get there before Veronica.

Oh God, oh God. That's me sitting on the bench below. How do I get back in? Will it hurt?

Something's pulling at me as if the body below and the part of me floating above are connected by an elastic cord.

Down, down. I'm transitioning from one world to another as though waking from a dream. Will part of me stay behind?

Focus, focus.

Smack. My spirit is dragged back into flesh and bone so fast the wind is knocked out of me. Blood rushes in my ears. My surroundings blur.

Cold, so cold. Can't move.

Don't panic. Breathe.

The mood of the ocean and texture of the air had changed, grumbling, stirring, electric, as if God were angry.

After thirty seconds of paralysis, I found myself bracing against the wind. Darn it was cold. Would Veronica show? Part of me hoped she would, the other part hoped she wouldn't. If she showed. My God, if she showed. That would prove this wasn't a dream, but real.

"Veronica," I called when she sprinted around the corner of the lighthouse.

She halted, put her hand to her mouth, then slid to the ground.

I ran to her and dropped to my knees.

"Just when I thought I was getting my head on straight," she said, "you offer me this."

"I'm sort of having a problem with it myself."

"*You're* having a problem?"

"If it's this easy to detach from the body and—"

"Easy? You almost blew my mind."

"Well, you know what I mean."

She looked at the moody ocean, then at the dark clouds. "There's a storm coming in. But...ain't it grand?"

"Yeah," I said. "Good thing you brought the Jeep."

✿✿✿

On the short drive to the house, we didn't speak; too many questions, too many improbable answers. After parking the Jeep, Veronica said, "Show me the labyrinth."

So, she'd been listening to my labyrinth spiel after all.

It started to sprinkle. No problem. We were both wearing water-proof jackets and could rush indoors if it turned into a downpour.

I led Veronica to the entrance of what I now thought of as a path of healing and prayer.

"You and your circles," she said, though not unkindly. "First the Native American Medicine Wheel, then the *Magick* Circle, now this."

"Hey," I said, leading her onto the winding path to the labyrinth's center, "the Magick Circle was Anne's contribution, which you've got to admit, helped us contact Antonia while in Big Sur. And this, well, I uncovered it, but I didn't build it. And once uncovered, I couldn't ignore it. You would've wondered at Anne's purpose in putting it here, too. My take is that these circles are human sanctuaries, like the Monarch Sanctuary for the butterflies."

"Truus would have a fit if she heard you right now," Veronica said.

"I know."

A wet mist swathed our hair, our jackets, and the concrete path.

"Will we need an *athame* to direct psychic energy and cut the doorway on our way out?" Veronica asked.

"No ceremonial daggers required," I said. "Just walk and allow for what comes."

"Okay then, while we're walking and allowing for what comes, please explain, to the best of your knowledge, what happened out there on the beach."

"You've got me," I said. "Teleportation. Out of body experience. They've done experiments at Stanford—"

"Spare me the facts that explain nothing."

"Maya tried it on me so—"

"You tried it on me. Which makes it okay?"

"Let's try contacting Maya. Maybe she can explain."

Veronica shrugged as if she couldn't care less.

I took her hand as we stepped into the labyrinth's center, not sure if I liked her this way, passive, accommodating. "Does this scare you?" I asked.

"What do you think?"

"I know the feeling."

Sprinkles turned to rain, but I was too intent on our mission to care. I concentrated hard, picturing a narrow tunnel leading from my mind to Maya's. "Let's sing the song she sang last Sunday."

"Sure, why not?" Veronica said, "in place of an incantation."

I hummed into the imaginary tunnel until the song lyrics arose from my memory.

The Lord stands knocking at the door to your heart,

A door that opens from within. Let him in.

Veronica joined in, her low, resonant, Mama Cass voice so like Maya's.

Hello sister, I know how you've been,

98

I know troubled times are upon you.
A third voice joined in. Maya!
Your tears I feel like rain, I want to ease your pain,
What will it take for you to turn to me?
When you leave here today, I'm with you all the way;
And if you need a friend, all you have to do is ask me in.
When the three of us reached the end of the song— *Let me in.* —
Veronica and I were both crying. We dropped back our heads and
let the rain stream down our faces. "God, this feels good," Veronica
said. So good in fact that time became timeless, and we soaked up
the rain with no sense of how long before making our way back out
of the labyrinth.

"First one out of the shower makes tea," I said as we stomped
through the back door and into the laundry room. We stripped off
our wet clothes and dropped them into the utility sink, our bodies
pink with cold and covered in goosebumps.

Veronica headed for her apartment in the basement. "Add a tea-
spoon of sugar to mine. And I'd appreciate it if you'd whip up a
salad."

For the second time since coming to Pacific Grove, she sounded
hopeful.

Chapter Sixteen

A S VERONICA AND I neared the yoga studio, I wasn't in a good mood. In fact, I was itching for a fight. After what happened last night, I wanted to talk, push for answers. Why, for instance, had Veronica been crying when I visited her in the basement, and why did she keep a pistol hidden under her pillow? Okay, so I could explain the pistol. She'd worked with the DEA in the past and was applying for a permanent job there, so she knew more about crime than I did and was therefore more cautious, more aware of what could happen. The crying part wasn't as easy to explain though I suspected it related to our father. *Her* albatross.

But Veronica wanted to go to yoga class. No yoga posture, no method of breath control, no power of meditation would put me at ease as long as Dr. Shane Donovan was around. The guy rubbed me the wrong way. He claimed to love Maya, yet wanted to take away what she valued most. How could he believe in his heart he was doing the right thing?

After parking the car, I reached behind the seat for our yoga mats. "About last night in the basement—"

"You shouldn't have been spying on me," Veronica said.

"Maya came to me telepathically and said she wanted to lead me to the place I visit in my dreams. She said she would try it on you next, but I told her not to. That if you caught on, you'd block her."

"I see. So, *you* experimented on me instead."

"I didn't think I'd be able to do it. Figured if I played along—"

"Let's drop it, okay?"

"If there's anything I can do..."

"Marjorie."

"All right. Subject dropped. And just so you know, this'll be my last yoga class. I can't stand being around that doctor friend of yours anymore."

"Okay."

"And I refuse to put up with anymore of yoga's physical torture."

"Fine with me."

I paused. Why was Veronica letting me off the hook without a fuss? "If Dr. Donovan asks us to lunch again, do you plan on going?"

"Nope."

"What if he wants to talk to us?"

"Then we listen."

"Where?"

"On the sidewalk outside the studio."

I eyed my sister as she slid out of the Jeep. Something was going on in that head of hers, and I wished I knew what it was. Maybe if I concentrated hard, I could read her—

Veronica smiled. "Can't do it, can you?"

I got out of the Jeep and slammed the door. She was blocking me out as I knew she would when she caught on to Maya's out-of-body experiment.

"Fool me once, shame on you," Veronica said. "Fool me twice—"

"Yeah, yeah, I get it." *Smart ass.*

On our drive over, the streets had been lined with marching bands and kids dressed as nectar flowers, striped caterpillars, and monarchs with pipe-cleaner antennae, so it came as a surprise that we'd arrived on time. And, despite the pre-butterfly parade crowds, we even got there before Dr. Donovan. I dropped my mat in a spot for two and began my meditative chant.

Even with my eyes closed, I knew when the doctor entered the room. I sensed his hesitation when he noticed that Veronica and I had chosen a new location without saving a place for him. I sensed his initial disappointment and, for a moment, felt sorry for him.

101

Sandra started with the Sun Salutation, and, before I'd even broken a sweat, she led us through postures with catchy names like Lotus Pose and Boat Pose. She didn't let up for an hour, encouraging us to stretch, bend, breathe, and sweat until I was pooped, which left me little time—or inclination—to fret over Dr. Shane Donovan.

When Sandra instructed us to lie on our backs with our legs straight and arms at our sides in the Corpse Pose, I was so grateful I nearly cried. My body relaxed, all thoughts passing from my mind like floating soap bubbles. "Come back to the breath, back to the breath, to the breath, the breath, breath..."

"Want to join me for lunch?" came a voice from above.

Sandra had emphasized that participants were not to interrupt one another during yoga practice. What was up with this guy?

"It's about Maya," Dr. Donovan said.

Oh, so that makes it okay? I stood and rolled up my yoga mat, wanting to tell him to pick on somebody else, that my sister deserved better, but then I recalled the gentle compassion in Maya's eyes when she'd told Veronica and me about her strong attraction to this man.

"No lunch today," Veronica said airily as the three of us walked to the cubby to pick up our shoes and keys. "But we'll join you for a walk if you like."

If the doctor was disappointed, he didn't let on. "Guess that'll have to do."

"East or west?" Veronica asked as we headed for the door.

"East," I said. Otherwise, we'd run into all those kids doing practice flights for the butterfly parade. The child in me wanted to join in on the fun, arms waving, antennae bobbing, but not with Dr. Donovan as a sidekick.

We'd made it to Forest Avenue before he glanced at Veronica and asked, "Have you convinced Maya to let me remove her birthmark?"

"Sorry, can't do," she said. "The choice is hers. You should know that."

His frown showed this wasn't the reply he'd expected. At least not from Veronica. "What made you change your mind?"

A moment passed before Veronica halted and faced him. "Force Maya's hand and you'll regret it."

"I know what's best for her. She'll thank me later."

A sudden memory hit like a haunting. My ex-fiancé, Cliff, and I standing at the site of the Lone Cypress on the 17-Mile-Drive near Monterey, where I heard the voice of my dead mother for the first time. I thought I was losing my mind and turned to Cliff for support, but his attention was focused on the condition of his camera, which had slipped from my hands onto the observation deck. "Damn it," he said. "I told you to be careful. See what happens when I listen to you." He'd insisted until the end that he knew what was best for me, and that I didn't know what the hell I was talking about.

Cliff and Dr. Donovan could've been clones.

"Continue on your current path, Dr. Donovan," I said, "and you'll lose Maya." He shook his head, but I wasn't done. "She knows her own mind, and I think that's one thing you love about her. You love her gentleness and kindness and the way she cares for others. Maybe if you think about it long enough, you'll realize you can love her birthmark, too."

The high-browed, I'm-a-doctor-not-a-philosopher look he presented me before turning to Veronica made me want to spit. "Maya's attitude contradicts all reason and common sense. She could have it all."

"She already does," Veronica said softly.

But the doctor wasn't having it. "Don't you want Maya to know what it feels like to be beautiful like you?"

"Let it be, Shane," Veronica said.

He shrugged. "Ultimately, she'll do what I say."

"And you're proud of that?" Veronica asked.

"I'm saving her."

"Damn it," Veronica said. "Mankind has started wars, destroyed nations, and murdered innocent people using that twisted logic. I'm

103

saving her. I'm saving my people. I'm saving my country.' Why not allow for her own perception of the truth?"

A thought nagged at me. Were my intentions toward Maya somehow superior to Dr. Donovan's? Protect or save? Where lay the difference? In my attempt to shield her from the man she loved, was I allowing for Maya's own perception of the truth?

"This is different," Dr. Donovan said.

"Yeah," Veronica said, "it always is."

Chapter Seventeen

IT WAS SUNDAY AND Maya was coming for a visit. Her only means of transportation, besides the generosity of friends, was an old mountain bike, so we'd arranged to pick her up after Mass at St. Mary's. As eleven o'clock rolled around, Veronica and I stood on the sidewalk between Central Avenue and the small portico entrance to the church. Organ music swelled from every gap, slit, and hollow of the building, announcing the end of Mass. We stepped aside for the parishioners streaming down the entry stairs and onto the church grounds, waving to and greeting perfect strangers as if they were close friends.

Since Maya was a member of the choir, we expected her to be one of the last to exit the church, but after a fifteen-minute wait and the clearing of all the Sunday worshipers, we grew concerned that she hadn't yet appeared. Veronica paced back and forth, shoulders back, hands on hips like a catwalk model. "She should've just told us where she lived."

"She must have a good reason for meeting us here," I said. "Bet she'll invite us over soon." Veronica was back to dressing *Victoria's Secret* style: black jeans, slinky snakeskin top, and black stilettos with four-inch heels. Seemed she'd grown tired of Anne's wardrobe after just one try. She'd fastened a black cardigan around her waist in case it got cold, which, in my opinion, occurred over an hour ago. I shivered just looking at her. I, too, wore jeans, the color of wheat, topped by a white cotton shirt. But instead of tying the arms of my navy jacket around my waist for future use, I was wearing the darn thing, not about to let the sleeves wrinkle or myself to freeze for the sake of fashion or vanity. What a sight, sisters identical in face and body, yet so different. Black hair and blonde. Slinky and status quo.

"Where is she?" Veronica asked, as though she expected me to see through the walls of the church. Okay, so, I'd spied on her once from the beach miles away, but that didn't mean I could—or would—do it again. Not worth the mental and spiritual strain.

"Um," I said, noting Veronica's growing impatience. I didn't want her walking off in a huff. "I'll go inside and take a look."

"Good idea. I'll wait out here in case she shows via a different route."

Maya was easy to spot, kneeling in one of the front pews, head bent in prayer.

Dear God, forgive me for asking, but what could Maya be praying for so intently? She's already an angel. I waited until she touched the tips of her fingers to her forehead, chest, and shoulders, before walking up the center aisle and sliding in next to her on the wooden bench. "Still coming for a visit?" I asked.

She turned, blinked, and rubbed her eyes as if waking from a dream. "Sorry. I had some catching up to do." Her eyes widened when she noticed we were the only ones left in the church. "Took longer than expected." She looked over her shoulder. "Where's Veronica?"

Concerned about her the glassy look in her eyes, I stayed put, prepared to catch her if she passed out and fell. "Outside, champing at the bit. If we don't get a move on, she'll probably go hide out in the Victorian's basement, her version of a man cave."

"Not without me, she won't," Maya said, pushing to a stand.

❂❂❂

Maya declared Anne's house too awesome for words and insisted on a full tour. As we moved from room to room, floor to floor, she gasped at the scroll and ivy-patterned wallpaper and carved moldings, the chandeliers, the brocade drapes, and the oriental carpets lain over wooden floors. I, too, was seeing many of the rooms for the first time. Besides my turret suite and the ground floor and basement, I'd pretty much ignored the rest of the house until now. When Veronica led us to her underground digs, Maya was transfixed. Who wouldn't be? The place had the floating-through-the-clouds look of a Hollywood depiction of heaven.

What impressed Maya most, however, lay just outside the kitchen door. "A labyrinth," she cried when we stepped outside. "I've been trying to get management to put one in at work for holistic empowerment, but the cost has been prohibitive. Let's walk it together."

Right off, the birds' companion calls sounded sweeter, the crows' caws less jarring, earthy sounds echoing the beat of my happy heart. Even the sulfury, briny ocean scent agreed with me as we weaved our way to the rose center and back out again, each at our own pace.

Maya was last to finish. "I hear they have a labyrinth at the Grace Cathedral in San Francisco," she said. "I'd love to walk it sometime. Will you join me?"

"Sure," I said, hoping this wasn't an empty promise. Vows, no matter how earnest, often go by the way of the wind, never to experience the joys of fruition.

Veronica walked over to the concrete bench stationed under a canopy of Monterey cypress and sat down.

"What's up with her?" Maya asked.

"Don't know. Let's find out."

As we neared the bench, Veronica patted the space next to her. "Squeeze in tight girls. Should be enough room for the three of us."

"Yeah," I said, "with half my butt hanging over."

"Don't be such a fusspot," she said.

I smiled. That was just the type of comeback Anne would've used. I wished she was here to share in our joy at being together.

Veronica waited for us to sit before sharing what was on her mind. "Maya, it's time you meet our father."

The impenetrable expression on Maya's face held the serene sadness of Michelangelo's Madonna of Bruges in which Mary appears to know of the hardships she and her son would encounter up ahead.

MARGARET DUARTE

"It'll be upsetting for you," Veronica said, "maybe even a shock, but..." She shifted her weight and stared at her palms. "He's an alcoholic, and..."

Maya took Veronica's hand, which appeared to be shaking. "I try not to, but I can pretty much read your mind. Even when we're not together. I think it has something to do with sharing the same DNA and having similar brain wave patterns, which makes our connection closer than with others. When you hurt, I hurt. When you're happy, I'm happy. So, I know how hard this is for you. I've tried sending positive vibes your way, but apparently haven't been all that successful."

"Telepathy between multiples is fiction," Veronica said.

"Then call it an unspoken knowing, without having to ask or explain," I said, remembering how I'd felt when Gerardo, my adoptive father, called me his little flower and told me he loved me, an intense empathy and bond rather than something mystical and unexplainable.

"Tell me about our father," Maya said, her voice a soft, tapering trill. "Did he share with you why he gave me away?"

"He didn't give you away," I objected. "At least not by choice. Antonia—"

"Don't excuse him," Veronica said from her end of the bench. She balled her free hand into a fist. "I'm so mad at him, I could wring his neck, but I've learned from experience it wouldn't do any good."

Maya released Veronica's hand so she could wipe the moisture from her eyes.

"The more I learn about the mess he made of our lives and his own," Veronica said, "the more sense it makes why he's so sick. But he's not too much of a drunk to tell us what happened. He owes us that much."

Maya looked at me in silent appeal.

I sensed the empathy and bond of our shared genetics, but the part about an unspoken knowing without having to ask failed me.

"He didn't raise you either, did he?" Maya asked.

"No," I said, glad we had that in common at least. This way she wouldn't feel as left out.

"I've waited a long time for an explanation," Maya said. "Guess another day or two won't hurt."

"You did hear me when I said he is an alcoholic?" Veronica said.

The expression on Maya's face remained calm. "I work with alcoholics every day. It's what I do."

The mist-filled air soothed my hot cheeks, and I felt an internal soothing as well, as if Earth's cool breath had penetrated my heart and mind. "Are you a nurse?"

"A social worker," she said. "I'm drawn to people with dependencies. When they see the mark on my face, their situations seem less hopeless. It brings out their empathy for others."

"About our father," Veronica prompted.

Maya slid off the bench and crouched in front of us. "I suspect there are a few things you need to know about his disease."

"I've lived with his damn disease half my life," Veronica said. "You think I need to know more?"

Maya smiled. "It's plain as the mark on my face that you both do."

"Me!" I blurted. "I just met the guy."

Maya took my hand in hers and squeezed it. "Let's start with Veronica, okay?"

"Okay by me," I said, ashamed of my outburst. Darn right, I needed to know more about alcoholism, if there was any hope of forming a relationship with my father. Veronica's best efforts at helping him battle his disease had proven inadequate. She needed to detach herself so she could get on with her life. Would I be able to do the same? Would I be able to stand by and watch the man who'd fathered me hit rock bottom, in hopes that he'd use it as a springboard to launch a recovery?

"How about we head inside to the kitchen," Maya suggested. "That way Veronica and I can talk while you brew us a pot of tea."

Good idea. It was getting chilly outside. Besides, Maya looked uncomfortable crouched in front of us on the damp pavement.

After leading the way in, I filled the teakettle with water and put it on the stove to heat. Meanwhile, Veronica and Maya settled at the dinette table in the breakfast nook. A burst of bassoon-like caws infused the lull in conversation, while the hum of the refrigerator and hiss of the teakettle filled the spaces between.

Into the orchestra of sounds, came the sweet cello of Maya's voice. "You've been amassing resentment, anger, and regrets for too long, Veronica. You're paralyzed by them."

"I'm tired of it all," Veronica admitted.

My hands shook as I poured boiling water into the ceramic teapot and added a bag of black tea.

"Your father has a right to do as he pleases," Maya said. "As do you."

"You're saying he has a right to drink himself to death?" Veronica asked.

"Yes."

"And get sicker until he dies or goes insane."

"Or feels enough pain to get help."

"I can't take that chance."

"Since when do *you* have control over your father's choices?" Maya asked, her voice soft, neutral. "Has all the yelling, crying, and counseling helped one bit?"

"No," Veronica said. "He rationalizes and justifies and convinces himself that lies are truths and truths are lies."

"You didn't cause him to drink," Maya said, "and you can't make him stop. Alcoholics are sick and therefore self-centered. He'll only quit if it's in his own best interest to do so."

Tears trailed down Veronica's face, which filled me with regret. It wasn't until I tasted salt on my lips that I realized I was crying, too. "You don't know how much it helps to have someone explain that to me," Veronica said. "I've tried so hard."

"I know," Maya said.

Knees shaking, I carried two mugs of steeped tea to the table, followed by creamer and sugar.

"Thanks, Marjorie," Maya said. She pulled out a chair and signaled for me to sit down. "Your turn."

Veronica stood and headed for the kitchen counter. She returned with another mug of tea. "Drink up, Marge. You might not be able to get it down later."

The warm liquid brought welcome relief from the salty taste in my mouth. What could Maya say that would make any difference at this point?

"You think that now you've finally found our father, you'll lose him," she said.

Her comment felt like a stomach jab, and I nearly spit up my tea. "I've waited so long."

"Me, too," she said. "Me, too. But losing him won't be that easy."

"What do you mean?" I said.

"Ask Veronica."

When I looked at our older sister, she gave me a sad smile. "Maya's right. He's not that easy to lose."

"Don't get sucked into his games," Maya warned. "You don't need his crumbs of affection, and what you do will never be enough."

I glanced at Veronica. She nodded.

"This all sounds so negative," I said.

Maya gazed down at her mug of tea, which was still full. "It is, I'm afraid. At times like this, it's best to use your mind instead of your heart. Feeling sorry for him and catering to his illness will only make things worse. For you as well as for our father. Actually, there's nothing wrong with the disgust you feel."

Disgust? Revulsion was a better word for the way I felt on first meeting him. To say nothing of the guilt I'd experienced since.

I set down my mug.

Maya reached out to steady it. "I mean it, Marjorie. You must find your own serenity. And rebuild from there."

Chapter Eighteen

HOW COULD MAYA REMAIN so calm? This would be the first time she would meet the man who had abandoned her as a child. Yet there she stood, more concerned about Veronica's and my well-being than her own. On my first meeting with our father, I'd had my head in the clouds, with thoughts of catching up and healing old wounds, an imagined scenario ungrounded in reality. But Maya knew about alcoholics, so she'd came prepared. Deliberate and thoughtful, she'd arrived intending to reach out to a man she had not imagined. Would it have made a difference if I had come with similar intentions and non-expectations?

Veronica rang the doorbell, then stepped back and lifted her chin. I did the same as I edged to the side of the entry, out of direct eye-shot of the man who would soon answer the door. Maya stood behind me, not hiding so much as staying out of the way.

The cottage our father had rented for his stay in Pacific Grove looked like a life-sized dollhouse, with its orange door and green trim. No one would guess that a depressed soul resided within. A bang came from inside, followed by a curse.

Veronica tensed.

I tried to think with my mind instead of my heart as Maya had suggested, but my heart was bouncing off the walls of my chest, making it hard to ignore. Our previous visit had turned into a disaster. So much anger, so much pain.

Maya put her hand on my shoulder.

Warmth coursed through me as if she had just dispensed a much-needed shot of serotonin. "Thank you," I whispered.

Bob yanked open the door, eyes narrowed, brows squeezed together, looking frightening, as people in pain often do. "Kicked the damn coffee table," he said.

At the sight of Veronica, his face cleared. "Oh, it's you."

"Hi Dad," she said. "May we come in?"

"We?" He peered past Veronica and grinned. "Oh hi, Marjorie. Long time no see."

Veronica edged past him and I followed, leaving him standing at the entry facing Maya.

I turned in time to see him slouch against the door frame. "Oh God," he said, before taking a deep, ragged breath.

Maya smiled. "Hi, Papa."

"I'm sorry," he said. "It wasn't supposed to be like this, please—"

"It's okay, Papa. Let me help you inside."

"You call me Papa after..."

"You *are* my father, aren't you?"

Bob wiped his eyes and allowed Maya to lead him to an armchair catty-corner to the sag-springed couch where I sat with a decorative pillow clasped on my lap. "You don't hate me?"

"You gave me life, Papa, and because of you, I have two beautiful sisters. Why would I hate you?"

"But your face..."

She smiled. "You mean, my gift?"

"Gift?"

Maya took Bob's hand and placed it over her birthmark. "It's hard to explain, but it's truly a gift."

Bob closed his eyes and his face cleared, as though he'd received a full dose of happy hormones—endorphin to block pain, dopamine to induce pleasure, serotonin to boost mood, oxytocin to enhance love. His breathing deepened, and he made no move to break contact with the source of such bliss and contentment.

"God. Maya," he said. "I feel... Oh my God, I feel..." He pulled his hand from Maya's cheek and looked at it as if it had become an instrument of healing, then pressed his palm against the stubble of his own cheek and held it there. "Could you... Could you make me feel like this all the time?"

"No, Papa, I can't."

"If I always felt this way, I'd..." He looked at the wide-bottomed decanter of liquor standing on the table with straight-up shiny impressiveness, apparently a replacement for the empty bottle of *Fat Bastard* chardonnay lying by its side. "My life would change, that's for sure."

Was it possible for our father to take that first step toward sobriety? Dared I hope?

Maya sat next to me on the couch positioned below a framed print of a ship navigating a stormy sea. Veronica had taken the wing-back chair to our left. The television was off, thank God, and the drapes drawn, giving the room a look of normalcy, unlike the people inside. "Are you going to run off like your two sisters did?" Bob, asked, motioning toward Veronica and me.

"If you want, you can reach me at any time."

"I don't know my way around Pacific Grove," he said. "Haven't been here that long. How about you come stay here with me?"

Maya's brow crinkled. "Are you sick?"

"No."

"Then why should I stay with you?"

"I'm lonely. I need you."

"When you need me, I'm not that hard to find. Pacific Grove is a small town."

Until then, Bob had concentrated all of his attention on Maya, so following her advice about saying little had been easy, though I had plenty of questions. Why, for instance, was he in Pacific Grove instead of in Maryland where he belonged? If he had traced Maya here, he would've known by now where she lived and worked, even met up with her and laid bare what was on his mind.

"I have three grown daughters," he said, "and none of them cares about me. Daughters should care about their fathers."

Veronica's shoulders tensed, but she said nothing.

114

I, too, said nothing, due to a loss for words. This man had no clue.

Maya crossed her legs, folded her hands, and rested her elbow on her knee. "Papa, please tell me the story of our birth and separation. I've waited so long."

Now, *that* caught his attention, at least to the point of ending his outburst of self-pity. It must've been the kind look on Maya's face and the way she'd said *Papa*. He stood and paced the room. "I could sure use a drink."

Veronica glanced at the decanter of liquor and upturned cocktail glass on the coffee table. I shook my head in sympathy—for my sister, for my father, for us all.

Maya said nothing, just continued to look at Bob with a serenity beyond my comprehension. He ran his hand over his stubbled chin and through his uncombed hair before sitting back down. "I suppose you want me to start from the beginning."

Maya nodded, her moral beauty so clearly etched on her face it was possible to forget that her birthmark was considered a deformity in this world of outward beauty.

Bob leaned forward, eyes closed, as if taking a mental trip into the past. How would his story compare to the one he had told Veronica, and later told me? "Thirty years ago," he said, "nine months before your birth, I came to Monterey on business… I'm a financial consultant, you know, a darn good one. You can ask—"

"Quit stalling," Veronica said. "We don't have all day."

He shot Veronica a pained look before continuing. "Having heard stories about the beauty of the 17-Mile Drive near Pebble Beach and the landmark of the Lone Cypress, I rented a car to check it out. That's where" —His voice caught, and he took a moment to compose himself— "That's where I met your mother. She stood facing the ocean, with the wind blowing through her long, black hair… Please understand. She was the most beautiful woman I'd ever seen. I couldn't tear my eyes away."

Maya's eyes crinkled in deep listening. "Go on."

"I don't know how long I watched her before she turned to leave—it could've been minutes, it could've been hours. But when our eyes met, my God." He smiled at Veronica for the first time since we'd entered the room. "Actually, she looked a lot like Vonnie."

Veronica frowned, her lips tight, as if she were withholding a silent scream. What was it costing her to hear the condensed, and possibly edited, version of our conception and birth, presented as a mistake that led to his addiction, with such remorse that it warranted an unconscious plea, if not outright request, for our forgiveness?

Perhaps Bob sensed her discomfort because he shook his head and refocused on Maya. "Except your mother's eyes were soft and caring like yours."

The implication was unkind, but likely true. Veronica's eyes often appeared cold and unfeeling. Like now. While Maya's could melt a glacier.

Our father said no more, just stared at the framed print hanging on the wall behind us as if pondering the ship's navigating secrets.

Veronica made a choking sound, but Bob didn't seem to hear, too deep into the lost treasures of the past.

"Were you married at the time?" Maya asked.

"Yes," he said, without averting his gaze from the print.

"To my step-mother, Elizabeth," Veronica said. "The selfless woman who raised me."

So far, our father had stuck to the same story I'd heard before, and it still made me want to curl up and cry. After Veronica and I met for the first time in Carmel Valley and discovered we were twins, she'd demanded an explanation from her father. Our father. And he'd shared all, except for one important detail. He hadn't mentioned Maya.

"Want me to go on?" he asked, giving Veronica a hard stare.

"Please do," Veronica said, her voice artificially sweet. She looked up at the ceiling as though it were the only safe harbor in this room of turbulence.

Bob refocused on Maya, more specifically, the birthmark on her face. "I extended my stay for another week, telling Elizabeth it was for business, and your mother and I ended up spending the entire seven days together."

He got up again, walked to the window, and looked outside. "Her name was Antonia Maria Flores."

"That's a beautiful name," Maya said. "How old was she?"

Bob leaned against the window frame. "Nineteen."

"Nineteen," Maya said. "And you didn't tell her you were married?"

"Not until later."

"Go on," she said, her smile wobbly.

"It nearly broke my heart to say goodbye. I know it broke hers."

Oh Mama. History just keeps repeating itself. I almost gave up everything for Cliff, and now I fear Maya will do the same for Dr. Shane Donovan.

Bob straightened, lifted his chin, and turned to Maya, his stance that of a man awaiting the verdict of an unsympathetic jury of three. "Nine months later, I received a telegram saying, 'I gave birth to triplets. Love Antonia.' I took the next flight to California."

"Triplets, is it?" Veronica said. "In your previous version of the story, you distinctly said 'twins.' Why did you lie?"

Bob ignored Veronica and continued. "Elizabeth and I hadn't been able to have children. We never checked into the cause, you know, if it was a problem with her or me. Turns out it wasn't me because—"

"You're veering off course, again," Veronica reminded him.

"That's the reason I couldn't leave you behind. I told Antonia I wanted all three of you."

"Including me?" Maya asked, sounding hopeful.

"At first, yes. Until..."

Something faded from Maya's eyes. Darn. What was he about to reveal? What further pain would it hold?

"How about Antonia? What was her response?" I asked, though I already knew the answer. The story was forever imprinted in my mind.

117

Bob hardly glanced my way. "She loved me and wanted me to be happy, but said she wouldn't give you up."

"And?" Veronica prompted.

"I told her I'd sue for custody. She had no income, lived with an elderly aunt, and her parents were both dead, which left her with little recourse."

"Dear God," I whispered. Though I'd heard this before almost word for word, a never-ending story, my gut twisted as if I were hearing it for the first time. So much for thinking with my mind instead of my heart.

"Antonia didn't scream or fuss, just cried," Bob said. "I couldn't bear it." The room became quiet. Dark clouds gathered in places concealed from our eyes, but no less recognizable. "Then the nurse held up one baby for me to see."

Please stop. Say no more.

"Shocked the hell out of me."

Veronica and I gasped. He was discussing Maya as if she were an object from the distant past, instead of a flesh and blood person in the here and now—his own flesh and blood.

Maya stared at him dry-eyed.

"Antonia told me she had named the child Maya, *Fallen Light,* and wouldn't give her up for the world. I was so relieved I agreed on taking only one of our daughters, the oldest and strongest, Veronica, *First Dawn,* and leave *Sunwalker* and *Fallen Light* behind."

Okay, so now he was discussing Maya as if she were a car delivered with a defect, *a lemon,* that could be returned to the showroom floor in exchange for a flawless model—Veronica.

"I promised to send child support for the other two, but Antonia said no. She wanted to cut off all ties, to never meet up again."

The other two? As a reminder that he was talking about Maya and me, I asked. "So, Maya and I stayed behind with Antonia."

Bob glanced at Veronica with a tenderness I hadn't noticed before. "You were preemies. Did I mention that? No? Your mother carried you to thirty-three weeks. About average for triplets. But you needed to stay in the hospital until you could do all the things full-term babies could do. Especially Veronica, since I'd be taking her home. You had to put on weight and be able to drink from a bottle and breathe on your own. That meant six weeks in NICU. Instead of flying home and returning for Veronica later, I stayed in a nearby hotel. Six weeks. Got that? Six weeks. With daily trips to the hospital. Keeping vigil, day after day, seeing your tiny bodies hooked up to IVs, listening to the beep of machines that kept you alive, unable to hold you. Because I wasn't listed as your father."

Bob turned his attention back to Maya. "Antonia made me promise never to mention *your* name again."

"Why?" I asked, since Maya wasn't asking. She reminded me of a mannequin the way she was staring straight ahead without a sign of what was going on inside. I fought the urge to wave my hands in front of her face saying, *Come back, come back, wherever you are.*

"Because" —Bob blinked as if waking from a dream— "with the help of an elderly aunt, Antonia planned on raising *Fallen Light* in the ways of her people, so she'd never feel ashamed of her disfigurement. Antonia said it was a gift, but that most people wouldn't see it that way. And would reject her."

"Like you?" I asked.

He wasn't listening. "Antonia's blood pressure was high, and she wasn't feeling well, which extended her hospital stay. The doctors said pre-eclampsia or high blood pressure was common in mothers after C-sections and multiple births. It wasn't until weeks after I'd returned to Maryland with Veronica, the hospital informed me of Antonia's death, due to a blood clot in her lung. It happened so unexpectedly she didn't have time to contact me. She would've let me know. She would've wanted Veronica and Marjorie together at least."

Bob paused and looked at me.

Parts of the story he now related were new to me. Besides never telling us about Maya, he'd never shared the part about our premature birth and prolonged stay in the hospital. Or his frequent visits there. I realized that he, too, had suffered, and I fought back a wave of pity.

"But it was too late, Marjorie. You'd been handed over to an adoption agency and adopted within weeks."

I didn't have to ask if he'd forgotten about the daughters he'd left behind, or about Antonia. His battle with alcohol told the rest of the story. He was stuck in the past due to regrettable choices.

"Can you ever forgive me?" he asked.

"Antonia already has," I said, knowing this to be true. "And she wants us to do the same, but" —I looked at my sisters and knew I couldn't speak for them. They would deal with this in their own separate ways— "I'll need time."

He nodded. "I'm so sorry."

Following Maya's earlier example, I got up and hugged our father with no other thought than to forgive. If I could. Then came an inspiration, be it sent by our mother or due to my own sense of the right thing to do. I dug into the pocket of my jeans and pulled out one of my most valued possessions: my mouse totem. Veronica had found it soon after arriving in Carmel Valley and had given it to an orphaned child named Joshua. Joshua later gave it to me.

"I have something for you, Father."

When I held the totem to the light, Bob's eyes widened. "Your mother's totem. She took it wherever she went. Where'd you get it?"

I looked at Veronica. She shook her head.

"It's a long story," I said, putting it into his hand.

He brought it to his lips. "My God, you don't know how much this means to me."

"I think I do," I said, realizing that the stone had come to him when he most needed it, after helping many others along the way. I turned to Maya. "You okay?"

"Pain is a great teacher," she said.

Chapter Nineteen

VERONICA WAS NOT IN good spirits the following morning. In fact, she was stark raving mad. We were seated in the enclosed sunporch on the north side of the house, the fog so thick we could barely make out the gazebo. She had claimed my wicker chair again and didn't seem about to relinquish it anytime soon. "I can't believe Maya left without telling us where she lives."

"She told our father she wasn't that hard to find," I said.

Veronica crossed and uncrossed her legs. "You seem rather calm about all this."

"You've been a good teacher," I said, holding back the smile that accompanied the memory of Veronica's cool, bad-girl act when I first met her.

Apparently, my remark didn't sit well with my sister. "What the hell's that supposed to mean?"

This time I didn't bother hiding my smile. "For starters, when we first met, you led me to believe you were a criminal, rather than tell me you were working with the DEA. And you appeared and disappeared without notice, giving me the cold shoulder to prevent me from asking too many questions."

No comment. Veronica's words were indisputably powerful, but the lack thereof, the space between, even more so. It suggested that she was listening, thinking, learning.

"And since we've been here in Pacific Grove," I said, "you've spent most of your time holed up in the basement, again distancing yourself from me."

The corners of Veronica's mouth drooped. "I didn't realize—"

"It's okay," I said, to prevent her from taking off in a defensive tangent. "You've taught me to be patient and try to understand. Until now, I've treated my adoptive mother and Morgan in much the same way. You've helped me realize how it feels. *Like shit.* Anyway, Maya said pain is a great teacher."

Veronica's mouth opened into a silent *oh*, the mist of her breath dissolving around her like a ghost of a scream. For a moment, her eyes looked vacant, then squinted in what appeared to be comprehension. The quietness between us filled with plaintive *coos*, which drew my attention to the aviary-sized birdcage standing nearby. Two doves with small heads, dull brown backs, and pale buffy underparts fluttered inside, a reminder that something wasn't right about this place. Who, for instance, was feeding the birds?

"Why do you think Maya's always so damn happy?" Veronica asked. "Do you think maybe she's" —Veronica released her right-handed grip on the armrest long enough to point at her temple— "not quite right in the head?"

I visualized the birthmark on Maya's face. She claimed it brought her joy, but I figured there was more to it. "Just the opposite, is my guess."

The mournful *coo WHO-o coo, coo, coo coos* of the doves made me weepy.

"And by 'just the opposite,' you mean...?"

Veronica was getting agitated again. What was bothering her to such a degree that she was losing her cool? Where was the emotionless sarcasm, the power, the strength?

"Maya's attitude is...I don't know...kind and selfless, which worries me. The world is hard on the saintly. Turns them into martyrs."

Veronica slammed her hand on the wicker armrest and practically leapt to a stand. "That does it. I'm going to do some research. Wanna come?"

I looked at the caged mourning doves, figuring both were male. From what I'd read their deep-perch-coos were solicitation calls. Female almost never sing. "Do you ever wonder who's feeding the birds?"

Veronica's eyes widened as if she'd seen a rainbow in the fog. "What birds?"

122

"Never mind," I said.

She lifted her hands and dropped them. A gesture of defeat? Hell no. Not Veronica. More likely a sign of frustration at my listlessness since moving into Anne's house. From the viewpoint of a woman so determined to achieve success with the DEA that all her behavior was directed toward that aim, my weak sense of self must be giving the impression of some kind of personality disorder.

"Do you want to find Maya or not?" she asked.

"Go on ahead," I said, wishing I could draw her into my world, even if it meant giving up my wicker chair. "It'll be good practice for you, Miss Undercover Agent." Then again, if I was hoping Veronica's kick ass personality was going to rub off on me, I had it wrong. I needed to get my act together, because neither she nor Maya could, would, or should do it for me.

Veronica's eyes brightened with purpose. Good. Mission and purpose brought out the best in her. "Practice, my foot. I'm curious as hell. And so are you. Don't try to deny it."

Something akin to excitement ignited in my belly, then rose to my forehead like a flame. "Where do you plan to start?"

Veronica smiled. "Not me, little sister. We. I figure we'll start by talking to Shane."

The flame in my forehead flared, then dimmed to a smolder. "That won't be until Saturday, so what do we do in the mean time?"

Veronica looked at the fog that veiled the windows. "Maybe I'll go hang out in the basement until then."

I flew to a stand. "Don't you dare!"

She grinned. "Gotcha."

"Brat." I pictured myself as a pear-shaped lute, with Veronica bent over me plucking, strumming, and muffling my strings. And darn, if I wasn't playing back the tune of her choice.

My mind started to race. What kind of research could we do on a gray morning such as this? Something indoors, where it was warm and quiet. I pictured a small table with a quilted cloth, surrounded by bookshelves. "I have an idea," I said, trying to sound casual, in-different. "There's someone I'd like you to meet."

Veronica fixed me with her icy stare, making me wonder if my eyes ever took on that frigid appearance. The answer had to be yes, since we were practically identical, yet I doubted I'd ever see anything but warmth streaming from Maya's. "Holding out on me again, huh," Veronica said, with the confidence of someone who knew me well after an acquaintance of less than seven months. But I wasn't about to tell her what. She'd find out soon enough. One more glance at the fog blanketing the exterior of the house and she said, "Okay, I'll play along. But we better walk instead of drive. It'll be safer."

Best add a sweatshirt to my current t-shirt and jeans, as well as a parka—and combat boots. "That'll be fine."

Veronica walked up to the birdcage and ran her fingers along its round wooden slats.

For a moment, the atmosphere turned liquid and a familiar tingling spread over my body. *Get with it, girls. You have work to do.* I leaned against the wicker settee for support. Work to do? Yes, but what?

"Hearing a voice again?" Veronica asked. She was accustomed to my little episodes by now, even had a few herself.

"Yes."

"A spirit who lives in this house?"

"I think so."

Veronica walked back to what had become *her* wicker chair and sat down, suddenly in no hurry to leave. "Well, I'll be."

❋❋❋

Veronica and I headed to town on foot, setting a fast pace, inhaling and exhaling the misty air, destined, it seemed, to continually walk in a cloud. When we entered the bookstore, Nessa was sitting at her table, sorting through a deck of cards. Not the deck I'd seen her work with before though. These cards looked like mini pieces of art. She glanced up and said something under her breath before standing, several cards still clasped in her hands.

"Veronica," I said, leading her forward. "I'd like you to meet Nessa. She does tarot readings."

"Hello, Nessa," Veronica said, edging up to the table and staring at the watercolor masterpieces.

Nessa shivered, and I didn't want to deliberate on what that meant.

"May I?" Veronica asked, pointing at the cards spread out on the quilted tablecloth.

Nessa shrugged, then gathered them up and placed them in Veronica's outstretched hand. Their eyes meet, and I thought I saw something flicker between them, though it was probably my imagination.

Veronica fanned the cards and pulled one from the rest. "Check this out, Marjorie. A woman with three heads."

Great.

She selected another even stranger card than the first—three screaming spirits swirling out of an old man's head. "Too cool."

While Veronica continued sorting through the deck, Nessa sat and looked on with what appeared to be forbearance.

Veronica sucked in her breath, recapturing my attention. "Look at this." The card she held pictured a woman, palms up, with a blood-red scar covering half her face. I caught Nessa looking at me. I looked away. Veronica slapped six more cards onto the table, face up, and pinned Nessa with a frosty stare. "What do they mean?"

"Sit down," she said, and we did.

Veronica pointed at the card on the table depicting a woman floating in a void, her long black hair swirling, her arms spread wide in appeal. "Looks like our mother."

Or you. "Nessa, do you know our sister, Maya?"

The lengthy pause after my question conveyed her reluctance to answer. "We're good friends."

Friends? What was going on here? "Why didn't you tell me this when we first met, or while you were doing my reading?"

She looked at me without a hint of apology, which should've

bothered me, but I was curious. Also, there was something about this woman I was beginning to like and respect. "Sometimes it's hard being in the position I'm in," she said. "I see things, but I also sense when it's best not to intervene."

"Then you know where she lives and works," I said, relieved that our search was over this soon.

"It would be best if you find her on your own."

So much for a quick end to our search.

Still staring at the six cards spread in front of her, Veronica said, "When we got here, you were working with a deck of cards that related to us. Which tells me you either knew we were coming or know a heck of a lot more about us than you're putting on. What's the deal?"

I stood, feeling lightheaded, as though the answer to Veronica's question would reveal more than I was prepared to take in. "Anyone for coffee? My treat."

Neither Veronica nor Nessa took me up on my offer, so I headed for the adjoining coffee shop. I needed a distraction. I needed caffeine. The aroma of brewed coffee and steamed milk grounded me. A good thing, because when I returned with my hot white mocha, Veronica and Nessa seemed to be at a stalemate, eyeing each other, neither giving an inch. I set my coffee on the table next to a card depicting a woman with two faces coming out of her forehead. "What do they mean?"

"Each person interprets the cards in different ways." Nessa said.

"Okay," I said, sitting down. "Fair enough." I turned to Veronica. "What do they mean to you?"

"Shit," Veronica said. "They're spooky as hell."

"They're called *Soul Cards*," Nessa said. "They're often used in therapy."

I lifted my coffee cup. "Want some? I offered before, but you didn't answer."

Nessa didn't seem to hear me. "Their powerful images evoke emotional and spiritual insights." She picked up the cards, shuffled them, and set them on the table in front of Veronica. "Think of an issue that concerns you."

Veronica gave an impatient nod. "Finding Maya."

Nessa grinned. "That'll do." She appeared to be taking a liking to Veronica. Who wouldn't? She was one of a kind. "Now pick a card and flip it over."

Veronica drew a card out of the deck's center and placed it on the table, face up. It was a picture of a blonde-haired woman looking into a mirror, her hand pressed against what she saw inside. Reflected back was an elusive female form, pale, thin, with a faint gleam in her eyes, her hand pressed against that of the blonde. I thought of Maya. This was something she'd do, see someone else's spirit while gazing into a mirror, offering her love and empathy. Veronica picked another card, this time of a person lying next to a pool of water looking in, only to see the reflection of someone else. "One more card," she said, slapping it onto the table next to the others. The image held the sad serenity of a religious icon, often depicted in statues of the Madonna.

"Well?" Nessa asked.

Veronica shook her head. "Well, what?"

"Maya works with the sick, like Mother Teresa," I said. "Which would explain the reflections in the mirror and the Madonna-like appearance of the card."

Nessa smiled, but said nothing.

I finished my coffee and got to my feet. "Thanks, Nessa, I know you're trying to help us, encouraging us to see what's right in front of us."

Veronica got up, still eyeing the cards on the table. "Yeah, thanks." She started to turn, then paused. "Almost forgot. How much do we owe you?"

Nessa looked at the cards Veronica had selected. "Are you kidding? If this helps Maya in any way…" She turned toward the bookshelf behind the table holding titles related to the metaphysical: *Astral Projection*; *Dreams that Come True*; *Return from Tomorrow*; *Adventures in Consciousness*. "She's all alone," Nessa said, "and…"

"What do you see?" I asked, placing my hand over hers. "If you care about her, and if you're that concerned, why not tell us?"

She met my eyes. "Because sometimes I'm wrong."

Chapter Twenty

THE ENDLESS FOG WAS getting to me as it was to Veronica. I felt blinded by it, Veronica stifled. In our search for Maya, we had ended up at a library computer on Friday afternoon, using the Internet to research recovery programs in Pacific Grove. We googled several facilities that treated people dependent on drugs and alcohol and came up with some promising leads. Soon we would act on them.

"I'm going to yoga class to talk to Shane," Veronica announced the following morning after breakfast.

"Go on without me," I said, unable to muster the strength—or will—for another encounter with Dr. Shane Donovan.

"Sure," Veronica said. "Let me do all the dirty work."

Talk about dirty work. From the kitchen table, I peered through the bay window into the October gloom—dark past breakfast, dusk before supper—reminding myself there was more weeding to do and wondering where to start. "I doubt Dr. Donovan will tell you where Maya lives. Seems everybody's trying to protect her."

"He'll talk," Veronica said grabbing the keys to my Jeep off the counter. "Don't expect me back anytime soon."

I shrugged, eyes droopy. The thought of pulling weeds under overcast skies lost its appeal.

A short nap was more to my liking.

"You can always explore the house some more," Veronica said on her way out.

"Yeah, right," I said under my breath, though the suggestion wasn't a bad one. We had toured all three stories and the basement with Maya, but the attic still remained a mystery.

I bent over the table, rested my head on my arms, and closed my eyes.

❂❂❂

I woke with a start.

Darn. I'd done it again, drifted off during the day. What was wrong with me?

I looked out the window for a clue as to how long I'd been out. Still morning. Better get a move on, or Veronica would return and I'd have nothing to show for during her absence. I got up and took the stairs, only to pause on the third-floor landing to catch my breath. Walking to town at a brisk pace was one thing, climbing three flights of stairs quite another. A door at the far end of the hallway opened to a stairwell leading to the attic. I climbed the narrow, curved stairs, expecting to end up in a space filled with old furniture and accumulated junk. Instead, I entered what appeared to be a well-equipped studio apartment. The ceiling was high with exposed wooden beams, yet there wasn't a cobweb in sight. A roughly hewn fireplace yawned across the south wall, the effect softened by a camel back couch and two matching armchairs upholstered in browns and creams.

A soft meow led me to the couch where a cat lay curled into a ball of contentment. It was a tabby, just like Gabriel, my backyard stray, who'd hitchhiked his way into my heart and now belonged to my-soon-to-be adoptive son, Joshua. Whom did this cat belong to? What did it eat?

It peered at me through half closed eyes, then treated me to a sharp-toothed, tonsil-exposing yawn. Its fur was clean, shiny, and free of mats. No sign of hunger. No sign of fear. I sat on the couch, giving the cat plenty of space, the intention being to encourage it to approach me, not bolt in fear. I leaned back and placed my hand midway between us, careful not to meet its eyes. "What are you do-ing up here all by yourself, little guy? Who's feeding you?" The cat pawed my hand. I waited. Another paw to my hand, followed by a series of finger sniffs. No reaction from me. It crawled closer, then stood and rubbed against my arm. Considering it safe to do so, I looked at the cat and gave a slow blink. It blinked back. "Don't you feel lonely up here all by yourself?" I asked, withdrawing my hand. The cat followed my hand as if it were a toy infused with catnip, then paused and stepped onto my lap. "Ah. Friends at last." I scratched its head. It kneaded my jeans.

Despite the fog, natural light streamed through the access window mounted on the roof, highlighting the glass-topped coffee table and the silver threads in the Persian carpet underneath. Why wasn't it warmer up here? It was at least seventy-two degrees outside, and with the sun hitting the roof from above, the room temperature should've been in the eighties. The windows were shaded, which had some insulating effect, and the house probably had good venting, but still. "Want to join me for a tour of the apartment?" I asked my new friend. "Or would you rather stay on the couch?" The cat made no move to vacate my lap, so I scooped it up and stood. "Okay, buddy. Let's start with the door on the left."

The door led to a room with a double bed backed by a walnut headboard. A cream blanket was stretched over the top mattress and tucked in with crisp hospital corners, as if the bed had been made under the tutelage of an Army Drill Sergeant. A topper, appliquéd with bright orange and black monarchs, lay folded at the bed's base. Another door led to a small bathroom with a shower, toilet, and pedestal sink. Next, I explored the mini kitchen which included all the basics, along with a cat feeder and litter box tucked into an open space below the counter.

No personal items lay strewn about, no shoes, no comb, no toothbrush. The apartment looked as neat and unlived in as those featured in magazine spreads. So, the question remained: Who was feeding the cat? If Anne had an upstairs boarder, she would've told us, and we would've seen him or her entering and leaving the house. Unless the boarder had a ladder and was making use of the access window in the roof.

"Yeah, right."

I eased the cat back onto the couch— "Bye kitty" —and headed for the stairs, feeling as if I'd invaded someone's private space, making me no more than an inquisitive snoop.

❂❂❂

I lifted my head from the kitchen table with no memory of getting there. I caught a whiff of vanilla though the oven was empty. Usually kitchen-task avoidant, I felt the urge to do some therapeutic baking. Maybe by following a list of step-by-step instructions, I'd regain a sense of control.

Forty-five minutes later, I opened the back door and welcomed my sister home with a platter of chocolate chip cookies in hand. And an announcement. "You'll never guess what I found upstairs."

Veronica snatched a cookie from the platter and bit into it before I'd even closed and secured the door. "Me, first."

She was right. News about Maya took precedent.

Veronica tossed the car keys onto the counter. They slid across the tiled surface and smacked against the backsplash. "Can you believe Shane wasn't going to tell me where Maya worked or lived?"

I eyed the keys, hoping she'd been kinder to my Jeep. "Told you so. He's wise to us."

"So, I promised to make Maya see reason about getting her face fixed."

"You didn't!"

"Had to get him to talk somehow."

"You lied?"

Veronica smiled and snatched another cookie.

What a convincing villain she'd make. If the DEA didn't work out for her, she could always try acting—the vixen with a golden heart. "I plan on telling Maya that the only reasonable thing for her to do is whatever the hell she wants."

"Sly," I said, wondering when Veronica had last eaten something solid. She'd lost weight and looked half starved. "So, you found out where she lives?"

"It's hard to believe. I mean, it's such a coincidence..."

132

"Come on. Out with it."

"She works with alcoholics, just like she said. The amazing thing is, she did so long before meeting Dad and knowing about his dependency."

"So, where does she—?"

"Near here, within walking distance of Monterey Bay."

"What's near here?"

"The treatment facility."

"Where she works?"

"It's non-profit, so the work doesn't pay much."

"I doubt that matters to Maya. So, where does she live?"

"You won't believe this."

What I did and didn't believe had undergone some major stretching in the past seven months. "Try me."

Veronica frowned. "In a yurt, like the one Anne camped in at Pfeiffer State Park, except larger. Nothing more than a glorified tent, according to Shane. She doesn't own a car and keeps only enough clothes on hand to wear between washings."

Maya had already told us that her only means of transportation was an old mountain bike. "Why?" I now asked, finding life without at least a closet full of clothes and a car difficult to comprehend. "Does she need money?"

"She gives it all away, says God will provide."

"Like God provides for the birds of the air that 'neither sow nor reap nor gather into barns,'" I said, quoting Matthew.

"And lilies of the field that 'neither toil nor spin,'" Veronica added, a sign that she, too, was up on some of the more familiar Bible verses. "Anyway, that's all I've got so far."

"Maya didn't give a clue about her minimalist lifestyle when she came to visit," I said. "In fact, she seemed impressed with Anne's house and all its amenities."

"Get real, Marjorie. Look at the way she dresses. She was wearing the same cargo pants and jacket both times I saw her. And they hardly looked new."

"Bet she'd look great in one of your vampy outfits," I said.

"My guess is she'd rather submit to torture than wear something of mine. Or yours. Now, tell me what you found upstairs."

"Talk about something hard to believe, the entire attic has been converted into a studio apartment with its own kitchen, bedroom, and bathroom. There's also a cat up there that looks healthy and isn't afraid of strangers. I wonder if Anne's got some kind of transient occupancy going on."

"We would've noticed if someone was staying up there," Veronica said. "Running water, creaking pipes."

"Not from the basement, you wouldn't, and I've been spending a lot of time outdoors."

"Or it's just an empty studio with a cat," Veronica said. "Maybe that's why this house is pest free. The cat's diet consists of mice and rats.

"Nope. There's a cat feeder full of food in the kitchen and no mouse or rat carcasses in sight. The place, including the cat's litter box, is spotless. If I hadn't vowed off using the phone while here, I'd call Anne to find out."

"You could always use your telepathic skills," Veronica said. "We could be dealing with a ghost here."

"The cat was real," I said, searching for a way to prove it. I checked my navy sweater for cat hair. None.

Veronica smiled. "Face it, Marge. This place is haunted."

Chapter Twenty-One

I HAD FINALLY GOTTEN used to the voices. Now I was seeing and smelling things as well. Doves in a giant birdcage; a cat that looked like my stray; the scent of vanilla. Good thing Veronica and I were visiting Maya today. I needed a diversion to get my head back on straight.

The familiar hum and cut of my Jeep's engine drew my attention to the back driveway. A door slammed and minutes later Veronica walked into the kitchen waving a stack of papers. I hadn't even known she was gone. "I went back to the library for information on the Guidepost Treatment Facility where Maya works." She swept the kitchen counters with her gaze, as if expecting a plate of freshly baked cookies to replace the one she'd wiped clean during our talk about the upstairs studio and cat. No go. Baking wasn't on my priority list right now.

"The Guidepost is headquartered in an old Victorian like this one," she said. "Just think, Anne could set up a similar substance abuse program here."

Anne, nurse, caregiver, and witch doctor, helping the weak and defeated. Right up her alley. "And we could help her," I said, knowing this wasn't an option.

"Sick people don't bring out the best in me," Veronica said, "especially when their illnesses are self-inflicted."

Veronica's comment about alcoholism being self-inflicted was harsh, but, yes, drinking was a choice, at least until addiction set in. To argue otherwise would mean our father was powerless to overcome his dependence.

Veronica wiggled the papers in her hand. "You've got to hear these testimonials. Some addicts sounded just like Dad before they turned their lives around. Do you think it's possible?"

"For Dad to turn his life around?"

Veronica read from one page, "'In twenty-eight days, I achieved sobriety, which is now leading me to the road of recovery and back to joyous living.'" She dropped her head and zeroed in on the ceiling, the muscles in her neck working as if fighting a private battle. She cleared her throat and said, "Hell, what am I thinking? Dad would never check into a facility like this. Too proud." She folded the papers and put them into her bag. "Plus, he likes drinking too much."

"Let's forget about Bob for now," I said, "and concentrate on Maya. Do you know how to get there?"

"Yeah, though the place may be off limits for drop-ins, to protect the identity of its patients."

"Let's ask for Maya and see what happens," I said.

"Won't know till we try."

❂❂❂

The Guidepost Treatment Facility appeared open and accessible, not at all the prison-like edifice I'd envisioned it to be. Plenty of parking, which meant visitors were likely encouraged to stop by to look up family and friends. The main house was as Veronica had described it, a large Victorian similar to Anne's, with a wraparound porch, even a turret.

"No wonder Maya likes it here," I said.

The grounds were carpeted in lush grass, edged by trimmed hedges and dotted with deciduous trees and evergreens. Pink and red camellias added to the mix, signaling "Welcome" more effectively than a sign ever would, no matter how well-crafted and lettered.

When Veronica and I entered the front office, the receptionist and people clustered around her desk stopped talking and stared. "Well, I'll be," said a man in tan shorts and a blue polo shirt. "I finally get sober, and I'm still seeing things."

"Oh dear," the receptionist said. "Oh dear, oh dear. I'm seeing the same thing, Pete, and I've been a teetotaler all my life."

"Are you Maya's sisters?" asked a meticulously dressed and

coiffed woman. She reminded me of my adoptive mother, only more cheerful.

Veronica and I glanced at each other and smiled.

"Heck," said Pete. "What a question. Not only sisters, but triplets. Good God, three Maya's. I call that hitting the jackpot."

"You sure are pretty," someone said, "Just like—"

"And, heeeere's Maya," Pete announced, imitating Johnny Carson's jovial sidekick, Ed McMahon.

Maya worked her way through the crowd—hugging, patting backs, and kissing cheeks—before greeting us with a wide grin. "What took you so long?"

I didn't answer, couldn't, not with that giant boulder in my throat. If Maya were running for office, she'd be a shoe-in. No one here seemed to notice—or care about—Maya's so-called disfigurement.

"You must love your job," Veronica said, sweeping her hand to include the room and all its occupants.

Maya considered the growing crowd and frowned. "Well, sort of."

Her fans booed, and my heart filled. Maya appeared to love, and be loved by, the folks at the Guidepost Treatment Facility. Unconditionally. How good was that?

"Could we talk in private?" Veronica asked, her voice raspy. "Or do we need to make an appointment?"

Maya scratched her head. "Guess I can make an exception for the two of you this once." She turned to the receptionist and sighed. "Would it be possible for me to take my lunch break early, Laura?"

Laura chuckled and waved her on. "Silly goose. Go on. Have a good time."

Maya led us through a side door into a small garden featuring a gazebo with two concrete benches. "Welcome to our facility."

"You're quite appreciated here," I said.

Maya's eyes took on the sheen of brilliant cut sapphires with liquid inclusions. "Some patients come to us near the point of suicide and are so inebriated they're hallucinating and having black outs.

Others...well, you get the picture. Every time one of them gets well, it's like a small miracle, for which we're forever grateful."

Neither Veronica nor I spoke, letting stillness do the talking, as it does so well. I closed my eyes and took in the scent of mown grass, ocean air, and coastal flowers.

"Would you like to attend one of our workshops?" Maya asked.

I lifted my shoulders and let them drop. Anything, if it meant getting closer to our sister. "Sure, why not?"

"Isn't there an issue of privacy involved?" Veronica asked. "I wouldn't want to piss off any of your patients."

You'd think we were seated in a cave rather than a slatted gazebo, the way Maya's laugh bounded and echoed back to us. "Are you kidding? Seeing double, even triple is nothing new to them. Plus, you may be healers. Genetics, you know."

Veronica tossed her hair over her shoulder. "That would be a new one."

Maya stood. "Come on. You can help me set up."

❁❁❁

I stared at the cards spread out on Maya's desk with a sense of déjà vu. "These look just like the Nessa's *Soul Cards*."

"Nessa?" Maya shot me a highbrowed look that reminded me of Veronica in her detective mode. "Did she tell you where I—"

"No," Veronica said after a quick glance in my direction. "She said we'd have to find you on our own."

Maya's laugh sounded like the ringing of bells announcing something sacred about to happen. "Remind me to thank her later." At our frowns, she added, "People often become more motivated in their search when information is withheld." She looked at Veronica and winked. "It brings out their detective skills."

"Our love for you is motivation enough," I said. "So please, don't hold out on us again. We've missed out on twenty-nine years together. Let's not waste another minute."

Maya frowned, but before she could express what was on her mind, a monarch drifted into the room through an open window. It landed on a *Soul Card* of a smiling woman, arms raised, as though releasing her will—and destiny—to something higher than herself. An angel in the illustration hovered above the woman, veiling her with its golden light.

"Soon you'll see monarchs all over Pacific Grove," Maya said, as though there were nothing out of the ordinary in what we were witnessing. I knew better though. I'd learned to look for messages everywhere. The trick was translating them into a language I could understand.

That's how the earth journey had been going for me, a journey I didn't instigate or relish, but continued to travel hoping to find a reason for being here, or at least a meaningful destination. Messages bombarded me from all directions, but in most cases, I lacked the ability to interpret them, except through hindsight when it was often too late. So, I wasn't about to let this butterfly's message go unheeded, as it appeared Maya intended to do. At least not without trying to crack the code. "Maya," I said in a low voice, so not to startle the butterfly. "What does it mean?"

I expected an evasive answer, similar to the one Nessa had given us when we'd quizzed her about the *Soul Cards*. Instead, she said, "Many profound spiritual experiences are highlighted by natural events."

"So, you, too, sense that the monarch's appearance means something."

"Open to individual interpretation, of course."

"Of course," I said. The butterfly lifted and fluttered back out through the window.

"It probably coincided with something you were thinking," Veronica said.

This from my cynical sister? "Are you calling it a coincidence?"

"Not a coincidence," she qualified, poking me in the arm. "I *have* learned something during my hibernation in the basement. What were you thinking just before the butterfly landed?"

"I don't remember."

"You said we'd missed out on twenty-nine years together," Maya said, "and not to waste another minute."

Veronica looked pleased. "Therefore, something about the butterfly must represent time."

"In what way?" I asked.

She scratched her head in pretense of deep thought. "Let me see now. The monarch larva starts out as a tiny caterpillar that eats until it's too big for its own skin. Then it sheds its old skin four or five times, growing bigger and bigger and sheaths itself into a cocoon which melts away, and then voilà! A butterfly."

"Thanks for the science lesson," I said. "So how does this bring us any closer to figuring out the butterfly's supposed message?"

Veronica looked at Maya and shrugged. "As Maya said, it's open to individual interpretation."

"In parts of Mexico," Maya said, "people believe the spirits of departed loved ones come on the wings of monarch butterflies. And the special places in which the butterflies gather, where the temperature is warm, and the butterfly is sheltered from the cold and the wind, are called 'magic circles.' We have two of our very own here in Pacific Grove."

Magic circles? I thought of the labyrinth and the medicine wheel and felt a surge of understanding well up inside, followed by hope.

At the sound of conversation and laughter in the hallway, Maya looked at the clock. "Oh, oh, almost out of time, and we still need to roll out ink for the touch drawings."

Chapter Twenty-Two

VERONICA AND I RETURNED to the Guidepost on Thursday. The grounds were awash in sunlight and the temperature a comfortable eighty degrees as if the Creator, in guise of the sun, felt indulgent, even generous, this day.

We spent the morning with Maya practicing a technique called *Touch Drawing* discovered by artist Deborah Koff-Chapin, the focus of the previous day's workshop. The drawings took only ten seconds to create, hardly enough time to formulate a thought. But, according to Maya, that was the point, to encourage patients to put their *feelings* onto the paper.

We dabbled small amounts of printing ink onto sixteen-by-twenty-four-inch plexiglass drawing boards, then spread out the ink with rollers and placed acid-free tissue paper on top. Next, we moved our fingertips over the paper, the pressure of our touch forming images on the backside. Each time we completed a painting, we lifted the paper from the drawing board and put it in a pile to keep them in order. Then we placed fresh sheets of tissue paper over the rolled-out ink and started a new painting.

"Some of my patients complete twenty or more drawings in a session," Maya said, "bringing beautiful images to life, while releasing painful emotions. Later, I use them as catalysts to encourage the participants to talk about themselves. This process often helps them tap into their own wisdom, to explore, understand, and resolve issues."

At times, I worked with my eyes closed. At others, I focused on the translucent paper, using not only my fingertips, but the backs of my fingers and palms of my hands to rub, sculpt, and record the images rising from within. This form of art, this drawing by touch, felt spontaneous and effortless, while at the same time, intense and dreamlike, as it gave expression to unexplored parts of myself. While placing a fresh sheet of tissue paper on the ink board, I recalled the Chumash pictographs I'd seen during our guided tour of the Ventana Wilderness six months ago. As I began to draw, the rock-art handprints of my Esselen ancestors came to mind, followed by another memory that took place on one of the last evenings of the tour before the weather turned bad. Softly, as if carried by the breeze, Dr. Mendez had recited the closing lines of Robinson Jeffers' poem, "Hands," which spoke of a multitude of hands and questioned whether the brown, shy people who painted them intended religion or magic with their sealed message.

"Time's up," Maya said.

I blinked and realized I was shaking.

"Wow, Marjorie," Veronica said, eyeing the drawing that had emerged like an underexposed negative through the tissue on my ink board. "A trail of hands. Mind if Maya and I add ours?"

I stared at my drawing and caught my breath. What thoughts and emotions, what inner wisdom, was my subconscious trying to express? "Sure," I said. "Though we won't be able to tell them apart afterwards."

"Are you kidding," Maya said as she pressed her hand onto the paper. "We came from one fertilized egg that split twice. Here's our chance to become one again."

"Not one," Veronica said, placing her print at the top of the trail of hands. "Our DNA may be virtually indistinguishable, but our fingerprints are *not* the same."

"Really?" I said, disappointed.

"We lose similarities in our looks, behavior, and health as we interact with our environment," Veronica said. "Starting in the womb."

"One, yet individual," Maya said. She pressed her thumbprint next to Veronica's printed hand, then next to one of mine. "Which explains why I was born with the gift of a birthmark and you two weren't."

142

I lifted the paper from the ink board with care, sensing that this physical expression of the unexplored held special significance I wouldn't understand until later.

☻☻☻

On Friday, the fog returned, dropping the temperature by a good ten degrees, yet the warmth of Maya's work radiated throughout the classroom. With Joni Mitchell singing "The Circle Game" in the background, Veronica and I—now well versed in the technique of *Touch Drawing*—stepped in to lighten Maya's load. We laid out fresh paper, rolled out ink, and watched as recovering alcoholics and drug addicts witnessed the beautiful lines and swirls that depicted their inner thoughts.

Maya's patients had unanimously voted to allow our participation in their group therapy sessions. "They consider you extensions of me," Maya told us, "and trust you'll honor their confidentiality."

Often the only sound in the room, as the painters concentrated on the movement of their fingers, was Joni singing about cartwheels turning to car wheels and the seasons going round and round. At other times, the room would explode with laughter and chatter as the participants held their artwork up to the light. I tried to imagine our father inspired in this way, but couldn't. He was literally and figuratively miles away. What would it take to bring laughter back into his life?

By day's end, Veronica and I rejoined Maya in the gazebo. We'd enjoyed her classes and her company for the past three days, but wondered if it might be best to allow her to continue her good work without the distraction of our presence. As the fog swirled around us, we suggested that we shouldn't come back.

Maya flew to a stand and threw up her hands. "We're making masks on Tuesday for Wednesday's Halloween party. My patients are expecting you. In fact, they'll be greatly disappointed if you aren't there. I insist you join us."

Glad for an excuse to return and continue bonding with Maya, I waited for Veronica's response.

"Um...okay," she said.

When we stood to leave, Maya clasped my hand between hers. "I'm taking vacation time, so we can be together for Thanksgiving."

"Awesome," I said, reluctant to leave this place of miracles.

Maya continued to hold my hand. Something appeared to be bothering her, something more urgent than our upcoming departure.

"Is something wrong?" I asked.

She shrugged. "It's probably nothing."

Maya was not a complainer. In fact, she was the most upbeat, optimistic person I knew. For her to even hint at trouble meant something was more than nothing. "Maya? What is it?" We'd been apart for twenty-nine years, drifting without one another's support. It was time to renew the bond with which we were born.

"Do you ever get the feeling you're being followed?" she asked.

"Sure. On the day you tagged me to the Monarch Sanctuary. It felt weird, but—"

"If someone's following you, it's probably Dad," Veronica said. "You've been keeping your whereabouts a mystery, which is like dangling a bottle of booze in front of his nose. He's probably spying on you."

"He barely seems capable of leaving his house," I countered.

"Don't underestimate him," Veronica said. "He's been spying on me for years. Which brings up the question. What's he doing here in Pacific Grove all by his lonesome, when he's got a perfectly comfortable home and a loving wife back in Maryland?"

Maya stared at Veronica, looking sad, yet thoughtful.

"Do you sense being followed here at the Guidepost," I asked, "or when you leave the grounds?"

"It's a feeling I get now and then while I'm riding my bike around town or walking on the beach. Nothing specific. Just a sense. I don't know. As I said, it's probably nothing."

"Why don't you come stay with us for a while," I said, feeling a surge of protectiveness. "We've got plenty of room. In fact, the place is palatial. I'll even do the cooking."

144

Maya laughed. "A long bicycle ride to work, though."

"We'll taxi you. No big deal. Or you can use my Jeep. Veronica and I get around on foot half the time, anyway."

Maya looked at the toes of her boots and shook her head.

"Damn it," Veronica said. "Now you've got *me* worried. Stay with us. At least until you're sure no one's stalking you. It would be safer and a lot more comfortable than that...that..."

Maya giggled. "So, you know where I live."

"A yurt of all things. You're crazy like Marjorie. Must be the blonde hair."

"It's located here on the facility grounds," Maya said, not in the least bit put out by Veronica's assessment of her choice of domicile. Want a tour? You'll envy me when we're done."

"I doubt it," Veronica said.

I thought back to my time in Big Sur, how I'd slept in a tent and never felt closer to nature—and to God. "I'd love to see it."

Maya led us along a winding path, bordered by yellow goldenrod, red Chinese lantern, white crocus, purple liriope, and pink cyclamen, limp due to the dripping fog. We approached a round structure with a latticed wall, topped by a circular roof that converged into a point. "Yurts are larger and stronger than tents," she said, "weather tight and economical to heat. Wait until you see it inside."

We entered the building through a small, framed door. The interior resembled a studio apartment, except round instead of square. A small kitchen to the left featured curved counters and cabinets that conformed to the arced wall. On the right, stood a slouchy blue sofa partnered with a worn, overstuffed chair and a veneer coffee table. Maya flicked on a floor lamp, its base the coiled tail of a snake, its rod the snake's body, and its shade supported by the snake's neck and head. "Ta da," she said. "My spirit power animal, symbolizing change, transition, and the shedding of illusions and limitations."

"It gets weirder and weirder," Veronica said.

Despite the second-hand and mismatched furniture, the yurt felt intimate and friendly.

145

"What's behind the bamboo screen?" Veronica asked.

"My bed. Want to see?"

As with the rest of her home, there was nothing frivolous about Maya's sleeping area. Though neatly made with white sheets and a faded blue blanket, the bed was little more than a full mattress and box spring on a steel frame—no bedspread, no headboard, no fluffy, shammed pillows. Next to the bed stood an upended apple crate, topped by a chipped ceramic lamp. The only piece of furniture in mint condition was the antique armoire. The overall effect was neat and economical, a delight to the eye.

"Comfortable, yes. Safe, no," Veronica said.

"It's perfect!" I said. "No squandering of resources, no degrading of the environment, no depriving the poor."

"Unburdened freedom," Maya said.

Veronica inspected the clear, acrylic dome at the crown of the yurt which looked like a giant skylight. "Can you see the stars at night?"

"Sure can," Maya said. "The cupola serves as a night light that helps put me to sleep."

"You have a hard time sleeping?" Veronica asked, her eyes narrowing like a concerned parent—or suspicious cop.

"I have dreams," Maya said. "Like motion pictures in my head, minus the plot and a happy ending. I can't stop them, so, I wave them on like pesky flies."

"Like the images in *Soul Cards*," I said, "created by feelings, not conscious thought."

Maya glanced at the ceiling, more opaque than clear due to the fog. "We can learn from dreams if we don't turn away from them in fear."

"You won't be seeing stars tonight," Veronica said. "Not with that cloud of fog clinging to your yurt like a wet blanket."

I thought of the tabby I'd seen in Anne's house. "You should get a cat."

"I've considered it, but—"

"How hard would it be for someone to break in?" Veronica asked.

"They lock the estate gates at night and check the grounds for intruders," Maya said. She pulled a cell phone out of her jacket and flipped it open. "I've got Nextel. We communicate by phone and radio. So, if an outsider sneaks in and causes trouble, I can call security for help."

"That's good," Veronica said. "Marjorie and I have sworn off phones while here, so we're difficult to reach."

"Wanna bet?" Maya said.

If she was referring to our telepathic experiment a week ago, I preferred not to count on it in case of an emergency.

"Anyway, why the fuss?" she said. "I've made it this far without help—"

"From us," I inserted, since she'd never say it. The thought of her being alone all these years saddened me. "Which is a darn shame."

"I'd love to get together as a family for Thanksgiving," Maya said. "I wonder if..."

"I don't think that would be a good idea," Veronica said.

"What wouldn't be a good idea?" I asked.

"It would only be for a few days," Maya said.

Veronica turned from her door inspection and sat on the sofa, sinking until her knees almost touched her chin. "He's a pain in the ass."

So, they were discussing Bob, our father. "We could put him up in one of the third-floor suites," I suggested.

"Or the attic," Veronica said. "With the cat and the Ghost Host."

"Ghost Host?" Maya asked.

"I found a cat in the attic apartment," I said, "that looks healthy and well cared for. I wondered who was feeding it. I meant to ask Anne, but—"

"She talks to Marjorie," Veronica said.

"Anne?" Maya asked.

"The Ghost Host," Veronica said.

The more we discussed the cat and the Ghost Host, the more

unlikely the situation seemed, but I refused to start questioning my sanity again. "I hear voices," I admitted.

"Of dead people," Veronica added.

"Only our mother until now, and our ancestor, Margarita Butron. One of whom you've heard, too, Veronica. So, don't point fingers."

"What a burden that must be," Maya said, the compassion in her voice almost bringing me to tears. "Do you see them too?" she asked.

"Sometimes."

Maya smiled. "If I get to meet the cat and you invite Papa, I'll stay with you during Thanksgiving week."

Veronica used the armrest to pull herself up from the depths of the sofa, then walked the circumference of the yurt before heading for the door. "What makes you think he'll come?"

"Leave it to me," Maya said, quite confident for someone who'd just met her father.

Chapter Twenty-Three

NO TOUCH PAINTING TODAY. Instead, we were making Halloween masks. The tables at the Guidepost had disappeared under reams of fabric, construction paper, yarn, feathers, glitter, and glue. Men and women of all ages, nationalities, and states of dress were calling out to one another as they sorted through the piles of inspiration.

The camaraderie of the participants proved beyond my comprehension as they practiced the communication skills they'd learned in rehab. Many of the people in the group had lost drug-using friends when they got sober, but here they were finding fellowship with others in recovery. The road to sobriety might be solitary, but it didn't have to be lonely. I couldn't picture our father joining in on the fun with such assertiveness and empathy. What made these people different? Once an alcoholic, always an alcoholic, or so I'd heard. Yet these patients seemed happy, even joyful.

I approached one of the scrap-littered tables, wondering where to begin, then picked up two black ostrich feathers and stared at them without a smidgen of artistic zeal. Next to me, Veronica was digging through a collection of materials with the passion of a garage-sale junkie. Brows knit, she inspected one exotic item after another, tossing most of them back and stacking the winners in a neat pile to the side. This mask-making business appeared to be taking on serious proportions. I didn't dare laugh, though the urge was strong.

Maya worked the room like a butterfly, settling here, then there, spreading the pollen of inspiration and enthusiasm before moving on. When she made it to our table, she laughed at the befuddled look on my face. I was still holding the ostrich feathers, unsure what to do with them. "Why don't you make two identical masks, one for you and one for me?" Maya suggested. "Then no one will be able to tell us apart."

Her beaming face incited a stirring in my chest, a prompting I couldn't ignore. I waved the feathers. They swayed like wispy black hair. "Identical masks," I said, energized at last. "Great idea."

When Maya moved on, I started my own excavation like an intern on an anthropological dig. Soon I, too, had a treasure trove of materials stacked to the side. I reached for the scissors and glue. Working on double-masks, double-fast, made hours pass like minutes. Veronica and the other crafters in the room faded into the background. Not only were Maya and I going to look alike, we'd look terrific.

Using myself as a model, I formed two masks out of poster board large enough to cover most of the face, thus Maya's birthmark. I painted them mint green and rimmed the eyeholes in hot pink outlined with black. Using an iridescent green fabric, I fashioned long, bejeweled, glitter-tipped fingers reinforced with construction paper and spread them over the face of the masks, leaving spaces for the eyes to peek through. Then I topped each mask with the ostrich feathers and a witch's hat made of black felt.

Although still struggling with her own creation, Veronica glanced over at mine. "Why'd you make two?"

"One for Maya, and one for me," I said, holding the masks up for her inspection.

Something passed over Veronica's face, which, I decided, had nothing to do with the quality of the masks.

"It was Maya's idea," I said. "She thought it would be fun to look alike. You know, minus the—"

"Oh." Veronica's hand went to her hair, a gesture so telling it made my heart hurt. Her hair, black as midnight, set her apart from her blonde sisters, and for once, it seemed to bother her. She nodded. "It'll be strange, not being able to tell you apart." She looked at her own creation and frowned. Without meaning to, I had trampled her enthusiasm.

Maya paused from her circulation of the room and stepped between us. "Goodness, Veronica, your headdress reminds me of our mother. The way I've always imagined her, dressed like one of our Ohlone ancestors. And your hair... It's exactly right. Long, black, and straight."

Maya was right in referring to Veronica's basket-like hat dotted with abalone shells as a headdress rather than a mask. Her face would remain exposed. "Will you be wearing any makeup?" I asked.

Veronica shook her head, lips tight. "You'll have to wait and see."

While I wondered what the rest of Veronica's costume would look like—a robe, a blanket of rabbit fur, a skirt of tule—Maya continued to stare at her headdress with the sharp-eyed look of an art connoisseur, which appeared to chase the clouds away. Veronica, our no-non-sense sister, smiled as if her project was just awarded a blue ribbon at the state fair. Silently, I thanked Maya, wondering if she knew what she'd just done. I doubted it. With Maya, it was all about service. She cared about people and wanted to make them happy with little regard for her own wants and needs. Yet, according to Maya, her wants and needs were being met splendidly. How could this be when she wasn't even trying? Something nagged at me as if there were a message here. Did it have something to do with love and service and releasing my own wants and needs for the sake of others?

"No," Veronica said.

I looked at her, startled. Was she talking to me?

"I don't think our mother would've worn a headdress like this."

"Why not?" I asked, relieved that she hadn't invaded my thoughts. "You'd think she'd be proud of her ancestry."

"Rebellion," Veronica said.

Yes, I could imagine our mother feeling rebellious of the old ways, as I'd rebelled against my adoptive mother's strict rules and the rigid ideas and belief systems that separated me from the rest of the world.

"It's probably what got her into so much trouble," Veronica said, "ditching all she'd been taught, without replacing it with something else."

Ditching all she'd been taught, without replacing it with something else. Veronica's words rang so true they left an impression like a clay handprint on my heart. Veronica was growing, as I'd been attempting to do on this journey Dr. Mendez had started me on.

Maya gasped when she shifted her attention from Veronica's project to mine. "Witch masks," she said, clapping her hands.

I thought of my good friend, Anne. "Not just witches, but healers."

"And we'll look the same." She held one mask to her face and said, "Only our eyes and lips will show."

We'd look the same all right. On the outside. We'd never look the same within. I could never give of myself the way Maya did on a constant basis.

A rumble of thunder came from outdoors and the room grew dark, which caused the crafters to stop what they were doing and look out the window. A heavy sheet of rain gushed from the heavens as if someone had torn a hole in the sky. We all watched, mesmerized by the spectacle unfolding in front of our eyes.

"Good thing the Halloween party will be inside tomorrow," I said. As much as I loved nature, the scene we were witnessing was a reminder of the invisible powers that surrounded us on October thirty-first, one of two times a year when the boundary separating the human and spirit worlds was most permeable.

"Hope the rain holds off long enough for the trick-or-treaters to get from house-to-house for their candy," Maya said, before turning to the group and announcing, "Cleanup time!"

Leave it to Maya to care about the little munchkins, ghosts, and goblins.

Veronica ended our chitchat with, "Yeah, let's clean up this mess and get home."

Maya giggled as she gathered up the scissors and glue. "Me to my comfy yurt, and you to your palatial mansion."

"You mean, to your sacred circle," I said, another case of my subconscious popping up and piping in.

Veronica halted and brought her hands to her hips. "Give me a square room any day. It's less confusing. All those round walls make positioning the furniture a pain."

"You're sleeping on a round bed in the basement," I reminded her.

"And I don't know if my head's facing up, down, or sideways."

"A round bed forces you to decide," Maya said. "What you believe to be real is real."

Veronica shook her head. "At least in a round room, in a square *bed, you* still know if you're facing up or down."

"See you later, girls!" I looked up in time to see the Ed McMahon impersonator we'd met on our first day leave the room along with several others.

Maya waved at his back. "Bye, Pete. See you tomorrow."

"He'll freeze in those shorts," I said.

"No way. Pete's from Holland. He thinks it's hot outside."

"What you believe to be real is real," Veronica said.

Chapter Twenty-Four

IT WAS HALLOWEEN NIGHT, and it wasn't raining. Instead, there was fog—lots of it. A perfect setting for this evening of ghosts and goblins. The swirling mists conjured up images of phantoms and graveyards, mystery and uncertainty. Maya and I were dressed alike in flowing black robes and black boots. Our masks were in place and our hair caught up in knots beneath our felt hats. Veronica, with her faux fur robe, basket hat, and makeup-free face, did a double take. "Couldn't one of you at least have worn a bracelet, so I could tell you apart?"

"That would've ruined all the fun," Maya said, followed by a pure, straight-from-the-gut laugh, the kind you hear in playgrounds and amusement parks.

"Aha! *Now* I know who's who," Veronica said. "Marjorie's laugh doesn't sound natural, like she's still learning how, but yours sounds like you've had plenty of practice."

Veronica was right. I didn't laugh much. Or sing or cry. What did that say about me? What didn't it say? I imitated Maya's laugh. It felt good. I tried it again.

"Maya!" called a man dressed as the Tin Woodman. He rushed toward me, his aluminum duct-tubed arms spread wide. "This Halloween party was a great idea." He wore a funnel hat and carried a fake silver ax. "It makes me feel like a kid again."

Maya laughed, which confused the Tin Man. His silver-painted face turned from me to her, then back to me. "Sorry, but I can't tell you two apart. You look and sound the same."

Costumed guests entered the Guidepost recreation room, loud

and boisterous, as if by masking their faces, they felt suddenly free. The overhead lights were dimmed, further illumination cast only by strategically placed jack-o'-lanterns and eerily lit skeletons and ghosts. Cobwebs, symbolizing progress, fate, and passing time, snaked from the ceiling and draped over cornhusks, black cats, and flying rodents and witches. A coffin, displaying a comatose Dracula, stood next to the restroom entrance for optimal exposure. I wondered how all the costumed guests could eat the vampire cookies and dragon-blood punch before their unmasking.

Laughter, games, fun. Hours became minutes. On Halloween, when the mundane and familiar turn magical, we can't help but see the world differently. And sometimes, if we're lucky, during one of these magical moments, we experience a breakthrough of healing and become acquainted with our true selves. Soon it would be time for our unmasking.

Near midnight, when the high point of the evening was about to unfold, a tall stranger entered the room. "It's Shane," Maya said, catching her breath. The latecomer's height and bearing were right, and he looked handsome in that flowing Spanish cape, cowl mask, and flat-brimmed sombrero, but Dr. Donovan wasn't invited, was he? "Did you know midnight on Halloween is the most powerful of Witching Hours?" Maya asked. I didn't. But the thought gave me hope. Maya could use some of those witchy powers to withstand the masked man with the sword.

Zorro scanned the room until he located Veronica. He approached her and struck up a conversation. Veronica—that traitor—smiled and pointed our way. Zorro said something, then shook his head. Veronica laughed, though I didn't think the situation the least bit funny.

The masked man, defender of the weak and oppressed, then headed our way as if he meant to carve a giant *Z* on our chests. He eyed us up and down, obviously waiting for one of us to speak and blow our cover. But neither of us said a word. "Very mysterious," he said, coming to a halt. "Are you going to make me guess who's who?"

Maya's continued stillness surprised me. This was a man she cared for. Why drag on the pretense? In a matter of minutes, she'd be directing the crowd to unmask, thereby revealing her own identity.

Zorro turned away from us, his cape draped around him like a funeral pall. "Might as well go back and talk to the only sane one of the three of you."

"That was close," Maya said, when he was a safe distance away.

"Why didn't you say something?" I asked.

"For the first time in my life, I feel like a fly on the wall," she said, "able to observe rather than be observed. Why would I give that up on demand?"

Tears welled in my eyes. "I didn't realize—"

She put her hand on my arm. "Don't get me wrong. Life is good. It's just that tonight, just this once, I want to experience what it would be like. No one's looking at my birthmark, Marjorie."

"I didn't think it bothered you," I said.

Maya chuckled. "Sometimes I wonder what would happen if I went along with the surgery. Would Shane look at me differently? Would his eyes mist over when he held me in his arms? Would he finally accept me for who I am?"

I doubted it, but didn't say so. The decision ultimately rested with her. Yet it worried me. I'd given up so much for Cliff, and it had never been enough. He'd wanted all of me, including my soul. Thank God, the voice of our dead mother had intervened before it was too late. Who would intervene for Maya?

The party wasn't much fun anymore, but I kept that thought to myself. Tonight meant a lot to Maya, and I wasn't about to dampen her mood with dire predictions, as my adoptive mother so often had. My concern for Maya came from a different place. At least I liked to think so. Anyway, I could be wrong. No use in writing a chapter in Maya's story before it happened. Maybe Dr. Donovan was the man she needed. Maybe he was part of God's plan.

Maya walked to the center of the room, her steps slow, as if she were about to set in motion an irreversible spiral of events. "Okay everybody. Countdown to midnight and your unmasking, starting now! Five... Four... Three... Two..."

"One!" people shouted from all directions, followed by tooth and finger-whistles and masks whirling into the air. Someone opened the outside door, letting in a welcome breeze.

Maya returned and asked, "Did you hear that?"

"What?"

"A sigh, carried on the wind."

Her words made me shiver. I wanted to hug her and tell her how much I loved her and how I'd been waiting for her all my life, but before I could do so, Dr. Donovan materialized at our side like a shadow. He gripped Maya's arms. "Never do that again. I don't like it."

I preferred him with his mask on.

Maya looked at me over Zorro's shoulder and winked.

I winked back. At least she had a sense of humor concerning Dr. Donovan's demanding ways, something I never had with Cliff. Would a sense of humor have made a difference?

The guests, temporarily unfettered by masks and egos, gathered around the treat-laden table. Maybe if I hurried, I could still get one of those vampire cookies.

"Please don't go," Maya said.

I hesitated. Something told me what was about to unfold wouldn't be to my liking.

"I want Shane to take a good look at you and then tell me if it would make a difference."

Oh God, Sis. Why are you doing this? What do you hope to accomplish?

"This isn't funny, Maya," Dr. Donovan managed between tight lips.

"It wasn't meant to be funny," she said, not at all cowed by his dark mood. "If my face were perfect like Marjorie's, would it make you happy, would it make you love me more?"

Although the doctor's eyes were a different color than Cliff's, the instant he looked at me, I saw my ex-fiancé. Both men simmered with controlled anger, judging and resisting when things didn't go their way. I met Maya's eyes and at that moment knew I, not she, was the second born. *Oh, little sister. Don't let him do this to you.*

"You're making a big deal out of nothing," the doctor said. "Cosmetic surgery is a procedure I've performed often. It'll change your life."

"And yours?" Maya whispered.

He looked like he might strike her. "Yes, damn it. Maybe without the growths disfiguring your nose and chin, you'll quit hiding out in that disgusting yurt of yours and spending all your time helping these...these..." He realized he was attracting attention and lowered his voice. "Maybe you'd buy some nice clothes and a car."

I was wrong about this man being just like Cliff. He was worse.

"You think I'd give up my yurt and all my friends?" Maya asked with an amused smile. "And buy clothes and a car?"

Maya's friends gathered around her, vampire cookies and dragon-blood punch in hand, as though sensing she needed their support. Dr. Donovan noticed and turned on Maya. "Look what you've done. Screwed up the evening for everyone."

"I don't think so," Maya said.

I smiled. She wasn't backing down.

She pointed at the table of treats. "There's plenty of goodies left folks. Don't be shy."

I took a step toward the table.

"No," Maya said. "Don't go."

I eyed the doctor, dressed in black rather than white. I didn't trust him. And tonight, it seemed, neither did Maya.

I scanned the room for Veronica. Our big sister didn't put up with bullies. Instead, she had a knack for cutting them down to size. Maya could use her support right now, as could I.

She stood in front of the Dracula's coffin, poking the amateur prop inside. I closed my eyes and visualized a tube of energy connecting her consciousness to mine. Then I sent a message through the tube—*Veronica, Maya needs you*—as if I were sending it through a paper-towel roll to amplify sound. Veronica stepped away from the coffin and glanced over her shoulder. *Over here, Sis.* She shook her head and covered her ears. *Come on. Come on.* Another shake of the head, then she looked our way. I curled my index finger, gesturing for her to come, then mouthed, *hurry*. She nodded. "Thank God," I whispered.

Dr. Donovan pressed his lips into a straight line and eyed Maya with what appeared to be pity.

"Hey Shane, what's with the long face?" Veronica asked on her approach.

"Maya's making a scene," he said.

Veronica looked at Maya and grinned. "Didn't think she had it in her."

"Damn it, Shane," Maya said.

My jaw dropped. Maya just said "damn."

Veronica clapped. "That a girl."

Maya's attention remained focused on the man she loved. "Would you rather I center my life on stuff? Would you rather I get all worked up over the cost of living and, as a result, miss out on living? Would you prefer to restrict the flow of good in my life and replace it with worry about all I lack?" She took a deep breath and her voice gentled. "Don't you see? My yurt allows me to observe all that's going on in the world. When it's raining, I see the drops splattering on the roof. When it's foggy, my ceiling becomes a cloud. When the sun comes out" —Maya lifted her face and closed her eyes as if she could feel the sun's heat on her skin— "I feel the touch of God."

Dr. Donovan regarded her in silence.

"Look around you, Shane," Maya said, her voice soothing. "See what's true. We have all we need."

"Are you through?" he said.

Maya smiled. "Yes, Shane, I am."

Chapter Twenty-Five

A LL SAINTS DAY PROVED to be as murky and chilly as Halloween had been. But instead of spending the morning in church commemorating every saint known and unknown to man, I sat hunched over my laptop at the bookstore—the heck with swearing off distracting technological devices—researching capillary hemangioma. The information was extensive, the colored pictures heartbreaking, but I refused to give up, hoping to find a way besides surgery to help Maya.

From my limited inquiry, I made a startling discovery—one that shouldn't have escaped Dr. Donovan. It was possible Maya didn't have capillary hemangioma, but instead, congenital vascular malformation, otherwise known as CVM. In most cases, hemangiomas were absent at birth, and our father had said Maya's face bore scars even then. CVMs, though, were present at birth, continued to grow into adulthood, and never went away. An MRI would differentiate between the two. Had Dr. Donovan requested one?

Continued reading disclosed that CVMs usually occurred during a child's embryonic development, which meant that during the time we'd shared our mother's womb, two of us had developed normally and the other had veered off course. The blood vessels under the right side of Maya's face had enlarged over time, causing the stains and malformations she perceived as a gift and Dr. Donovan saw as an aberration.

Treatment of CVMs included laser therapy, sclerotherapy, selective embolization, surgical debulking, and compression garments. But none of these sounded promising in turning my sister into the physical beauty Dr. Donovan wanted her to be. The surgical debulking treatment, for instance, was described as complex and multi-staged and could result in complications. Even when successful, it required ongoing management. In other words, it was possible for Maya to become a lifetime patient and encounter a situation inferior to the one she lived with now. What was Dr. Shane Donovan thinking?

CVM, according to my reading, was rare and occurred in only one percent of all births. Therefore, it wasn't always properly diagnosed and treated. The misdiagnosis of Maya's condition as infantile hemangiomata, otherwise known as IH, might explain why the doctors hadn't attempted to remove her defect while she was a child. Hemangiomas could be alarming, but most didn't require treatment. The majority disappeared in a few years, leaving behind a patch of shrunken elastic skin, the appearance of which could be improved by plastic surgery after the child had grown.

By the time I left the bookstore with all my notes and downloaded research, I was trembling, and by the time I got home, my legs barely supported my weight. I entered the kitchen, set my laptop on the counter, and headed for the basement in search of Veronica.

She wasn't there. "Darn it, Sis. Why aren't you ever around when I need you?" I considered walking the labyrinth to calm myself, but no, I needed to talk, not walk. Our father's house wasn't far away, just a few blocks down Lighthouse Avenue. Too bad Veronica and I had created a false distance between us.

❂❂❂

"Please be home," I whispered, as I waited for a car to pass before crossing the street. My father's rented cottage was up ahead. I could tell by its orange tiled roof.

I was no longer trembling. In fact, I felt amazingly calm. Ridiculous, since I was seeking the support of a man Veronica had warned me couldn't be trusted. For Maya, though, I'd do it. Attempting to help should count for something. I walked up the concrete walk, took the three steps to the front porch entrance, and knocked on the door.

Bob answered and didn't look drunk. Dressed in slacks, polo shirt, and sweater, he appeared ready to go out.

"Did I pick a bad time?" I asked.

He checked his watch before replying. "What's up?"

"I need to talk to you about Maya."

"Might as well come in," he said with the enthusiasm of a snail.

"Are you certain it's okay?"

The frown on his face said it wasn't. "Sure, why not?" He backed into the living room and held open the door, looking over my shoulder as though expecting a visitor other than me.

"Dad," I said, addressing him as close to Maya's *Papa*, as my still-closed heart would allow. I was here to ask for his help, so the least I could do was treat him as if I cared. Which I did. Not in the way I'd first imagined, but as one flawed soul reaching out to another, knowing we weren't meant to travel this life journey alone. "Maya has this friend," I began. "His name is Dr. Shane Donovan, and he wants to perform surgery on her face."

Bob's eyes brightened. "Surgery?" He clapped and gave a hoot. "God Almighty. My baby girl will be as beautiful as her sisters. Then I can get on with my life."

Baby girl? So, Maya *was* the youngest. I filed this information in the back of my mind while trying not to grimace at his words. I detected self-interest in his reaction, almost as if he cared more about picking up the shards of his broken life than the wellbeing of his youngest daughter. Maya's outer beauty seemed more important to the men who claimed to love her than whom she was inside. "Remember when you touched her face?" I asked.

His smile faded. "Sure. Why?"

"How did it make you feel?"

"Good, I guess."

"You said if you could always feel like that, you'd never need to drink again."

"I did?"

Veronica had warned me about our father's blackouts, how

162

sometimes he didn't remember things that happened only minutes before. I felt the emptiness Veronica must've experienced so often well up inside of me, where it threatened to overwhelm all my good intentions.

For an instant, his face turned ugly. Then he laughed. "My baby girl comes here for one lousy visit. One. Then, instead of coming back to check on her *papa*, she hangs out with a bunch of addicts and alcoholics."

How did he know where Maya hung out? From what I remembered, she'd shared little about herself with him. It had taken effort on Veronica's and my part to find her, so Bob must've put in an effort, too. Okay, so I'd hit a dead end. Time for a new tactic. "You said our mother wanted to train Maya in the ways of the Native American, so she wouldn't feel shame about her birthmark, but see it as a gift."

Bob gave a hollow laugh which only compounded the emptiness I felt inside, a hunger for the love, compassion, and hope Maya had revealed to be within reach, if only I knew how to access it. "Gift?" he said. "In this world, what matters is how you look, who you know, and how much you earn."

"What did you do with mother's mouse totem?" I asked.

"Totem? You mean the rock? Uh..." He patted the pockets of his slacks. "It's around here somewhere." He scratched his chin. "Last time I saw it..."

I gave the room a visual search and spotted the totem on the floor next to the coffee table. I picked it up and gripped it in my closed hand, tempted to keep it. What if he lost the totem for good next time, my only physical contact with Antonia, all the memories it held?

"It must've fallen out of my pocket," Bob said. "Give it to me."

My eyes burned. Parting with one of my most valued possessions had been hard enough the first time. Parting with it a second time, for a man who had no clue as to its value, was nearly impossible.

Give it to him, Sunwalker.

"Mother," I said under my breath.

It will find its way back to where it belongs.

I opened my hand, exposing the stone—and my heart—to my father.

He snatched the stone and shoved it into his slacks pocket.

"Maya works near here," I said.

"As if I didn't know. What do you think I've been doing since my arrival in this do-nothing town? Living it up with the butterflies? Your father's no slouch."

"Have you been following her?"

"Following?" he sputtered.

Moisture trickled down my back. The room was stifling. I had to get out of here.

"I wouldn't stoop that low," he said, avoiding my eyes.

"Then how do you know where she works?"

"I have my sources. She might as well live in Fort Knox, the way she's surrounded by faculty and security."

Wow. When it came to the two most important men in Maya's life, she was on her own. Thank God, she was further along in the self-understanding and discovering of life's purpose departments than I was. So, why did my concern for her outweigh my concern for myself?

Chapter Twenty-Six

RAIN AND FOG DISTORTED each day of the following week, and my attitude became distorted as well. I saw shadows everywhere and couldn't shake a nagging feeling that something was off. Veronica grew impatient with my distrust of Dr. Donovan. "What's with this doctor shit?" she demanded. "His name is Shane. Got that? Shane. He loves Maya, and he wants to help her, except she's too damn stubborn to let him." With all her newfound wisdom, Veronica was blind to the darkness I sensed in the doctor. No matter how hard I tried, I couldn't get Veronica to see past his handsome face and the medical jargon he spewed about what was best for his beloved.

In my concern for Maya's safety after she'd shared her suspicion of being followed, I started hanging out at the Guidepost. As a result, I became acquainted with the terrific ways the facility helped those debilitated by drugs and alcohol. Maya's work dealt with the final stages of the drug and alcohol recovery process, which kicked in after the patients had completed the drug abuse rehab program. She provided the newly sober with a network of support to assist in making sobriety last and facilitate in rebuilding new lives.

Maya made each patient feel heard, accepted, and loved. Her work with those who'd strayed off course like the veins beneath her birth marked face electrified me. Maya and I functioned like two parts of a whole, and the patients accepted me as one of their own. For the first time in my life, I comprehended the deep joy of selfless service. Maya helped me internalize what all those encrypted messages from our dead mother and life's lessons had failed to do. That it wasn't about me. A voice from deep within kept whispering, *I can do that.* Not that I could come close to attaining Maya's almost magical touch with her patients. Our hands may have looked alike, but our fingerprints weren't the same, unique expressions through which the Creator made His presence known. As His good poured through me to others that week, I felt as though I were contributing in a way that mattered. I sensed a new passion and purpose emerge of opening doors for those muted and suppressed, helping them heal through inclusion. The only thing subtracting from my joy was that Veronica and our father weren't there to share it. I suspected time was running out. For what, I didn't know.

On Sunday, after Mass at St. Mary's, Maya dropped the news I'd dreaded. She was considering surgery to remove the mark on her face. After a moment of shocked silence, I lectured her on all I'd learned through my research, and then, with little thought to her feelings, I warned her about the possible complications. When that didn't seem to faze her, I reminded her of how the birthmark brought her peace and happiness and how it inadvertently helped others. I explained it was wrong to give in to Dr. Donovan and if he wasn't happy with her now, he'd never be. She smiled. Just smiled.

On my return home, Veronica cornered me in the kitchen. "What's the deal with you running off and hanging out with Maya practically day and night?

"I'm worried about her, especially now that she's considering surgery."

I was about to repeat the lecture I'd forced on Maya, but Veronica stopped me dead. "Seems to me you're jealous of our sister."

No words could've hurt more, but what terrified me was...they could be true.

❂❂❂

Three days of stormy weather followed, days I spent holed up in my turret room—sleeping. Rain battered the windows; thoughts battered my mind. I feared both would never stop. I wanted to call Morgan. Veronica had already broken our no-phone-use pact by calling the yoga studio. Emergency? Hardly. Telling Morgan about meeting my birth father came closer to my definition of an emergency. Plus having a second sister, being a triplet, one of three! Morgan knew why I was here. I'd shared all, via a series of long, weepy phone calls, after I'd left Big Sur for Pacific Grove. I just about begged him to demand I come home, tell me he couldn't do without me, that no one was holding me back but myself. His reply? Not what I wanted, but what I needed. "I want you here," he said. "Joshua wants you here. We all do. But you have to finish what you started. I'd love to pull you into my arms and make it all better, but we'd both regret it in the morning." He then encouraged me to follow my heart and repeated his vow to wait for me.

I'd heard it said our personality is like the cologne we wear, our character what we *really* smell like. I'd tried Anne's "Rich Hippie" organic perfume. Smelled good, but it wasn't me. Calling Morgan now would confirm that I hadn't yet traveled far enough on my road to independence—that I still needed someone else to tell me what to do. And I didn't like how that would make me smell.

I love you, Morgan. Please don't give up on me.

❀❀❀

On Thursday morning, I woke to fog, minus the rain. I pressed my face into the pillow, allowing sleep to tug me back, greedy to extract from it more of what I needed.

"Meow." The sound was loud, drawn out, sweet.

"Meow." Something landed on the foot of my bed, the weight reassuring.

"Meow." The weight edged closer.

I shifted onto my back and stared as the tabby from upstairs brought its face close to mine. "Hey, kitty, what's up?" I asked, still groggy from the respite of sleep and comforting thoughts of home. "You look just like my stray, Gabriel, but fatter." I scratched its head. "Someone's been feeding you well." The cat settled onto the pillow next to mine and purred like a windup toy. I stroked its warm, shiny fur, amazed at how much solace a cat could bring. The cat yawned.

"Do you have a name?" I asked. It looked at me as if prompting me to guess. "Forget it. I'm not good at guessing games. How about a nickname? Like Chip, for instance, as in chocolate chip cookie." The cat's stare gave nothing away, a talent I envied. I'd attempted to hide my feelings for years now and failed. Big time. "Are you Anne's cat?"

Chip's head jerked toward the door. Seconds later, a woman rushed into the room. "There you are, you little monster." She shooed the cat off the pillow. "How many times do I have to tell you to stay off the bed?"

"Jeez!" The upstairs boarder. And I was meeting her for the first time half-dressed and with bed-head hair. "It's okay about the cat," I said.

She shook her head and tsk-tsked. "Naughty thing."

"Are you staying in the attic apartment?" I asked.

She smiled, apparently unperturbed about walking into my bedroom without a knock or invitation. "His name isn't Chip," she said, eyeing the cat with knit brows. "He can be such a nuisance."

"So, what *is* his name?" I asked, sitting up to get a better view. She was thin, emaciated even, and wore a silk shirtdress, along with what appeared to be an authentic strand of pearls.

"Raphael," she said, "like the angel.

"My tabby's name is Gabriel, like the other angel."

She smiled. "God's messengers."

I wondered at the coincidence. Then again, for the past eight months my life had been full of coincidences. Dr. Mendez called these occurrences synchronistic, coincidences that weren't coincidences, but meaningfully related.

"Why are you still in bed?" the boarder asked, reminding me of my adoptive mother. "Could be a sign of depression." She eyed me with narrowed eyes. "No reason for a lovely girl like you to be depressed. A waste of time if you ask me. Life's too short for all that needs to be done during our short stay here on this earth without wasting hours in bed."

I stared at her, transfixed. What a feisty old woman.

She turned to leave. "Come on Raphael. This young lady needs to get up and get moving. There's much for her to do."

"Wait," I said.

She looked at me over her shoulder.

"What's your name?"

"Christine, Marjorie dear. It was nice speaking with you."

"Umm, Christine..."

She left behind the scent of vanilla and her words planted in my mind. *This young lady needs to get up and get moving. There's much for her to do.*

I jumped out of bed and grabbed my robe, hoping to waylay the mysterious visitor before she made herself scarce again. I wanted to ask her how she knew my name and how she managed live upstairs without us knowing.

Still struggling into my robe, I rushed out of my room and slammed into Veronica. She was the first to recover. "What's the big hurry?"

"Did you see someone coming out of my room just now?"

"Like who? Santa Claus?"

"Sorry, Veronica, not now." I headed for the attic stairs. "Please, oh please, don't disappear."

"Hey, Sis," Veronica said from close behind me. "You freaking out on me?"

I halted. Freaking out? Oh, God. She was right. I was freaking out. I turned and gave her a clumsy hug. A sob followed, then another.

Veronica patted my back. "I came here to check up on you, not make you cry."

"It wasn't you," I said, realizing what my subconscious had known all along. "I think I just saw a ghost."

Veronica pulled away with an abruptness that left me feeling unanchored, then gave me a smart-ass smile.

"Before you start feeling all smug and superior," I said, "remember, you've seen the dead, too."

Veronica frowned and stepped back. "It took the combined effort of you, Anne, and me to provoke Antonia into showing herself. Even then, she was more vapor than form."

Frustration flowed through me like stale air, so unlike the joy I'd experienced at the Guidepost with Maya. "Hearing voices coming out of nowhere is easier to accept," I said. "We hear the invisible all the time, but" —I shook my head to avoid bursting into tears— "seeing the invisible is—"

"Different," Veronica said, her voice sympathetic.

She led me downstairs to the parlor and pressed me into the warm embrace of a tufted-armchair, then drew the matching ottoman in close, sat, and leaned forward. "Okay, talk."

"I think it's the boarder."

No knitting of brows, no smirk, no long exhale. "Yes?"

"The cat came into my room this morning, you know, the one I told you about, and" —I took a calming breath— "a woman followed it in."

Veronica took my cold, shaky hands in hers and rubbed warmth back into them. It felt so darn good, I managed a smile. "She knew my name and told me the cat's name was Raphael. She also told me to get up, that I had things to do."

"Maybe you were halfway between sleep and wakefulness," Veronica said.

"You mean, experiencing some kind of transitional state? No, it was more than that."

I wished the old woman would walk in at this moment with a plate of cookies, introduce herself, explain that she'd been away for a while and was happy to meet us, and then tell us Anne said to say hello.

"I thought you'd adjusted to your psychic abilities by now," Veronica said, releasing my hands and rubbing her forehead.

I got up and walked through the open archway into the dim foyer. Only enough sunlight filtered through the stained-glass panels around the front door to prevent the need for overhead lighting, as if the brightness of the real world was too much for the room to absorb.

"You could always make an exception to our no-phone rule and call Anne," Veronica said, following me out of the parlor. "It might help to have someone besides me to talk to, since I'm as clueless as you are. Or you could..."

I approached the crystal ball on the foyer table. If I couldn't make an exception for Morgan, there'd be no exceptions at all. "Could what?"

Veronica rubbed her hands up and down her jeans. "Talk to Maya."

I ran my hand over the crystal ball, noting its clarity, its smoothness. Anyone could pick one up these days for less than forty dollars, yet how many people actually owned one? Why hadn't our mother reached out to Maya the way she'd reached out to Veronica and me? It made no sense. Nothing made sense. "I doubt Maya hears voices."

"Maya communicated with us telepathically," Veronica said, "which ranks right up there with hearing voices."

"Yes, but..." I marched back to my chair in the parlor and sank into its rolled, comforting arms. "I just don't know."

"Okay, so how about you, Maya, and I form a circle and call on Antonia," Veronica said leaning against the heavily framed archway between the foyer and parlor. "Like we did with Anne in Big Sur. If that doesn't work, we'll forget all the psychic stuff and phone Anne. This is her house. She should be privy to any ghostly boarders."

I took in the elaborate details of the ivy-patterned wallpaper, brocade valances, and fringed lamps, so warm, so reassuring. "At least *this* ghost seems happy and well-adjusted."

Veronica snorted. "If she's so happy and well-adjusted, why isn't she in heaven where she belongs?"

Chapter Twenty-Seven

WHILE VERONICA ATTENDED YOGA class, I spent the morning wandering about the house looking for a ghost and a cat. They weren't inclined to exposing themselves, however. Of course not. That would put me out of my misery. It was highly inefficient, the way my so-called psychic abilities worked. I sensed things at the oddest moments, hardly ever when expected. Spirits talked, I listened. Spirits appeared, I watched. After which they'd go on their merry way, scattering puzzle pieces all over the place, always leaving out a key few. I used to like puzzles.

By noon, I called it quits. I hadn't come to Pacific Grove to chase my tail, or sit around and mope. Antonia had urged Veronica and me to meet with our father for a reason, which included discovering the secret they'd kept from us for too long. We were triplets, not twins, and had a beautiful sister named Maya. I wasn't about to waste another week without enjoying her company. She'd promised to spend time here during Thanksgiving week if we included our father. In four days would be the big day. What better time for a family reunion?

A sudden vision of my adoptive mother had me leaning against the stair rail for support. How could I consider a family reunion without her? "Oh Mom," I whispered, the back of my eyes burning. "We've never spent a Thanksgiving apart." She would plan and fuss, adjusting and perfecting her turkey and stuffing recipes: fresh turkey versus frozen, hen versus tom, apple and walnut stuffing versus the one with garlic and sweet peppers. It had been tough for her to keep the tradition alive after my father—her foremost fan and critic—died. How could she go on without me?

I sat on the top step of the second-floor landing and took deep breaths. If I called her, she'd interfere. She'd demand I come home, stop this foolishness. Her way of showing love was to regulate my life, which I would no longer allow. "God bless you, Mom," I said, my chest banded in pain. "I'll make it up to you some day. Promise."

❂❂❂

It was Tuesday, the day before Thanksgiving. Maya was already here. Our father would arrive soon. Veronica and I had helped Maya settle into the bedroom suite across the hall from mine, and we were sitting at the kitchen table discussing where Bob would best fit in.

"I still say we put him in the studio apartment in the attic," Veronica said.

"It's probably haunted," I grumbled. "He'd freak out."

"I doubt it," Veronica said. "He's not a sensitive like you."

"True," I admitted, "and it would give him more privacy."

It was early yet, and the backyard was still in shadow, but there was no fog. I stared at the brick sidewalk leading to the garage. Several birds were pecking into its crevices, finding their breakfast there free for the taking. "Coffee anyone?" I asked, getting up to pour myself a refill.

Veronica held up her nutritional drink. Chocolate today. "I'm fine."

I glanced at Maya's glass of water, sitting on the table untouched. "Last chance for a cup of hot java."

She shook her head. "No thanks."

"How about some hot chocolate?" I persisted.

A blank stare. "No thanks."

I shrugged. Coffee wasn't as healthy as water or a nutritional drink, but for me it was one of life's simple pleasures. And this morning, I was all for simple pleasures.

"So, where's the cat?" Maya asked.

I set my coffee on the table and headed back to the counter for the homemade chocolate chip cookies I'd baked for our Thanksgiving guests. Veronica frowned as I handed a cookie to Maya as if the offering offended her. "I haven't seen or heard a damn thing," she said, implying she'd searched the entire house, which I knew she hadn't. "In fact, things have been quite normal around here, considering the house belongs to Marjorie's friend, Anne. She's a witch you know."

"A very generous witch," I said. "One who not only provided a roof over our heads, but a wealth of information about yoga and the nutritional supplements you've been living on since our arrival."

"Hold it," Veronica said. "I wasn't criticizing Anne. I met her, too, remember? And I think she's great."

"Anne?" Maya asked.

"Yes, Anne Bolen," I said. "You know, this is her house."

"Shane has a sister named Anne," Maya said, her face tilted as if she were asking a question instead of making a statement."

"Oh," I said, not about to delve into one of my least favorite subjects: Dr. Shane Donovan. "Back to your question about the cat. I saw it for the first time in the attic in what I call the studio apartment. Then Thursday morning it jumped onto my bed."

Maya giggled. "Nice wake-up call."

"Better than a rooster," Veronica said.

"Then a woman came rushing in. She said her name was Christine, and while I was sitting there with my mouth hanging open, she lectured me about still being in bed. I tell you, she sounded just like my adoptive mother, ordering me around as if I were a kid. The really frustrating part is that before she took off she called me, 'Marjorie,' and I didn't have time to ask who she was and how she knew my name."

"She's a ghost," Veronica said, trying to stifle a yawn.

The left side of Maya's face paled, even more so than usual. "Shane had a great aunt named Christine. In fact, the armoire Shane gave me once belonged to her. She raised him from the age of five and died soon after he graduated from medical school, just before he started his general surgery residency."

Veronica eyed Maya, her mouth forming a silent oh.

Anne had never mentioned having a brother. Or an aunt. In fact, she'd rarely mentioned her personal life at all. Nope. I wouldn't believe it. Not without proof.

"He mentioned being raised in a big house," Maya continued, looking around her with renewed interest. "That it was crammed full of antiques and that the armoire wouldn't be missed. Do you think this is the place?"

The coffee wasn't settling well. My throat and chest burned.

"Wild," Veronica said. "Shane living here? Let's call him and find out."

"We agreed on emergency phone use only during our stay here," I said, still pushed out of shape about her ditching our agreement to sign us up for a yoga class. Okay, so we hadn't made it official with a notary and thumbprints next to our signatures. But she'd broken her word, without explanation or apology, which probably ran along the line of doing it for our own good.

Veronica stood and headed for the sink with her empty glass. "Okay then, you two wait for Dad while I go visit Shane."

"But you don't know where he lives," I said.

She winked at Maya. "Do now."

Before I could respond, someone knocked on the screen door.

"Damn," Veronica said. "Dad's here."

I smiled. "Looks like Dr. Donovan will have to wait."

Veronica snorted. "Still calling him doctor, huh?"

Maya looked back and forth between us, then rose to answer the door. "Papa," she cried, taking his hand and pulling him into the kitchen. "Welcome. Welcome."

Bob looked around, wide-eyed. "This kitchen is so white."

Maya gave him a hug. Not a short two-second hug, but a solid, seven-second bear hug with a tight squeeze. "Where's your suitcase?"

"In the car. I wanted to make sure you girls meant it about me staying here." His gaze settled on the plate of homemade cookies. "Chocolate chip, my favorite."

"Give me your keys," Veronica said. "I'll get your bagga...stuff."
It sounded like she'd been about to say *baggage* before catching herself.

Bob fumbled in his coat pocket. "You sure?"

"Positive," Maya said. "We have so much catching up to do."

He handed Veronica the keys, but his eyes remained fixed on Maya.

"Would you like some coffee?" I asked, having second thoughts about inviting him to stay, though there was no going back now.

He looked at me for the first time. "Coffee?"

I held up my empty mug. "Tastes great with chocolate chip cookies."

He turned to look out the back door. "Here comes Veronica with my bags."

"Hold it with the coffee, Marjorie," Maya said. "Let's take Papa to his room first."

"But we never decided for sure—"

"The studio apartment," Maya said. "It's in the attic, right?"

I nodded. What was the big hurry?

Veronica entered the kitchen carrying two exquisite brown leather bags, a reminder that our father was a wealthy man, a fact easily forgotten given the poverty of his existence. "Here's your stuff, Dad," she said. "Gotta go."

Bob blinked, then scowled. "Go? Where?"

"You haven't even moved in yet," Veronica said, "and you're already butting into my business."

Bob lifted his chin. "I thought you'd want to stay and visit for a while."

Veronica backed out the door. "All right if I use your car, Marjorie?"

"Sure," I said, upset with her for being so difficult. The least she could do was try to be civil. This was supposed to be a time for bonding, for giving thanks as a family.

"Tell Shane hi for me," Maya said, and I wondered if she'd relayed this message for our father's benefit, to clue him in, make him feel involved.

He picked up on it immediately. "Shane?"

"Dr. Shane Donovan," I said. "Remember, the man I told you about?"

His expression cleared. "The guy who's going to fix Maya's face?" He turned to Maya, and I held my breath. "I'm so happy for you, baby. Finally, you'll be as beautiful as your sisters."

Maya smiled. "Come on Papa, I'll take you to your room. The attic room, right, Marjorie?"

"No," I said. The attic room belonged to our ghost boarder and her cat. "Give him the turret suite above mine. The temperature's more consistent there and it'll save him from climbing an extra set of stairs."

"Chicken," Veronica said, with a farewell wave.

I waved back. Soon we'd hear more than I wanted or needed about Dr. Shane Donovan. "Dear God. Please don't let him be Anne's brother."

Chapter Twenty-Eight

THE NEWS VERONICA BROUGHT home that afternoon wasn't good; at least not from my view. The rest of the family thought it fabulous. "Just think," Maya said. "Shane's your best friend's brother and once lived in this house. Isn't that amazing?" Veronica thought Dr. Donovan's kinship to Anne was an awesome coincidence. Bob couldn't quit grinning. To him, the doctor, like Santa, bore only gifts and goodwill. Trouble was, we were about to celebrate Thanksgiving, not Christmas, and I didn't believe for one minute the doctor's concept of goodwill included pure, unconditional, and self-denying love.

I was so tired of coincidences, I wanted to cry. Why couldn't life run smoothly for a change, allow us to spend a few days together without incident? Picturing Dr. Shane Donovan as Anne's brother was impossible for me. My mind couldn't stretch that far. So, I let it go.

What I couldn't let go, though, was the hope that having my family together under one roof would cause a loving and permanent bond. Sure, the four of us had different outlooks on life and therefore different agendas, but we could work around that, compromise, learn from one another. Personal growth includes acknowledging one's own character deficiencies. I didn't need Dr. Mendez to remind me of that. I, for instance, distrusted Dr. Donovan's judgment and intentions, but that didn't give me the right to decide what Maya should and shouldn't do. I was acting and sounding like my adoptive mother, pushing *my* agenda instead of stepping back and honoring my sister's right to freewill. Maya hadn't asked for my advice. She hadn't invited me in. When did caring cross into interference? For the sake of peace, I needed to back off and mind my own business, even if that meant watching her make a decision with which I disagreed.

I could sure use Antonia's advice now. Why hadn't she made her presence known, if not to the others, at least to me? I'd half expected some form of communication between us on Halloween night, when the veil between the human and spirit worlds was particularly thin. But no. Of course not. That would've been too predictable, too easy. So why not now? Wasn't this family reunion what Antonia had been striving for, the reason she'd come back from the grave?

After delivering the startling news about Dr. Donovan, Veronica made a quick retreat into the basement. Maya and Bob headed to the parlor for a chat. Which left me in a house that suddenly seemed too small. I slipped out through the back-porch door and made my way to the labyrinth, my hands reaching into my fanny pack for my mouse totem, before realizing it was no longer there. I wondered if Bob had lost it again, then pushed the thought from my mind.

Instead, I concentrated on the call of the resident birds staying behind to winter in Anne's backyard—the high, whistled *fee-bee-bees* and raspy *chick-a-dee-dees* of what my field guide identified as Chestnut-Backed Chickadees and the noisy *kwesh* and *check* notes of the Western Scrub Jay. Birds hopped and swooped between the branches and needles of the conifers above and the dense foliage below with sharp *chinks* and *musical pur-lees*. Sparrows and kinglets landed on the labyrinth as if urging me on with *ohh-dear-mees* and *look-at-mes*.

According to my research, the walk from the labyrinth's entrance to its center represented purgation, where one attempts to release, empty, and let go of the need to control. I took a deep breath and entered the circle. This was supposed to be a nurturing experience, taken at a slow pace, no rushing through to capture the prize in the center. Under the guidance of the birds' wheezy trills and warbles, I concentrated on the intricate path, allowing my worries to fade and my intuitive mind to surface. The route was long and illogical—six semi-right-angle turns, twenty-eight U-turns—yet a trek I could safely get lost on, secure in knowing it would ultimately lead to the right place. So, it came as no surprise that the first clue signifying I was anywhere near my destination was being there, in the place of illumination, meditation, and prayer. A woodpecker called from above *wake-up, wake-up, wake-up* as I set down my marker stones and opened my mind and heart to what awaited me in the labyrinth's center.

Your struggle has only just begun.

This wasn't what I'd expected. Advice from my subconscious, yes. Dire predictions from my birth mother, no. I'd thought my stay in Pacific Grove was about over, that soon I'd be headed back home. Antonia, however, was never the bearer of good news, her specialty, throwing out new and unexpected challenges. "What struggle?" I asked, unable to keep the irritation out of my voice. "We found Bob. We found Maya. They're both here now. What more do you—"

Be strong, Sunwalker. The end is near.

"The end?" I cried, the sound of my voice muffled by the gathering mist. Even sheltered under massive evergreens, the keen edge of a penetrating breeze sliced through my clothes. "Less than five minutes ago, you said the struggle had just begun."

You will not be alone.

"Of course, I won't. I have Veronica. I have Maya. I have Dad."

No response from my mother.

I snatched up the marker stones and dropped them into my fanny pack, trying not to be angry. I'd come to the labyrinth to open my mind and heart, not shut them down. The counterclockwise walk out from the center symbolized the act of taking what I'd received there into the world, along with a renewed sense of empowerment and strength. As I retraced the steps I'd taken in, I tried to digest and integrate Antonia's words—*The struggle has just begun. You must be strong.* Instead, bitterness swelled in my chest like an expandable water toy absorbing four hundred times its weight. Why bother? As far as I could tell, she'd spelled out more disaster. As I stepped out of the circle, accompanied by the bold descending *caw* of a crow, she imparted one last message. *In the end, all will be well.*

❂❂❂

"Where's Veronica?" Maya asked when I came in through the back-porch door.

"In the basement," I said. "Hibernating." Maya cocked her head and looked at me as if I were a rare species not conducive to our environment. "Okay. That wasn't very nice, was it?"

"Hibernating works," Maya said. "Do you think she'd mind if I joined her?"

I shrugged. The anger I still bore my mother had shifted to Veronica, which wasn't fair. She'd done nothing wrong. "Guess the only way to find out is to ask her. She made it clear she didn't want *me* down there."

"Does she bite?"

"A little," I said, smiling. "But it doesn't hurt much. Only in the heart."

"She's been through a lot, hasn't she?" Maya asked.

"You mean because of our father?"

"He'd be a hard person to live with."

"Yes."

"You turn to nature to remember who you are, Marjorie, and Veronica has chosen the isolation of the basement."

"And yoga," I added.

"Nature is full of small homilies, isn't it?"

I laughed. "And sometimes, I even understand one of them." Maya seemed so wise, so caring, so advanced in her spiritual search. "I gather you find yourself by serving others."

She smiled so gently, I felt drawn to her light. "With God as my guide."

"I wonder who guides our mother," I said. "Does God reach out to her, too? I mean, from where does she get the wisdom, or inclination, to counsel me as she does? My adoptive mother tries to bend me to her will, while Antonia goads me to stand on my own two feet.

181

Then she turns around and encourages Veronica, who's broken free of her oppressive father, to go back and face him. I don't get it."

"Maybe because our father knew the secret, she wanted him to share," Maya said.

I shook my head, confused. "Why didn't she come right out and tell us about you instead of requesting we meet with our father and reopening old wounds?"

"Maybe there's more to the secret than my existence. Antonia knows Veronica has to face her father before she can overcome the inner barriers that limit her."

"Yet she had me escape my adoptive mother."

"Do you hate her?" Maya asked.

"Truus? No. I love her very much."

"Well, then your case isn't the same as Veronica's. Veronica will never find peace as long as she's bound by hate. She has taken her father's abuse in silence and anger and is now looking within for her part in it. She's bleeding inside, Marjorie, crying out in her own sarcastic way. As a result, she's incapable of seeing the bright side of anything. She's in danger of losing compassion. Whereas your problem has more to do with fear, the fear of standing up for what you believe in, the fear that you might fail. We all respond to life's challenges in our own unique ways."

While Maya spoke, I wondered what life challenges she had experienced. If I asked, I doubted she'd tell me. And even if she did, she'd give it a rosy cast. "Maya," I said. "How do *you* deal with the fear?"

"I replace it with what I want and then expect it to be true," she said. "Life moves in the direction of our thoughts."

"Okay. Done," I said with a cocky grin.

Maya gave me the thumbs up. "That's it then."

My grin grew wider. Couldn't help it. She had that effect on me. She made even the ridiculous sound credible. "But nothing's changed."

"Of course, it has, silly. Once you get the idea implanted in your mind, everything falls into place. The people and circumstances you need will be drawn into your experience just when needed."

"Okay," I said. Arguing with Maya would be pointless. I didn't possess her wisdom, a wisdom she'd gained through experience.

My quick compliance didn't fool her though. She grabbed my shoulders and looked into my eyes. "One more time. Implant what you want into your mind." I closed my eyes and pictured Antonia happy, rising into the heavens. I pictured Bob, sober. I even tried to picture Maya without her birthmark, but couldn't. When I reopened my eyes, Maya was staring at me. She didn't say a word, just stared. Then, "You've put yourself in line with a much larger mind. Now let *It* do what *It* does so well."

Looking back at my sister, I sensed warmth glide over me, warmth no less miraculous than what comes from the 4.5-billion-year-old star we call the sun. "How do you do that?" I whispered.

She smiled. "I'm genius."

"Maya? Tell me what you said to our father?"

"I certainly didn't tell him what to do."

"I wasn't implying—"

"I know you weren't, dear. Deep inside, he's a kind, gentle person just aching to be free. There's more good in him than bad. If we concentrate on the good, we'll call more of it forth."

"I like that," I said. "It makes sense. But what did you say to him?"

"I listened and sent him my love. Instead of worrying about the things that divide us, I concentrated on what unites us."

"Antonia?"

"For starters, yes. I assured him he didn't have to make himself loveable. That we already loved him."

"Did you tell him about the work you do?"

"Yes."

"What did he say?"

"Not much. But he listened, which was a good sign."

"That's it?"

"No. I told him there was nothing wrong with him."

"Why'd you tell him that?"

"Because it's true. I told him to forget all those negative thoughts that have caused him pain over the years, that all he needed in order to heal was right inside of him, ready to be activated. I also referred him to an exclusive outpatient drug rehab facility in Maryland that specializes in dual diagnosis and holistic therapies."

A sob rose in my throat, light but not hollow, like a pain-infused bubble rising from the depths. "Can his addiction be overcome?"

"Believe it to be true," she said.

Chapter Twenty-Nine

IT WAS THANKSGIVING MORNING, and I needed to go shopping. Bob was up in his third-floor suite and Maya and Veronica were in the basement. If I didn't buy a small turkey and some side-dish fixings before the markets closed, we might as well kiss off having a holiday dinner.

With the grocery store practically deserted, I carted through the aisles for the items on my shopping list and make it through check-out before noon. My purchases included boxed stuffing mix, instant mashed potatoes, canned gravy, yams, and cranberry sauce, ready-to-serve pumpkin pie, and a four-pound, maple-brined turkey breast.

Truus would've been horrified.

I put the turkey breast in the oven at two o'clock and headed for the dining room to set the table. The china hutch provided lovely white linens—so neatly folded, they didn't need pressing—fine white china, sparkling crystal stemware, and gold flatware. I decorated the center of the table with an assortment of candles snatched from the parlor and a ceramic turkey I'd purchased for half off at the grocery store.

Gauging by the mouth-watering aroma wafting from the oven, I figured the turkey breast was coming along fine, so I prepared the yams with brown sugar, pineapple, and marshmallows and slid them into the small side oven to bake. The boxed stuffing, instant mashed potatoes, and canned gravy took only minutes to prepare. The trick was keeping them warm until dinnertime. The center of the stovetop served as a warming zone. Problem solved. I placed the cranberry sauce on the table, put a chilled bottle of apple cider on the side-board, lit the candles, and dimmed the chandelier.

Time to change clothes and call in my guests.

❍❍❍

Veronica swept into the dining room as though walking the red carpet instead of a hardwood floor covered by a pastel-hued area rug. She wore a long-sleeved, taupe maxi dress with matching sandals and a gold choker, another outfit likely filched from Anne's wardrobe.

It took me a minute to adjust to the sight of Maya. She was dressed in a clingy black, mini dress, her hair a mass of hairspray and curling-iron curls. *Tomboy to princess. Wow!*

I looked down at my jeans and sequined top. "Jeez guys, you could've warned me."

"Paybacks are a bitch," Veronica said, with a secretive smile.

I assumed she was referring to the way Maya and I had teamed up on Halloween with identical masks, leaving her out in the cold, so I kept silent.

"Smells good in here," Bob said before taking a seat at the south end of the table. "You've been busy." He'd come to the table shaved and suited. What a transformation. No wonder he'd stolen our mother's heart.

"Yeah," Veronica said, choosing the high-backed armchair on the north end of the table. "Busy like Martha in the Bible."

This wasn't a compliment. As I remembered the story of Martha, she complained to Jesus that her sister had left her to serve alone. "Tell her to help me," she said, to which Jesus replied, "Martha, Martha, you are worried and troubled about many things. But one thing is needed, and Mary has chosen that good part, which will not be taken from her."

I had a pretty good idea who represented Mary in our little family saga.

If I allowed it, Veronica's offhanded crack would ricochet in my head for weeks and decimate my self-image. Instead, I practiced a technique Dr. Mendez called neuroplasticity and tweaked her words into something positive. *Don't sweat the small stuff.* Humbled, but not shamed, I sat in the chair to our father's left. "Who wants to say grace?"

"I do," Bob said. He waited for Maya to take the remaining seat at the table, then crossed himself and said, "Lord, thank you for my girls. I thought I'd lost them, and here they are." He paused to clear his throat. I kept my eyes closed, not wanting to invade the privacy of his exposed heart. "Thank you for the food on this table. It was prepared with love. And thank you, dear Lord, for the forgiveness I sense here tonight."

"Amen," we voiced together.

Before anyone picked up their forks, Veronica said, "Sorry about the 'Martha' comment, Marjorie. I appreciate you doing this. Otherwise Thanksgiving would've come and gone without notice." She turned to Maya. "When our little sister here smelled the turkey, she transformed into a whirlwind, insisting that we dress up to suit the occasion, and to honor you."

I felt limp and weepy. "It's like a dream come true," I said, trying to bypass the lump in my throat, "having us all together like this, all dressed up and—"

"I'll toast to that," our father said, holding up his empty glass.

I froze. Was he expecting alcohol?

Maya picked up the bottle of sparkling cider from the sideboard and filled our glasses. "Veronica, could you please lead us in a toast?"

"Sure," she said with a half-smile. "Since I've already thanked Marjorie for putting this meal together and since Dad has already said grace, I'd like to announce that my sojourn in the basement is over."

"Hear, hear," I said, raising my sparkling cider.

"Hold it. I'm not done," she said, motioning for me to put down my glass. "For the next week, I plan to hang out with you, my family. Then I'll inform the higher-ups who'll be deciding my fate with the DEA that I want to go back to school, nights, for training in mental health nursing. If I get accepted into the basic training program at Quantico and pass muster, I hope to team up with another special agent and help people who need medication and treatment in place of or in addition to jail. Maya convinced me that many of the drug-related problems in our society are mental health issues, which, if caught and treated early, may prevent criminal activity. Sometimes more is needed to fight the war on drugs than a badge and gun."

Wow, Veronica would push herself to the limit by taking on evening classes in addition to DEA training. From what she'd shared with me, only a handful of the thousands of applicants with impressive credentials made it through the selection process as special agent recruits. "That's awesome," I said. If her dream became a reality, Veronica's compassion would have a chance to bloom.

"And I've broken our pact about not using the phone during our stay here," Veronica continued.

"Again," I said softly.

"I called Ben. We're getting married after my fate with the DEA is decided."

No one responded, including me. Ben, *Gentle Bear*, Mendoza would be my brother-in-law at last. What had changed Veronica's mind? During our time in Big Sur, she'd admitted that love scared the crap out of her.

I looked at Maya, and the gentle expression on her face was my answer. Something she'd said to Veronica must've penetrated her fear of commitment and opened her heart.

"Well, don't all congratulate me at once," Veronica said.

"If you love him, I'm sure he's a great guy," Bob said. He'd loosened his tie and was unfastening the top button of his shirt.

"I can vouch for the fact that Ben loves Veronica," I added, noticing the sheen of perspiration on Bob's forehead. *Oh God, please let him be reacting to Veronica's announcement. Not the lack of alcohol.* "Though she's put him through hell."

"*Me* put *him* through hell?" Veronica sputtered. "No worse than what you've done, and are still doing, to Morgan."

My mood brightened at the mention of the man I loved. She was right. I'd put Morgan—and myself—through hell. But that would soon change. I couldn't wait to introduce him to Maya. It was time she saw what true love in a relationship involved. And Joshua, oh my gosh, what a kick he'd get out of meeting a third identical sister. He'd melt Maya's heart, as he had mine.

"Earth to Marjorie," Veronica said.

"Yeah, yeah," I said, "you made your point."

The food wasn't half-bad, though just about any menu item would've been acceptable as long as it brought us together in thanksgiving. While the candles flickered and we ate our meal, I felt myself swell with contentment and good will. Maybe it had something to do with the way the house seemed to coddle and nurture its occupants. Or maybe it had more to do with the fact that we were engaged in the moment instead of dwelling on our painful pasts.

At the close of our meal, I stood with reluctance, hesitant to disturb this fragile sense of unity, fearing this meeting as one would never be repeated. "Anyone for pumpkin pie with whipped cream?"

Bob groaned and rubbed his stomach. "Maybe later."

Veronica picked up her plate and flatware and handed them to me. Guess I was on cleanup duty, too. *Every family needs their Martha.* Then she turned to our father and smiled. "I agree with Dad. Later would be nice."

Wow, Veronica just agreed with our father. Dared I hope that hate could turn into acceptance, if not outright love?

"Same here," Maya said, getting up to help.

The doorbell rang.

"Expecting anyone?" I asked no one in particular.

"Who'd be calling on Thanksgiving?" Bob asked. "No one has manners anymore."

"Maybe it's a homeless person who needs something to eat," Maya said. "You wouldn't believe how many people go without a meal on Thanksgiving. We have plenty left to share." Before anyone could respond, she rushed out of the room and into the foyer.

Bob shook his head. "Must be a result of her humble upbringing."

Veronica looked like she was about to say something, then seemed to think better of it.

"We can all learn from her," I said. "Happiness comes from giving."

Bob stood and headed for the foyer. "Okay, I'll give you that, but she still shouldn't be out there on her own. It could be someone up to no good."

I agreed with my father and appreciated his concern. It showed he was making progress in the father-daughter department after all the years of neglect. He hadn't yet left the dining room, though, before Maya was back. "Look who's come for a visit." Her lips were moist and rosy, her eyes bright as sapphires. She looked like an angel.

When Dr. Donovan entered the room, Bob broke into a smile. You'd think President Bush had just come for a visit.

"The place still looks the same," Dr. Donovan said with a shake of his head. "Crystals, candles, stodgy drapes." He loosened his tie and blew out a breath.

I glanced at Veronica and tried to gauge her reaction as she stared at the jumble of leftovers and dirty dishes on the table. Even the crystal had lost its luster.

Who had invited the doctor to our family affair? I doubted it had been Maya, which left... From across the table, I met Veronica's gaze. *How could you?* I mouthed. She looked away.

Maya introduced the doctor to our father, who became animated, as if a puppeteer had gotten the hang of how to manipulate his strings.

I blew out the candles and cleared the table, then washed and dried the china, crystal, and flatware. When I reentered the dining room to put them away, Veronica, Bob, and Dr. Donovan had retired to the parlor. Maya followed me into the kitchen, her face a moist and feverish pink. "Papa says he's ready for pumpkin pie now."

"Are you okay?" I asked, grabbing a napkin to wipe her forehead.

"Sure, why do you ask?"

"Cause you look hot and bothered."

She looked over my shoulder as I dabbed at her face. "It bothers me to know Shane needs me in a way he doesn't yet realize."

I thought of Cliff and figured it was time I shared. "I once knew someone who had a similar effect on me," I said. "I thought I loved him, and maybe I did, but whenever I was with him, something didn't feel right. He claimed to love me, but..."

By the dazed look in Maya's eyes, I realized she wasn't listening, so I pulled her into a tight hug. "If you ever want to talk, I'm here."

"Thanks," she said. "Is the coffee ready?"

I released her slowly, hoping she'd open up before it was too late.

"Tell you what," I said. "You can take in the pie, and I'll take care of the coffee."

Maya looked into my eyes. "I know you don't like him, Marjorie."

"You're darn right, I don't. But I'm not the one deciding, you are. It's like what you told me about our father."

Maya's eyes widened. "How does this compare?"

"You said all we could do was offer him our love and support and encourage him to trust his inner guide." I cut a piece of pumpkin pie and put it on a plate, then topped it with a squirt of whipped cream and handed it to my sister.

When she reached for the plate, I squirt a dab of whipped cream onto her nose. She squealed at my foolishness, then wiped off the cream and smeared it onto my face. I pointed the can at her. "Back off." She squealed again, this time followed by laughter. "What does your inner guide tell you to do?" I asked.

"I don't know."

Another squirt of whipped cream. It hit her on the forehead. "What does your inner guide say?"

"That you're crazy," she said, looking down at her dress to check if I'd inflicted any damage.

I put down the can. "Fair enough."

We were still laughing when Veronica charged into the kitchen. "What's the hold up."

❂❂❂

After serving coffee and pie, I hightailed it back to the kitchen with the excuse of having more cleaning up to do. To my surprise, Veronica and Maya followed with an offer to help.

"The men are talking about the boost it was for New York City to have three of the World Series games played there after the terrorist attacks on the World Trade Center," Veronica said, "even with the Yankees falling to the Diamondbacks in game seven. I love it when strangers bond over sports. Anyway, thank you again for what you did tonight. It was the kind of Thanksgiving I've always dreamed of. Just wish our mother could've been here to share it."

"Maybe she was," I said.

"I wish I could've gotten to know her," Maya said with a sigh.

I took off my apron and looked through the window to the backyard. The sun had set and the light was fading fast. It was also wet and foggy. "Maybe you still can."

"Marjorie…" Veronica said, with a note of warning.

"How?" Maya asked.

I continued to look out the window, wondering if what I was about to suggest was crazy, especially with Dad and Dr. Donovan nearby. "Veronica, do you remember the circle we talked about forming to call on Antonia?"

"In the labyrinth?" she said. "Sure."

"Want to give it a try?"

She looked down at the gown she wore. "Dressed like this?"

I pulled a small flashlight out of Anne's junk drawer. "For what we're about to do, changing clothes won't be necessary."

We slipped out through the back-porch door. With luck, Dr. Donovan and our father wouldn't even notice we were gone.

192

Chapter Thirty

I UNLOCKED THE DOOR to the backyard shed and stepped inside, barely able to distinguish one fuzzy form from another until the beam of my flashlight turned silhouettes and shades of gray into recognizable objects. "I remember seeing some insulated shirts hanging from hooks on the wall next to the rake and shovels."

"There're probably full of cobwebs and spiders," Veronica said, "but don't mind me. I'd rather be bitten by a spider than ruin this dress."

I found the man-sized shirts and shook them to clear them of intruders before handing one to each of my sisters and donning my own. "Flannel on the outside, fleece on the inside. Can't beat that for warmth and comfort." On the way out of the shed, I spotted a flashlight/lantern combo poking out of a cubbyhole and exchanged it for the one I held, amazed at the intense light it projected when I turned it on.

Veronica pulled the plaid shirt over her taupe gown. "Seems Anne's just about prepared for everything. She'd make a good Girl Scout."

Maya laughed. "Isn't 'Be Prepared' a Boy Scout motto?"

"Actually, the motto's shared by both," I said. "Though it's impossible to be prepared for everything."

"Like spirits from the other side," Veronica said. "And alcoholic fathers."

I could've added another example to her list—Dr. Shane Donovan—but kept it to myself.

Since the three of us had walked the labyrinth before, we rushed through the step of preparation, taking deep, centering breaths. "Antonia, your daughters have come together at last to complete the circle as you asked us to in Big Sur," I said, stating our intention.

We were pressed for time. When Dr. Donovan and our father grew tired of talking about 9/11 and the World Series, they'd come looking for us. The tight beam of the flashlight pierced the darkness and swirling fog, revealing only small sections of the path in front of us. We walked in silence, making right-angled and 180 degree turns along the eleven circuits of the labyrinth, before reaching its center.

"Now what?" Veronica whispered. She was shivering, as were Maya and I. Our shirts, though insulated, couldn't completely block out the cold—or our nervous anticipation.

"We join hands," I said, "and wait for Antonia."

When Maya's hand met mine, I noticed it was trembling. I figured it was in reaction to the cold until she said, "I think Antonia has tried to reach me, too, but I ignored her." Her hand tightened. "The way I was raised by our mother's people, it's no big deal to hear voices. Native Americans believe voice-hearers reveal messages that have spiritual significance. So, it wasn't like I thought I was going crazy when Antonia spoke to me. I just didn't want to be bothered."

"I don't blame you," Veronica said. "She can be a real pain in the ass. If Marjorie hadn't set me straight in Carmel Valley, warning me that the voice I was hearing might be our mother's, I would've ignored her, too."

Maya released a puff of air, which could've signaled relief. Or maybe she'd been holding her breath. "I've gotten good at blocking her, creating what might as well have been a wall of concrete between us. It may take more than our combined efforts to blast our way through."

"If I hadn't listened to our mother," I said, "I would've never gotten to know the two of you, so I plan on listening until she stops talking."

"Let's cut the regrets and get this over with," Veronica said. "It's frickin' cold out here."

In typical Veronica fashion, she'd ticked me off. If she thought for one minute, I'd lead a let's-talk-to-our-dead-mother session with unwilling participants, she had another think coming. The chance to set her straight, though, was taken out of my hands. "What the hell are you doing out there?" Dr. Donovan yelled from the back-porch entry.

"Talking to our mother," Maya called back. "Wanna join us?"

The screen door slammed, followed by double footsteps, which meant Bob was joining us, too. Talk about it being impossible to be prepared for everything.

"This should be interesting," Veronica said under her breath before announcing, "We're in the labyrinth."

Interesting? I called it a disaster.

"Labyrinth? What's that?" Bob asked.

Although it was the last thing I wanted to do, I walked across the path of the labyrinth and intercepted Dr. Donovan and our father on the brick steps leading to the latticed porch entry. "Come on, I'll show you."

Our father drew in his breath when the beam of my flashlight revealed the mandala-like circle to our right. "It looks like some kind of maze."

"In a maze you get lost," I said, quoting the bookstore clerk. "In a labyrinth, you find the way."

"How?" he asked.

"Through prayer and meditation." I led him to the break in the circle marking the entrance. "Consider the labyrinth a journey to your center."

Dr. Donovan didn't follow. My guess was that he hadn't moved over ten feet from the back door. "I can't believe you unearthed that damn thing," he said, his voice sounding strained. "It was Anne's idea to install it. I fought against it. Named it for what it was. No more than a New Age resurrection of the occult." He cleared his throat before continuing. "Anne said the labyrinth represents the womb, the Earth Mother, a coiled snake. Can you believe it? She

195

talked about the Black Madonna, Isis, Sophia, Artemis, and the divine mother as if they're all one. Said they hold special significance to women of today. She used to meditate there for hours."

Bob squinted through the swirling fog at Veronica's and Maya's dark figures in the labyrinth's center. "Maya said if I learned to meditate, it could ease my dependence on alcohol."

With my back to Dr. Donovan, I couldn't see his expression, but his resistance to approaching the labyrinth conveyed all I needed to know. Let him try to inflict his will on all four of us, especially our father, whom he was trying his darndest to impress.

"What do you mean, communicate with your mother?" Bob asked.

I'd wondered how long it would take for Maya's comment to sink in.

"Sometimes she talks to us," I said.

Bob blew out his breath. "That's crazy."

"You've got that right," Dr. Donovan said, indicating he hadn't yet cut and run.

"It's true," Maya said. "All three of us have heard her. I'm so grateful she helped bring us together. I want to make it up to her if it isn't too late. That's one reason we're here."

Bob entered the labyrinth behind me. "What do I do?"

"Just follow me," I said.

As we worked our way to the center, I didn't explain what we were doing. It was getting colder, and we were pressed for time. Maya and Veronica made room for us when we stepped onto the six-petaled rose in the heart of the labyrinth, symbol of human and divine love. We formed a tight circle and joined hands.

"What now?" Bob whispered, the warmth of his body next to mine reassuring. In this space surrounded by darkness and swirling mist, I could almost forget—and forgive—all his shortcomings as a father.

I didn't know what to do next, but wasn't about to admit it, not after coming this far. "Come on, Antonia," I whispered. "Now's your chance."

Bob must've thought I was praying, because he said, "Amen."

Veronica chuckled. Maya squeezed my hand. "Antonia," I said, trying to keep the pleading out of my voice. "Come to us now. Let us know if the circle is complete."

"I think she's been trying to contact me, too," Bob said, "but I thought it was the alcohol."

Veronica blew out her breath. "Give me a break."

I could only guess what Dr. Donovan was thinking while we huddled in the labyrinth's center with a flashlight pointed at our feet. Having a skeptic as an audience was distracting, even with fog and darkness obliterating his form. "Okay Mother," I said. "We're here to listen."

After a short silence, punctuated by dripping mist, chirping crickets, and Dr. Donovan's loud sighs, Veronica slapped her thigh. "Spit it out, Antonia. I'm tired of your games." To my surprise, she then started to cry. "If we can help you, tell us what to do. Anything to get things back to normal."

Bob's breath hitched in his throat.

This séance wasn't going well. So much for serving as a medium. I sucked at it.

Dr. Donovan barked out a laugh, which sheared through the dark like a knife. "No wonder Maya's screwed up. It runs in the family."

I could tell by the sudden tension in my father's body that his high esteem for the doctor had dropped a notch or two. Santa had taken off his red suit and was actually Ebenezer Scrooge.

"I'm sorry for inviting him," Veronica said, her voice unsteady. "I thought bringing in an outsider would help break the ice, keep things light."

"Growth can be messy," Maya said before I could say something I'd later regret.

Veronica grunted. "You call this growth?"

The wind kicked in, the fog shifted, and stars and a half moon appeared. Then it started to drizzle. "Shit," Veronica said.

"Ready to go in now?" Dr. Donovan asked, his sugarcoated voice grating on my nerves. The man was a nuisance.

Rather than reply, Maya broke into song.

Mothers are a special breed,

Always near when you're in need,

Even when you can't reach out and hold them,

A mother is a special friend,

The love she gives can never end

A mother's love has no end.

And just when the rain started pounding down in earnest, our mother spoke.

First Dawn. Sunwalker. Fallen Light. You were together in my womb. Now you are together again. If only for a short while.

"What else is new?" Veronica said.

Her words expressed pain, and I figured our mother would know that. No need to intervene. Rainwater ran down my face and the legs of my jeans, and I wondered about the damage to my sisters' gowns.

Maya jerked her hand from mine. "Did you feel that?"

"Feel what?" I'd been thinking about the rain, so had paid little attention to what else was going on in our surroundings. The wind died to a whisper; rain fell like tears.

"Do you think I pissed Antonia off?" Veronica asked.

Was that regret I heard in her voice? "I doubt it. She's on to you by now."

Veronica released her breath.

I was no longer aware of the cold. If it hadn't been for my soaked shirt and jeans, it would've felt like I was taking a warm shower.

"Why'd you call me *Fallen Light*?" Maya asked.

Bob started to answer, but Antonia beat him to it.

Light fallen from the heavens.

You shine on everyone you meet.

For the first time since I'd met her, Maya lost control. Her sobs ruptured the stillness. "Thank you for that, Mother." She stepped out of the labyrinth's center and took the path leading out. "I thought it meant something else."

About to follow her, I hesitated at our mother's next words. *All will be as it should be.* Another riddle explaining nothing.

"She's quite a woman, that mother of yours," Bob said with what sounded like relief.

Instead of taking the winding path to the labyrinth's exit, Veronica and Bob cut across it in their rush to get back to the kitchen. Since I was holding the flashlight and didn't want to leave Maya alone, I followed her the long way out.

By the time Maya and I entered the house, Dr. Donovan had left for home. Not that I blamed him. Witnessing what had just transpired on this precipitous Thanksgiving night would've tried anyone's patience. Let alone a man who had none.

Chapter Thirty-One

THE PARTY WAS OVER.

It was Friday morning and our father had already returned to his rented cottage and his lonesome life. I wondered if his thirst for a jigger of scotch was why he had appeared so jittery, so eager to hightail it out of here.

Alcohol is a mighty ruler.

Maya, though, seemed reluctant to leave. "I want you and Veronica to know..." She shook her head as if reconsidering what she was about to say. "Could we sit down somewhere?"

I gestured toward the kitchen table.

"No." She twisted her hands and looked out the window. The sun was rising, its light penetrating the darkness, but without enough passion to break through the clouds. "Let's go to the sunporch. It's cozy in there."

I didn't need telepathic powers to know something was wrong.

Veronica wore a smile that suggested she knew something I didn't.

What you believe to be true, is true, said a familiar voice.

So, our mother was still with us. Had she come into our lives for an extended stay?

"Thanks, Mother," I said under my breath.

Maya claimed the wicker chair and glanced at the birdcage. "What's the empty cage for?"

Veronica dropped into a slouch on the settee. "Phantom birds."

"Oh," Maya said, dismissing the enclosure as though it were glimpsed on the side of a road and easily forgotten. "Sit down, Marjorie. You may be the only one to disagree with what I'm about to say."

I pulled a cushioned ottoman from behind a potted fern, positioned it next to Maya, and sat down, wondering about the doves. How odd that I was the only one able to see and hear them. "Guess I've been out voted on something." *Please don't let it be about the surgery.*

"Yes," Maya said, "by the most influential voter of all. My heart."

I knew what was coming. "So, you love him that much, huh?"

Maya smiled. "All reason and logic say Shane's wrong for me and I'm wrong for him. My birthmark presents a challenge and therefore an obstacle to his happiness and spiritual growth. What I'm about to do may change all that, though not in the way he, you, or anyone else may expect."

"You remind me of Antonia," I said. "She also talks in riddles."

"I don't mean to." Maya folded her hands on her lap. They were unadorned, the hands of a person without vanity or pride. Yet, if what I suspected was true, she was about to submit to cosmetic surgery.

Veronica shifted in her seat. Her smug smile had changed into a frown. "You're doing it for *Shane?*"

Maya tensed, then touched her face and sighed. "The real Shane, the man I love, won't emerge and transform until I do."

"Tell him to go jump in the lake," I said, jerking to a stand. I wanted to punch the daylights out of Dr. Donovan. Whom was he trying to fool? Fixing Maya's face wouldn't change a darn thing. She'd still be whom she was, and so would he.

"What can it hurt?" Veronica asked, frowning in my direction. "She'll be killing two birds with one stone, right? Helping Shane and helping herself."

I eyed the ornate wicker cage. It was swaying. She'd be killing two birds with one stone all right.

"Speaking of talking in riddles," Veronica said. "What's your problem with surgery besides that it might make Maya prettier than you?"

Maya gasped.

Yes, Veronica certainly had a way with words.

I walked up to one of the porch windows and stared at the abandoned birdbath and gazebo, hating myself for repeating the information I'd already shared with her about the possible complications of surgery, but doing it anyway. "For one thing, the surgical treatment of CVM is not simply cosmetic, like a face lift or tummy tuck. It's complex and multi-staged and may require ongoing management. And there could be complications."

My emotional offensive evoked no response. Probably for the best, because I had worse news to impart, something I'd held back before. "There's also a possibility of substantial morbidity." It shouldn't have been necessary for me to share what I'd learned on the Internet, but my guess was that Dr. Shane Donovan hadn't provided Maya with this information, which likely meant no pre-op consultations.

"Morbidity?" Veronica said. "Talk about a worst-case scenario. Don't you think you're carrying your objection to surgery a bit far?"

I continued to look outside, unable to bear meeting either sister's eyes while delivering what I knew. "Maya could look worse for a while." The pain in my chest made me want to curl into a ball, but that would only weaken my case. "I can't believe Dr. Donovan hasn't discussed this with you."

"Shane, damn it. His name is Shane," Veronica said.

What difference did it make what I called him? He was about to affect my sister's life in a way that was irreversible. "And she could still retain a scar that would be cosmetically unacceptable to—"

"Shane," Veronica interjected, punctuating the name with a slap to her thigh.

Looking from one sister to another, I sensed no support for my arguments. "You're already beautiful, Maya," I said, my voice a whisper. "Why put yourself through all that?"

"Would you do it for Morgan?" Veronica asked.

"He'd never ask that of me."

Veronica snorted. "Oh, please."

"That's why I'm engaged to Morgan not Cliff. To Cliff, it would've mattered."

"You're comparing Shane to your ex-fiancé?" Veronica asked, her voice pitched high.

This time, I slapped my thighs, the resulting pain nothing compared to the painful throbbing in my chest. "Thanks to Antonia, I realized Cliff was wrong for me and would've hurt me in the end." I knelt in front of Maya and took her hands into mine. "Please think about this before it's too late."

"Okay," Veronica said, "If our mother clued you in about Cliff, why hasn't she done so with Maya about Shane?"

I released Maya's hands and sat on my heels. "Maybe that's our job."

"Or maybe you're wrong," Veronica said. "Maybe Antonia knows Maya is stronger and wiser than either one of us. That she doesn't need dire warnings and advice. That she can take care of herself."

Maya leaned forward and placed her hands over mine. It felt like a kiss. "This isn't about me, Marjorie. It's about Shane. I see a way to help him."

Shane! Who gives a rat's ass about Shane? My teeth clenched on the words unsaid.

"And help our mother," Maya added softly.

Our mother? How in blazes would her surgery help Antonia?

"Marjorie," she said, before I could put my question into words. "I appreciate what you're trying to do. In fact, it warms my heart to know you love me that much. But let me ask you something. When it comes to the path you've chosen for *your* life, who do you count on to make the final decision?"

"Not Cliff," I snapped. "Not even Morgan. I've learned the hard way to count on myself."

"Would you appreciate it if I tried to interfere?"

"No," I said, knowing where this was leading and not liking it one bit.

"Then please, don't interfere with mine."

I stood and backed up a step. "Even if I'm sure you're making the wrong decision?"

Maya smiled, and I swear I saw a halo radiate from the top of her head. "Do the people who love you most agree with all you do?"

I thought of Truus and how she'd reacted when I told her of my plans to go to Big Sur to contact my birth mother. I'd listened to her arguments. I'd seen the hurt on her face. She thought I was crazy, that I was giving up all I'd worked for, and that I was losing my faith. Even Morgan had tried at first to persuade me to stay home where he could watch over and protect me. Instead, I'd struck out on my own, without consideration to what it would cost myself and those who loved me. I looked at my little sister and hated the answer I had to give. "The people who love me most tried to stop me."

I walked up to the birdcage. Neither Veronica nor Maya seemed to notice when I unlatched the door. In confinement, the doves stayed safe and protected.

I was about to set them free.

"Maya, would you like me to drive you home?" Veronica asked.

I felt the light pressure of someone's hand on my shoulder, but I didn't turn around.

"I'm asking for your understanding," Maya said, "not your agreement."

For the first time, I knew, really knew, how Truus must've felt when she discovered I'd left for Big Sur in the middle of the night without saying goodbye.

Despite her warnings.

Maya and Veronica left the porch, and I listened to the doves' hollow *coos*.

They hadn't left their cage, apparently preferring to stay where they were.

I slumped onto the wicker chair, still warm with the memory of Maya's body, and closed my eyes. Maybe if I nodded off for a while, the pain would go away.

❂❂❂

I awoke to the sound of *cooing*, which surprised me, because it came from above my head. Had the doves escaped after all?

I stood and walked up to the cage.

It was empty.

Looking for a sign of the free-flying birds, I noticed someone sitting in the rocking chair at the far end of the porch. Even in shadow, I knew it wasn't Veronica. "Christine," I said, breaking into shivers. "Is that you?"

"Why yes, child," she said, sitting quiet as death. "I notice the doves are out of their cage."

"I let them go," I confessed. As if she didn't know.

"Yes," was all she said.

"Will Raphael attack them?" I asked in sudden concern.

"It's a little late to worry about that now."

"You're right." I waited for the onslaught of guilt that didn't come.

"Don't they sound nice, though," she said.

The cheerfulness of their *coos* was unmistakable. Sometimes the freedom to choose is worth the cost. And the doves had chosen to be free.

Christine considered me, then, to my relief, she began rocking in her chair. "You've been through quite an ordeal today, haven't you?"

I walked up to her, my heart throbbing as though warning me against what I was about to do. Entreat a ghost for understanding. "A man named Dr. Shane Donovan may ruin my sister's life, and there's nothing I can do about it."

Christine smiled. "Sit down, dear. I'd like to tell you a story."

Chapter Thirty-Two

AS THE SUNPORCH GREW darker and chillier, I waited for a dead woman to tell me a story.

What you believe to be real is real, I reminded myself, in part to keep me from running out of the room in fear for my sanity and in part because it was true. I believed Christine was real, therefore she was. I dragged the ottoman from the other end of the room to where she sat rocking and settled down. "My tale may seem rather dull," she began, "but I'd appreciate it if you would listen to the end. Some of life's lessons are meted out slowly, one morsel at a time, spanning generations, not through high drama."

I nodded, eager for her to relate what she knew, a woman who had passed to the other side and didn't talk in riddles. Why couldn't my mother do that?

"In 1920 my parents, David and Charlotte Hart, still newlyweds, decided to build the house of their dreams. They wanted a safe haven for their future children, a place where the little ones could grow and play free from the discomforts and evils of the outside world. In a way, they were attempting to do what the good Christian people of Pacific Grove had once tried to do, isolate themselves in an ideal world."

"Sounds heavenly," I said.

Christine nodded. "My parents, like the early residents of Pacific Grove, wanted to create a slice of heaven here on earth. In the early 1880's, Pacific Grove was a retreat rather than a town, a safe haven for the gentle, refined, cultured, and pious. Community leaders banned cards and dice and intoxicating beverages. They also forbade dancing. They set a curfew to keep people under eighteen indoors and out of mischief after nine in the evening. And then, to keep out those who might contaminate their community, they erected a fence encircling nearly the entire retreat grounds."

"Only to become insular and secluded," I ventured.

"I gather you see where this is leading."

"Unfortunately, yes," I said.

"When my parents built this house, they made certain every nail, shingle, and pane of glass, contributed to the whole, all the while praying for guidance from on high."

"In a way, they succeeded," I said, remembering how tranquil the house had made me feel when we'd first arrived, promising peace and protection, as if welcoming me home.

"Beyond their hopes and dreams," Christine agreed. "My sister, Karen, and I loved this house. In fact, we were obsessed by it. We became fitful and restless whenever we were forced to leave, be it to attend a church social, visit an amusement park, or visit a friend."

"Like precious doves in a gilded cage."

Christine paused from her story while my words hung in the air. Then she shook her head and continued. "Karen and I regressed mentally and physically each time we left the house, so we were home schooled by our mother. The only way she could get us to mingle with outsiders was to host parties and sleepovers with the neighborhood children."

"It's hard to imagine," I said.

"Too late, my parents realized their mistake. Karen and I had become incapable of functioning when it came to the unfamiliar and unknown. We were in heaven, all right, content with our little world. But we were also in hell."

The drawn-out *coo WHO-o coo, coo, coo*s of doves filled the quiet that followed as though lamenting Christine's words.

"You didn't sing," I said. "Like the female doves."

Christine paused her rocking and looked out the window. The growing darkness created a curtain of sorts between the house and the street. "Those who've found love don't need to sing." She sighed, then continued. "When Karen and I reached our teens and still showed no interest in exploring the outside world, our parents resorted to counseling."

"To no avail."

Christine looked at me as though she'd forgotten I was there. "At which point, they gave up and became our caretakers."

I gasped.

"Don't get me wrong, we weren't invalids by any means," Christine assured me. "Karen and I fed and clothed ourselves, and we kept each other amused. We cooked lavish meals for our parents and their guests, and we polished and cleaned until the house sparkled from top to bottom. All was well. As long as we didn't have to leave."

"Which worked out okay until your parents died." It was all so predictable. And sad.

"That's when we were forced to change or die." Christine stopped rocking and looked at me with eyes that suddenly appeared as dead as she was. "I changed. Karen died."

"Dear God," I whispered.

"But I'm getting ahead of myself," Christine said with a shake of her head. "Out of necessity, I became my sister's as well as my own connection to the outside world. For one thing, I had to plan our parents' funeral, with the help of the family lawyer, of course. Then there were bills to pay and all those necessary trips to town. I ventured to the post office, the bank, the grocery store, and to the doctor when Karen became ill. For the first time, I was forced to step into the flow of life."

"And when Karen passed away, you were all alone."

Christine looked at me and smiled. "Actually, no. After Karen's funeral, our lawyer informed me that I still had family on my mother's side, two orphaned cousins once or twice removed, alive and well, but even lonelier than I. He asked if I would take them in."

"Anne and Shane," I guessed.

Christine nodded. "And they saved my life."

As I waited for the story to continue, I wondered at life's uncertainties—and miracles.

"Yes, Marjorie. They were indeed miracles. Anne was seven and Shane five. They were so cute and well mannered, thank the Lord. Anne was the social butterfly. She loved people and couldn't wait to go to school. She wanted to become a nurse. Shane was quieter, more intense. His dream was to become a surgeon. To my relief, both children were not only prepared to face the world, but eager to help those in it.

"Needless to say, life changed after that. My once constricted world burst open, everyday a new discovery. I became a room mother, a teacher's aide, even a soccer mom. And with the money willed by my parents, I put both Anne and Shane through medical school."

"But all didn't run smoothly for Anne," I said, having discovered this during our time together in Pfeiffer State Park. At Christine's raised brow, I explained. "She told me things while we camped in Big Sur."

Christine sighed. "That's just it. By allowing them to go out into the world and join the flow of life, I couldn't protect them from other forms of pain and suffering. However, if asked to choose between the way I and they were raised, which do you think they would prefer?"

"The life of freedom. Without fences and cages."

My ghostly friend nodded.

I heard the whistle of dove wings from behind me and turned to watch the doves fly unimpeded. "Christine. You and the birds are dead, so why are you still here?"

When she didn't answer, I looked back to where she sat. The rocker was still, her eyes closed, her liver-spotted hands folded on her lap, then, "The house still has us under its spell."

"You can't move on?"

"Not without Karen."

"But Karen's not here," I said.

"Oh, yes she is, my dear, but she won't show herself while you and Veronica are around. She's afraid, you see."

Fear, such a debilitating force. "My mother's having a hard time leaving this world, too, so I guess we're in the same boat. We're both trying to help someone move on. What I don't understand is why I can see you while others can't."

"Your mother and I exist in a realm beyond space, time, and matter, my dear, and you've found a way to visit us there. Veronica could too if she tried, but that's another matter."

"How?" I asked.

Christine shook her head. "Language can't explain it so you would understand. Any attempt would be inaccurate."

"Try anyway," I pleaded.

She considered me for a moment before proceeding. "Nothing really changes when we die, at least not in the way you think. We aren't separate beings, but one. Most of us, in an attempt to gain control over our lives, develop ego, which helps us in the material realm of the body, but hinders us in the spiritual realm of consciousness. You, for instance, strive for order. You want everything in its place. You fret. You plan. You look for answers. It would work better if, instead of asking whom you are and wondering in what direction your path ought to go, you learned to live the questions. Maya, for example, has learned to ignore her ego-mind and listen to the *One Mind*. She's not looking for how to get where she's going. She's already there."

Learn to live with the questions. Easier said than done. "The lesson being?" I asked, wondering how Christine knew all this about me and about Maya, whose visit had been short.

"That you learn to live the rich experiences the world has to offer, instead of trying to get back to where you came from."

"How about Shane?"

"Shane hasn't let go of his ego and possibly never will. His desire to control is too strong."

"And how will Maya's ability to ignore her ego-mind and listen to the One Mind help save her?"

"She doesn't need saving, Marjorie. She has learned not only to let go of her ego, but also of herself. She is free from the bonds of space and time."

"Unlike the rest of us."

"Yes," Christine said. "Unlike the rest of us."

I looked at the woman who had transported from another realm and understood the mystery of our oneness, but still hadn't learned to let go.

How difficult that must be.

So, how had Maya freed herself from the restrictions of ego while thriving in the material world? Her birthmark, was my guess. Her deformity had restrained her ego enough to help her discover her deepest strength and weakness. Love.

"Look at love long enough and you will become lovely," Christine said.

There wasn't anything left to say, so I bent forward to take Christine's hand. She shook her head, no. "I'm denied the comfort of physical touch in the walkway between worlds, but that doesn't prevent me from taking pleasure in the way you've touched my soul."

I stood, intending to head to the kitchen for dinner, but felt the urgency to add, "Your parents meant well."

Christine smiled. "Yes they did, my dear. But they would not allow us our divine right to bring something better into our lives. They loved us into a living death."

Chapter Thirty-Three

THE BELL AT ST. Mary's tolled, announcing the commencement of Mass, and although rain pelted the church's high-ceilinged roof, I sat dry underneath in what resembled an upended hull of a massive fishing boat. I'd come to hear my sister sing, hoping her voice would guide me to that place beyond space and time where my ego would stay behind and we could become one.

The organ burst forth, filling the alter, the pews, the church's every nook and cranny with vibration and sound, and when Maya started to sing, I embraced the swelling wave and tried to stay afloat as she swept me away.

When life has got you down and you need a friend...
You need somebody to turn to, but there's no one there.
You've got to face the pain, but you know you can't.
You feel like crawling inside yourself, and staying there.

My body remained planted on the wooden bench, but my spirit lifted with the words of the song, higher, higher. *Yes, Maya. I've found a friend. You. You're there for me when I feel like crawling inside of myself. I love you and want to get to know you better. We were separated for too long.* I wanted to tell my sister these things. I wanted to spend the rest of my life near her. If not in the same town, at least close enough for frequent visits. Veronica, Maya, and I had found each other at last. We had so much catching up to do.

Well, you've got someone.
You've got somebody to hold you.
You've got somebody to help you through,
If you'll only make a place

For Him in your life.

I knew what the song meant. To make room in my life for God. But I wanted Maya in my life, too. A flesh and blood person. Was that so wrong? Would God, the Great Spirit, punish me for thinking this, for wanting this?

Make a place.

Make a place, in your life.

The song ended too soon. I wasn't finished absorbing it, responding to it.

I've made a place for you in my life, Maya. God will understand, because I've made a place for Him, too. But don't make me choose. Because, God forgive me, I would choose you.

As Mass continued, I slipped out of St. Mary's. The rain had stopped, and the ferns and bushes and sidewalks and trees looked shiny and smelled like a freshly scrubbed house on cleaning day. So many birds, some I recognized from Anne's backyard, some not, with their *seet-seet-seet-seet-turrrrs* and *zir-zir-zir-zir-see-sees*. The water flowing in the channel across the street sounded like wet wind. On any other day, I would've marveled at its calming stream sounds and the bent and twisted eucalyptus that smelled of mint, pine, and lemon. But not today. I walked four blocks down Central Street and was about to cross Grand Avenue when I heard someone call my name.

Nessa, the palm reader, waved and hurried in my direction. I pointed toward the gazebo in Jewell Park. "Yes," she called, breaking into a run.

We took a seat on the bench in the small shelter. "What's up?" I asked.

"My blood pressure," she said, breathing hard. "Probing tarot cards and people's palms all day is bad for the circulation."

I grinned. With that ponytail and baseball cap, she looked like an eighteen-year-old. "It could lead to an early grave, that's for sure."

I expected that she would avoid eye contact as she had while performing my tarot reading. Instead, she subjected me to an intense gaze. "When we last talked alone," she said. "I told you not to fight your abilities, not to shut that door."

"Yes, I remember."

"That was hypocritical of me. I've been doing the same. I know things I haven't been sharing."

"I figured as much."

"Something's about to happen to Maya."

I always wondered what it would be like to be put to the rack, stretched until my joints popped out of their sockets. Now I had a good idea. I covered my stomach with both arms and bent forward, feeling like I might puke.

"And Maya knows," Nessa said.

I tried to straighten, but couldn't. I pointed toward St. Mary's. "Can you believe, she's in there singing her heart out as if she doesn't have a care in the world?"

Nessa sighed. "Aside from work, singing brings her closest to God."

Knowing how Maya's voice affected me, I could imagine how it must feel to have such vocal range and control.

"The question is, do we interfere or let things take their course?" Nessa said. "It's a hard call, especially when it involves someone you love."

She must've noticed the question mark in my eyes because she added, "Yes, I love your sister. She's been a good friend—the best. She's helped me through some tough times."

I said nothing. What was there to say? Christine, our house ghost, had told me a story about interference, how we couldn't protect people from the consequences of living life to its fullest. Life involved risk. It involved pain. It involved death and rebirth.

"I also love Shane," Nessa added, startling me out of my thoughts.

Shane? What was wrong with the women in this town?

The unfocused look in her eyes and her sad smile confirmed that she was serious. "Shane and I are long-time friends. When I introduced him to Maya and he saw the birthmark on her face, he became obsessed with turning her into the beautiful woman he envisioned. She presented a textbook case for the amazing things cosmetic surgery can do…change people's lives. He didn't expect to fall in love with her. I didn't expect it either."

"As a trusted friend, maybe you can convince him to find someone else to love and leave Maya alone."

Nessa shook her head. "His love for your sister goes beyond the birthmark on her face. I'd go so far as to say it's unhealthy in a spiritual sense, the kind of love that's hard to re-direct. I believe he cares for her deeply, but not in the way she needs to be loved. He's hell bent on taking away what she values more than life."

"Who are we trying to fool?" I said. "Her feelings for Dr. Shane Donovan guarantee she won't listen to us. Plus, we have another problem. Veronica and our father think the surgery is a good idea. They're encouraging her to go ahead with it."

"Yes," Nessa said. "Veronica gave me the impression of being strong and opinioned when I met her. In fact, I felt chilled. Don't ask me why. It happens that way sometimes. My body reacts, and in time, my mind catches up. When Veronica pointed out the card of a woman floating in a void, she thought it depicted your mother. My take is that it depicted her. She's searching and begging for help, but is too proud to ask."

"How about the card of the woman with her hand pressed against the mirror while looking inside?" I asked.

"You've probably already come up with your own interpretation. Mine is that it depicted Maya. And the image reflected back signified you, offering your love and support."

"How about the person looking into the pool of water and seeing the reflection of someone else?" I asked.

"Also, Maya. When she looks at her reflection, she sees you and Veronica and senses your pain. She knows what your individual searches are costing you."

"How do *you* know all this?"

"Some of it comes to me in the same way knowledge comes to

you, from a dimension we know exists but may never understand. However, Maya told me the part about knowing your pain. She knows Antonia's haunting has caused you to leave your adoptive mother, your fiancé, your friends and your hometown. She knows the pain you felt at your birth father's abandonment."

"Hold it," I said. "Maya shares that pain, too. As does Veronica."

Nessa put her hand on mine. "Let me explain. Maya knows about your adoptive father, Gerardo, and how you lost him to cancer. She knows about your adoptive mother, Truus, who stifles you with her love. And she knows about Cliff, your ex-fiancé, who ruled your life in a way similar to the way Shane rules hers. She knows about the voices and how they sent your life into a tailspin. She also knows about Morgan."

"By reading my mind?"

"Through her dreams. It wasn't just your birth mother you've heard crying during the past nine months. It was also Maya."

"How?"

"She was raised by an elderly aunt of Antonia's, old enough to remember and practice the traditions of the Esselen. Her Indian name was *Dreamcatcher*, and she noticed early on that besides having a facial deformity, Maya had psychic abilities. To prevent startling her or making her feel like a freak, *Dreamcatcher* directed Maya's inner eye toward something safe, something everyone does nightly."

"Dreams," I said.

"Yes."

"So how do her dreams differ from ours?" I asked.

"Each morning, *Dreamcatcher* helped Maya relive and interpret her dreams, so she wouldn't forget them."

"So, it's possible that Veronica and I also have significant dreams, but forget them on waking."

"Not only possible, but probable." Nessa brought my hand to her right cheek. "You told me you saw yourself with a horrific scar on your face."

"Yes," I said, shivering at the memory. "I thought I was seeing myself. Instead it was Maya."

"That's how dreams work for her. She sees you in her dreams."

A gust of wind carrying pinpricks of rain penetrated the gazebo's lattice and struck us from behind. We jumped, squealing like teens. "My car's parked at St. Mary's," I said. "Want a ride home?"

"My house is closer than your car." Nessa positioned the bill of her cap so the gathering rain would trail down its sides. "It's hard to watch a person you love make decisions you disagree with, but selfless love demands you let go and allow, no matter what the consequences."

Water gathered in my hair and dripped down my face. "I'm having a hard time with that. I still think there's something we could do."

Nessa started to turn away, but stopped and gave me a soggy hug. "Pray."

I hugged her back. "I doubt I have much pull with whoever's in charge."

"Maya does," Nessa said.

We ran in opposite directions, Nessa toward the churning ocean and I toward St. Mary's, the little red church by the sea.

Chapter Thirty-Four

"WHERE'S MAYA?" I ASKED Veronica two days later, trying not to panic. "I just came from the Guidepost. They told me she'd taken the rest of the month and all of December off."

Veronica glanced at her left wrist though she wasn't wearing a watch. "Probably checking into the hospital about now."

Good thing I was sitting down. It was also a good thing I hadn't yet eaten, because even on empty, acid flowed into my throat as if I'd contracted gastroesophageal reflux disease. I couldn't bear to look at Veronica. Instead, I focused on the damp scene outside the kitchen window. It had stopped raining, but the sun hadn't yet pierced the clouds on this climactic day. "Which hospital?"

Veronica started to pace, a sign she wasn't as calm as she pretended to be. "Don't know."

"Can you find out?"

"Probably, but I won't."

My abdominal muscles contracted. Nausea was setting in. "Why?"

Veronica stopped pacing and planted herself in front of me, hands on hips. "Because if I do, you'll interfere."

Tired of feeling like a jerk, I'd already decided to step back and allow Maya to get on with her life. "Sounds like it's too late for that. Shouldn't we at least be there to support her? We're family. She may need us."

The working of Veronica's jaw made it clear she was having second thoughts.

Someone banged on the back-screen door. "Veronica. Marjorie." It was our father.

"I called a doctor friend of mine in Maryland," he said when I let him in, "and there's more to the removal of CVMs than Shane led us to believe. There may be complications."

I held back the response, *I told you so*. "She may already be in the hospital."

"I want to be with her. She may need me." The redness of his eyes differed from the times I'd seen him before, as if he'd been crying. His hands still shook, but his carriage and the firmness of his jaw suggested alcohol wasn't foremost on his mind.

"And what do you propose to do for her?" Veronica asked, her tone mocking.

Bob's eyes turned into watery pools. "Show her my love, as she showed me hers." He looked at me as if pleading for understanding. "Even though I abandoned you and Maya as babies, she didn't judge me. I owe her for that. And so much more." I wanted to say I hadn't judged him either, but that would've been a lie. "She told me I was made in God's perfect image. Can you believe it? She said to focus on this truth, that this was all that mattered." His eyes shone with what appeared to be worship. I recognized the look. I'd seen it in the eyes of Maya's patients at the Guidepost, as I suspected mine had shone when in Maya's presence.

I hugged our father and patted his back. "And she was right."

Veronica's mouth twisted in wry concession as she aimed cold blue eyes his way. "Seems I'm outvoted. Did you bring your phone?"

Bob pulled away from me and fumbled inside the pocket of his corduroy jacket. "Yeah. Right here."

Veronica reached for it, foot tapping. She was going to call Dr. Donovan. Thank God.

After Bob handed over his phone, Veronica shook her head and left the room.

He turned to me, his hands opening and closing at his sides. "I should've listened to you, Marjorie. You're a lot like Maya. You know how she feels inside. I" —his face contorted as if his throat were burning like mine— "was only thinking of myself, wanting her to be beautiful like her sisters, so I'd no longer feel guilty. But it's not that simple, is it?"

"No," I agreed. "Not by a long shot. But if it makes you feel any better, no matter what you and I would've said or done, Maya would've gone ahead with the surgery, anyway. All we can do for her now is what she did for us. Love her without judgment."

Easier said than done.

"You really think so?"

Before I could answer, Veronica charged back into the room and slammed the phone on the counter. "Shane's not answering."

"Maybe they're already in surgery," I said.

"Don't say that," Veronica snapped.

Though tempted to ask why the sudden change of heart, I didn't see the benefit in fueling her anger, or even worse, burdening her with guilt. The guilt I freighted on my shoulders was enough for both of us. Too bad it wasn't as easily disposed of as junk mail.

Our father picked up the phone and slid it back into his pocket, making me wonder a second time if I should break my self-imposed restriction about using mine and call Morgan. Unplugging from pervasive technology for the sake of self-preservation and sanity had its merits, but being off-the-grid could be highly inconvenient.

Before I had a chance to retrieve my phone from upstairs, Veronica opened the door and said, "Hope the Jeep's gassed up, because we'll need it."

"It's full," I said, grabbing my purse and keys. *Forgive me Morgan.* "Maybe Nessa knows where Maya is."

"Who's Nessa?" our father asked.

❂❂❂

Nessa wasn't at work either.

"She went to the hospital to visit a friend," the clerk said from behind the counter.

I motioned for my father to get out his phone. "Do you have her cell number?"

The woman pondered my request with a frown. "I'm not sure she'd want me to impart that information."

"It's okay," I said, hoping I didn't look as helpless as I felt. "We're good friends. In fact," —I turned to point at Veronica— "the woman she's visiting is our sister."

The clerk's eyes widened. "You mean Maya? Oh, you're the triplets." I nodded.

Her lips softened into a near smile. "Well, in that case..." She opened a drawer behind the counter and shuffled through it, causing her mood to sour again. "The lack of people's organizational skills around here is appalling."

I tried to bring back her smile. "Not Nessa's I hope."

"Heaven's no. She keeps her stuff locked away in that Pandora's box of hers. As if we'd mess with her tarot and *Soul Cards*." She shivered. "Those eerie things."

I copied Nessa's number from the scrap of paper the clerk held out, then reached for Bob's phone. "Keep your fingers crossed, Dad."

Nessa answered on the third ring, sounding winded as if she'd been running.

"Nessa, thank God. This is Marjorie. Where's Maya?"

"I don't know. Shane pulled a fast one on me and, it seems, on you, too. I'm calling all the local hospitals."

"Will they tell you if she's a patient there?"

"If I ask for her by name, they will. Unless she or Shane has instructed otherwise. I was about to call Community Hospital off Holman Highway. If that doesn't pan out, I'll be checking with Mee Memorial in King City."

"Why don't you tell her to use her psychic skills?" Veronica asked.

By the silence on the other end of the phone, I figured Nessa had heard Veronica's smart aleck remark.

Bob gave Veronica a dark look, but she shrugged it off. "We're wasting time," she said. "Ask Nessa what can we do?"

221

"Nessa, we want to help, but don't know the area."

"Call Natividad Medical Center in Salinas and Salinas Valley Memorial, then let me know what you find."

"Will do." I gave her our father's cell number in case she located Maya first.

❍❍❍

Nessa and I kept in touch by phoning back and forth during our search for Maya in local hospitals. With no success. The day was almost over, and we were discouraged and hungry.

Since it was one of the few restaurants I was familiar with and it was nearby, I suggested we meet for dinner at the Tinnery. Too late, I realized how it would remind me of our last meal there with Dr. Donovan. Even then, I had sensed that his relationship with Maya would lead to a situation not to my liking.

The waitress came by for our orders just as Nessa's phone belted out a jarring version of the "Mexican Hat Dance."

"It's Shane," Nessa said.

When she answered, the rest of us leaned in close to listen.

"I'll give you a few minutes to decide," the waitress said, sensing our change in mood with the intuition of a seasoned server.

"Yes, yes." Nessa's voice sounded tense. She listened to Dr. Donovan for what seemed a long time. She glanced at us, then away. "Dear God." She pulled the phone from her ear long enough to check the time. "Okay. Yes. I understand. It's five-twenty. If we hurry, we can be there by nine." She ended the call and fumbled for her purse. "She's at Saint Francis Memorial Hospital in San Francisco. Let's go."

We dropped our menus and a tip on the table, rushed out of the restaurant, and piled into Nessa's Bronco.

"Shane told me he chose Saint Francis Memorial because its medical equipment is top-notch and it has plenty of trained personnel in case of an emergency," Nessa said as we headed up Ocean View Boulevard toward Highway 1. "Maya's surgery went well, better than expected. There will be more surgeries, according to Shane, because the procedure is tricky, but Maya got through this one without a hitch and was resting peacefully. Then, about an hour ago, her blood pressure spiked and fluid began accumulating in her lungs. She started mumbling about *no-man's-land* and wanting to see her mother."

See Mother? Oh no you don't, Sis.

"She lost a lot of blood during surgery, but not enough to warrant her present condition, which Shane likened to a high-output cardiac state. And...

"Dear God. He said for us to hurry."

Chapter Thirty-Five

DURING THE THREE-HOUR drive from Pacific Grove to San Francisco, I tried to rein in my anger at Dr. Donovan for performing a complex surgical procedure on my sister for the sake of aesthetics rather than medical necessity. Everything I'd read about congenital vascular malformations cautioned that candidates for surgical removal and reconstruction were rare. Experts advised that multidisciplinary assessment, including MRI and CT scans, and at least six months of non-operative compression treatment precede all interventions. Even the preferred surgical strategy of debulking came with the risk of hemorrhaging. Few lesions could be completely cured. In fact, surgery could stimulate the lesions to re-grow. Add to that, the recommendation that all surgical strategies required the involvement of multidisciplinary teams—not just a doctor of one—and Dr. Donovan's behavior made me question his competence.

"Maya was born with the most aggressive and difficult anomaly to treat," I said as Nessa navigated the streets of San Francisco. "Yet Dr. Donovan is treating it as if it's as easily dealt with as fat reduction through liposuction."

No response.

Okay, I got it. No one wanted to hear any more of my rants.

At any other time, I would've enjoyed being on top of Nob Hill in San Francisco, but not with Maya lying in ICU, mumbling about no-man's-land and asking for our mother. Nessa, the palm reader who was fast becoming a friend, proved to be an excellent driver under stress. And driving in San Francisco definitely provoked stress, regardless if one was sightseeing or racing against time. As we pulled into the visitor parking lot at Saint Francis Memorial Hospital, she called Dr. Donovan to let him know we'd arrived. He instructed us to meet him at the emergency entrance.

The moment he saw us, Dr. Donovan rushed forward and pulled me into his arms. *Me?* Before I could object, I felt his body tremble. "God," he said, "this can't be happening. My beautiful Maya." Despite wanting to call him a selfish fool, I returned his hug. Just as Maya would've wanted me to. I looked at Nessa over the doctor's shoulder and noticed her pallor. How difficult it must be to see her friend suffer in this way.

"Maya's waiting for us, right?" Veronica asked in a voice that trembled.

Dr. Donovan released me. "Sorry. I lost it for a minute there." He shook Bob's hand and gave Veronica a swift embrace, then turned his gaze on Nessa. "Thanks for coming."

She nodded. "Let's go."

He led us through three corridors, then up an elevator and through more corridors, calling to mind a well-lit, much traveled, and confusing maze, and I wondered if I—or Maya—would ever find our way out. He opened the door to a room in ICU with a warning, "Don't be alarmed. Her face is heavily bandaged, and there are tubes."

A beeping sound came from the heart monitor, which I hated right off. I also hated the room's muted yellow light and the smell of disinfectant. But most of all I hated seeing my sister in that hospital bed, bandaged almost beyond recognition, when two days before, she'd been singing her heart out at St. Mary's.

Bob sank onto the chair next to the bed and took Maya's hand. "We're here, sweet angel."

Her eyes fluttered, but remained closed.

Dr. Donovan's breath hitched in his throat. "She's only lightly sedated. Her choice, not mine. She said she wanted to have her wits about her when you arrived." He backed toward the door. "I'll give you some time alone."

It took all the strength I could muster to fight the fear building

225

up inside. I reminded myself that, limited by human ignorance, I didn't know God's plan for Maya, nor for Dr. Donovan. I only knew what *I* wanted, which was for Maya to get well and remain in our lives for the next sixty years. I imagined the good times we'd have. The laughter we'd share and how we'd help one another learn from life's difficulties, large and small.

I lowered myself onto a chair against the wall, then closed my eyes and envisioned Maya singing in the choir.

Hello sister, I know how you've been,
I know troubled times are upon you...
Maya, I pleaded, *not yet. Don't leave us now.*

"Marjorie?" Maya said, her voice a whisper.

Legs unsteady, I approached her.

Bob rose and signaled for me to take his chair.

"I saw you in church last Sunday," she said so softly I had to bend in close to hear.

"Your voice" —I paused to clear my throat and blink back tears— "took me to heaven."

She sighed. "I'm glad."

From heaven to this. Why?

"Will you forgive me?" she asked.

"Forgive you? You don't need forgiveness? I love you. Even if you don't do what I say."

"Love *him*, too."

Though I knew to whom she was referring, I asked anyway. "Love who, Maya?"

Her blue eyes looked radiant against the white of the bandages. "He's a bit assertive, but—"

Assertive! How could an otherwise smart and well-adjusted woman not see Dr. Donovan for what he was: willful, controlling, opinionated, aggressive—obnoxious?

"You're judging him again," Maya whispered, her lips barely visible through the layers of gauze. "I see it in your eyes."

I realized how it must hurt for her to talk with all those bandages crisscrossing her face. I had to get her to stop. Anyway, what more was there to say? My opinion of the doctor was beside the point right now. The important thing was for Maya to regain her strength and get well. We'd have a big party after her hospital release. Go on trips together. Get married, have children.

"He loves me," Maya said. "That has to count for something."

I jerked to a stand. The chair tipped and would've crashed to the floor if Bob hadn't caught it on time. *Look what he's done to you,* I wanted to say. But to what end? Maya requested that I see through the eyes of forgiveness and love. Her eyes. Which was like asking me to live life perfectly, something I found impossible to do.

Bob put his hands on my shoulders, and Veronica came to stand next to me. Neither said a word. The back of my throat was heavy with tears. I dabbed at my eyes.

Veronica handed me a tissue, a gesture so caring that I knew she, too, had changed during our short stay in Pacific Grove.

"If we were all the same," Maya said in her soft, kind voice, "the world would stop."

I needed to shut up and back off, or she'd talk herself into exhaustion.

"Don't fight against what is," she said. "There will always be grief, pain, and trouble. Use them to help strengthen your path and your mission."

I wanted her all to myself. I wanted to feel her warm body while I had the chance. I wanted to be part of her life and for her to be part of mine. I was a vampire, a manipulator, no better than Dr. Donovan.

What a jerk.

Maya took a shuddering breath, a sign of what all this talk was costing her. "Go. Your role is not at my side. You'll know what to do when the time comes."

Did I hear right? Did she want me to go? Not just shut up and back off, but go? What if she turned for the worse while I was gone? No, I wouldn't allow myself to think that. She'd be fine. No use is weighing the situation down with negativity. I glanced at our father and noticed his tears.

Maya reached for my hand. "I've sown many seeds, but won't be around to watch them grow."

"Don't talk like that," I said, despite my determination to keep quiet. "You'll be okay, better than ever. Dr. Donovan said so. Anyway, all those seeds you planted need your special touch, the unique thumbprint you were born with."

She smiled. "Nah, they'll know what to do."

Unable to hold back the tears any longer, I whispered, "We need you."

"Atta girl," Maya said. "Every time you experience a little death in your life, allow yourself to cry."

I kissed her hand. It felt cold. According to the heart monitor, her blood pressure was still high. Yes, I needed to leave, even if it was one of the hardest things I'd ever had to do, so she could regain her strength, get back on track. My chest ached. You'd think I was having a heart attack. How could anyone experience such pain and live?

"I don't feel it anymore," Maya said.

Again, I knew to what she was referring. She no longer felt the bliss provided by her birthmark. "Is it possible to pull up that feeling from someplace else?" I asked.

Through the holes in the bandages that allowed for her eyes, I saw she was crying. The bandages were performing double duty, absorbing her blood—and her tears.

The birthmark that had started out as an irritant, a grain of sand inside an oyster shell, had transformed into a beautiful pearl that had enriched many lives.

"You can live without it," I said, "like the rest of us do."

Maya turned her bandaged face to locate Veronica, then reached out with her free hand. "Where's my powerful warrior?"

Veronica's face crumbled as she, too, gave in to tears. It seemed even warriors had their limits. She took Maya's hand and bent in close to whisper, "Shane says there's nothing wrong with you."

"Shane lacks the inner eye."

"But there's nothing physically wrong with you," Veronica persisted. "Just relax, heal up, and get better. Then you and Shane can marry. Better yet, you, Marjorie, and I can have a triple wedding. Imagine that."

"Antonia and I will be at your wedding," she said. "We'll see you in our dreams."

"Quit talking like that," Veronica said, swiping at her face with her hand. "You're getting better and that's that."

Before Maya could respond, Dr. Donovan re-entered the room.

Veronica stepped back so he could approach the bed. When his gaze met Maya's, the charged atmosphere between them practically gave off sparks.

I let go of Maya's hand and backed away.

"Not yet," Maya said, reaching out to me.

I took her hand and held it to my cheek, then looked at Dr. Donovan and tried to compare him to Morgan. But my hostility made it impossible.

"Shane loves me," Maya whispered. "Don't punish him for that, Marjorie. Forgive him for me and for his sister, Anne."

Dr. Donovan raked his fingers through his hair. "Maya. Please. There's nothing wrong with you. I've performed hundreds of surgeries without a single mishap. Have you so little faith in me?"

Nessa stood at the foot of the bed, offering her silent support. I wondered at a friendship such as hers, looking on with love and no thought for herself.

Maya must've been in my head again, because she whispered, "Nessa, take care of Shane for me."

Dr. Donovan jerked and looked at Nessa.

"It's okay, Shane," Nessa said. "I understand."

He shook his head. "I'm glad somebody does."

Although it about killed me to do so, I kissed Maya's bandaged cheek and said goodbye. For her sake, not mine. She needed to rest. My presence would prevent her from doing so. I might never see her again, but she'd told me to go. If it was God's will, she would recover and come home with us. Otherwise...

I couldn't stand by and watch her die.

"Think of me when you next walk the labyrinth," Maya said, releasing my hand.

My thoughts jerked back to the day Maya, Veronica, and I had finished walking the labyrinth at Anne's house. "I hear they have a labyrinth at the Grace Cathedral in San Francisco," she'd said. "I'd love to walk it sometime. Will you join me?"

"Sure," I now said, as I had then.

Please God don't allow this to become an empty promise.

I turned to Veronica. "I'll be in the waiting room."

Brave words.

I only made it as far as the elevator before I sank to the floor, my trembling legs unable to support another step.

Chapter Thirty-Six

HOW IS IT THAT I had lived twenty-nine years without being aware of Maya's existence, yet after only two months of knowing her, I couldn't seem to function without her? I couldn't eat. I couldn't sleep. And while part of me wanted to stick by her side every waking moment, the other part reminded me she'd asked for me to go.

On our first night in San Francisco, Nessa, Veronica, Bob, and I had checked into the Commodore Hotel on Sutter Street. During the days that followed, we'd drifted apart, each finding our own ways to cope, which was a shame, because we were hurting inside and could've used one another's company. We ate separately, slept in separate rooms, and filled the time in our own separate ways.

Nessa, I assumed, was busy comforting Dr. Donovan. When Veronica wasn't with Maya, she was probably working out at the gym two blocks from our hotel to prepare for the brutal physical test up ahead if she was accepted as a basic agent trainee with the DEA. As for our father... Well, the Commodore had a bar, purportedly one of San Francisco's finest hot spots.

I dealt with my hurt by wandering the streets.

On Wednesday, I stuck close to the hotel and hospital as though held back by a magnetic force, which limited my explorations to Sutter Street. I walked in a daze, weaving in and out of stores, browsing over books, home accessories, and punk-rock ware before heading back to the hotel, tired and empty-handed. *Are you okay, Maya? I need a sign. Don't you dare leave me without giving me the opportunity to say goodbye.*

The following day it rained, which put a halt to any reflective walking. So, while Maya lay in ICU, I sat in the theatre, watching movies, one after another, until the plots, characters, and settings became indistinguishable and mimicked the conditions in my life—where Maya became the heroine of every story and I cried that the hero couldn't save her.

On Friday, I walked up Pine to Powell and caught the cable car to Union Square—the heartbeat of San Francisco, a place of fashion, dining, and theatre. The square's shimmering white Christmas tree should've inspired a joyful swelling in my chest. And the giant red stars on Macy's storefront should've at least elicited a small expression of wonderment. Instead, I turned my back on the festive holiday glimmer of San Francisco's premier shopping district and walked back to Powell as fast as the crowded streets would allow.

Forgoing the cable car, I leaned into a brisk uphill walk, passing a bookstore without a second glance, feeling dead inside. By the time I reached California Street, I was panting from the exertion of the climb. I eyed the cable car, yet with heart pounding and knees aching I turned left and continued walking. From the complimentary hotel map I'd stuffed into my coat pocket, I knew California Street intersected with Jones, Leavenworth, and Hyde, all downhill streets leading back to Sutter, which, in turn, led back to the hotel. Just a little more exertion and I'd be home free.

I labored past the Fairmont Hotel, nearing Nob Hill, then caught sight of a building that brought me to a halt. It loomed in front of me and stretched into the sky like a giant porthole to heaven. The Gothic Cathedral, with its soaring vertical lines, horizontal cornices, balconies, and circular rose window, drew me. And before a directive had formed in my mind, I climbed the concrete steps and walked through the bronze-and-gold-plated doors into the vestibule bay. The cathedral's interior looked dark and intimidating, until I caught the sheets of light streaming through the tall stained-glass windows in the west wall. What a magnificent contrast, light and shadow, with grainy patches between. The hallowed space was so quiet, I could hear my own footsteps and breathing. The pain in my knees and chest lightened. Peace settled over me.

After dipping my fingers into the holy water in the baptismal font at the nave entrance, I made the sign of the cross and marveled at the vaulted ceiling. At least ninety feet high, it resembled the underside of an overturned boat the size of Noah's ark. I could understand the concept of a boat bearing the people of God through the storms of life, but one that was upside down? It reminded me of the ceiling of St. Mary's in Pacific Grove.

Had I stumbled into another Episcopalian Church?

Something familiar lay stretched out on the floor to the right of me; a carpet replica of the labyrinth in Anne's backyard. Maya's request flooded my mind. *Think of me when you next walk the labyrinth.* "You bet," I said, blinking back tears. An unseen hand had guided me to the Grace Cathedral to fulfill a promise I'd made to my sister.

The labyrinth, an invisible thread to the Source, offered what I needed at the moment—guidance. Did I understand what I was about to do? No. The remunerations of the three-staged labyrinth experience—release, receive, and return—hadn't emerged for me yet. But I entered the opening in the perimeter of the circle with full trust that I'd learn something I needed to know.

I'd read that belief is the bridge between our world and the beyond, belief without evidence to prove that something is true. Was my belief strong enough to span the gap between me and the unknown where the revelatory potential of Maya's life and possible death could emerge?

As I walked along the singular path toward the center—no tricks, no dead ends—I concentrated on my breathing. *Let go. Open your heart. Leave your troubles behind.* My feet became steady as if they'd repeated this pilgrimage to the center so often they'd grown familiar with every turn, and with every step, my anger and blame edged closer to forgiveness—for Maya, for Dr. Shane Donovan, and for me.

On reaching the heart of the labyrinth, I sat on its rose center and dropped my face into my hands. I pictured myself in the center of my medicine wheel, with colored stones marking the four directions, a sacred place where my mind could find rest. I longed for Antonia, who'd first contacted me there. She, too, had been crying.

"Where are you now, Mother? In the hospital with Maya? Please watch over her for me."

Although I wanted to stay longer—to connect with the Divine as many labyrinth walkers had professed doing here—I needed to leave soon to reach the hotel before dark. A thought came unbidden. *Eternity in an hour.*

I stood and weaved back along the path I'd taken in—then the path of *release,* now the path of *return*—where I needed to implement and bring into my life what I'd received in the center. But what had I received there? My mind came up blank. What had I missed? If nothing else, the path to the exit would give me time to readjust to a world I didn't want to face.

Out of the corner of my eye, I glimpsed a fellow walker on the two-way path I was on. No surprise. The labyrinth was open to all as a tool for adding a mystical dimension to life. The walker moved in and out of my peripheral vision while maneuvering the twists and turns of the labyrinth. I heard laughter, which made me smile. Laughter released endorphins.

A familiar voice came from behind me, quoting the Twenty-Third Psalm. *I walk through the valley of the shadow of death. I will fear no evil because thou art with me.*

I looked over my shoulder.

The walker wore a mask identical to the one Maya and I had worn on Halloween, with the same flowing black robe.

I laughed. I cried. "Maya, is that you?"

No answer. Just a smile that looked just like Maya's. And mine.

"Oh Maya, I thought you were going to..." I looked at the church entry. "Where's Veronica? Where's Bob? How'd you get here?"

The walker put a finger to her lips, then waved for me to move on. "Okay," I said, though it almost killed me to do so. I had so many questions. Like how she'd recovered to the point of being released from the hospital, how she'd known I was here, and who'd taken the time to drive back to Pacific Grove to dig up her Halloween costume?

I wanted to pull her into my arms, tell her how happy I was that she was back and how much I loved her. But she'd been through hell and needed time to experience the labyrinth and gain from it what she could.

Tonight, I would call Morgan, tell him we'd discovered why Antonia had urged Veronica and me to meet with our father. I'd wanted for Maya to be a surprise, but now realized I'd almost waited too long. If she had died, Morgan would never have met her.

I couldn't bear the thought.

My body was shaking. I strayed off the path as though my feet had lost the sense of direction so clear on the way in. My nose started to run. I used the sleeve of my jacket to mop it. When I reached the exit, I turned. But Maya was no longer there.

I sank to my knees, as if hit head-on by an invisible object, uncertain if I'd survive. "Maya! Oh my God, Maya."

I felt the warmth of a hand on my shoulder. I jerked around. "Maya!" But it wasn't my sister.

Disappointment shot through my numbed body and jolted it back to awareness. "I'm looking for my sister," I said to the priest eyeing me with concern.

"Maya?" he asked.

"Yes. Do you know her?"

He shook his head and gave me a hand up. "I heard you call her name."

"I'm sorry," I said. "I didn't mean to make a scene. But she was just here...in the labyrinth, and I was surprised, because when I left, she was in the hospital...in Saint Francis Memorial...in ICU, and I thought she was dying. But there she was walking the labyrinth quoting the psalm of David...and I wondered how she got here."

Running out of words, I looked at the priest and wondered aloud, "Are you real?"

He smiled in such an otherworldly way that although he said, "Yes," I wasn't sure.

"I shouldn't have left her alone at the hospital. I left because she asked me to. Actually, she told me to, but I shouldn't have." My voice sounded hard and bitter. "I should've felt the bed as if I were in it, I should've felt the bandages as if they were on my face. I should've talked to her, comforted her, and reassured her. I should've told her what a good person she was..."

He held out his hand. Cupped in his palm was the mouse totem I'd given to my father. "I found this in the center of the labyrinth and wondered if it was yours."

"My mouse totem," I said, finding it hard to breathe. How had it gotten there? *Maya?*

The priest smiled. "I gather the stone holds special significance."

"Dear God, yes," I said, taking it from his hand. I closed my eyes and held it to my chest. *Thank you, Maya.*

"Follow me," he said, "and we'll pray for your sister. I know just the place."

"Father." The swelling in my throat made it hard to speak. "I think she's dead."

He motioned toward the front of the church. "There's something in the South Transept I'd like you to see."

"The organ?" I asked.

He smiled. "Although it's one of the oldest surviving organs in California and is rolled out of its glass case for concerts, that's not what I want you to see."

"The stained-glass windows?"

"You're getting close. But not just any windows. I believe what I'm about to show you will also hold special significance."

We paused in front of a spread of windows featuring the Old Testament patriarchs, Moses and Abraham.

"Magnificent," I said.

"Look at the window below," he said.

A bubble of hope rose from deep inside. "The window displayed the Twenty-Third Psalm, with the verses Maya had quoted in the labyrinth."

"Step closer," he said. "The key verses are in the medallions."

236

"The medallions. Yes, I see them. My God, there it is." *I will fear no evil for thou art with me.* "That's what Maya said. I heard her. She was here."

"Sometimes the images people see in the labyrinth come from the subconscious mind," the priest said.

"You don't understand, Father. Maya and my sister Veronica and I are triplets. We're very close..."

He shook his head and looked at the window of Moses with the Ten Commandments. "Even so."

Now would be the time to tell him about my dead mother and how she talked to me, but I held back. I didn't want to see his kind face turn stern and solemn. I didn't want him to bless me against evil spirits or tell me I was messing with things best left alone.

Then I blurted it out, anyway. "Father, sometimes I see and hear the dead."

To my surprise, the kind look on his face didn't turn to condemnation. Continuing to gaze at the window, he said, "As a spiritual leader, I'd be the last one to say what you're seeing and hearing isn't real. If nothing else, it's real to you. Did Maya seem happy?"

"Yes, Father. And that makes me wonder... Where do people go when they first die if not to heaven or hell?" *No-man's-land?*

Instead of answering my question, he asked one of his own. "Are you looking at Maya's situation as it actually is?"

"Excuse me?"

"It seems you're seeing it as something tragic."

"Yes, Father. I think she's dead."

"Yet, you said she was laughing and quoting the Twenty-Third Psalm. How do you think she was feeling?"

"Happy."

"Only happy?"

"At peace. Free."

"And would you deny her that?"

I didn't answer.

"You're grieving for your loss, which is only natural, as long as you don't get lost in the pain. You mentioned another sister."

Unbidden, my heart leapt. "Veronica."

"Where is she now?"

"Probably in the hospital with our father."

"Suffering?"

"Probably very much."

"Do they fear death as you do?"

I started to protest, but realized he was right. No matter what I'd heard about the afterlife, it still frightened me. "Probably."

"The three of you are clinging to Maya. But it's only by letting her go that you can make room for what comes next."

His statement swirled in my mind but didn't take hold. "Next? What comes next?"

"If you'll bear with me, there's something else I'd like you to see." I nodded and he led me back through the South Aisle of the church and through the Vestibule Bay to The Chapel of St. Francis. Before me rose a brilliant glass window, depicting birds soaring between leafy branches. "It's referred to as *The Love of Nature of St. Francis* window," the priest said. "The mosaic is called *The Tree of Life*."

"St. Francis," I said, thinking of the hospital where Nessa, Dr. Donovan, and my family were likely gathered in pain.

"Are you familiar with the prayer of St. Francis?" he asked.

"Yes," I said. "Though I don't have it memorized."

"While I refresh your memory," he said, "I'd like you to think about Maya, about yourself, and about what comes next.

"Lord, make me an instrument of your peace," he began. "Where there is hatred—"

"—let me sow love," I said.

He smiled and continued, "Where there is injury—"

"—pardon."

"Do you get the picture?" he said.

I nodded. The prayer was coming back to me, not in my voice, but Maya's.

Where there is doubt, faith.

Where there is despair, hope.

Where there is darkness, light.

Where there is sadness, joy.

"Oh, Divine Master," the priest said, "grant that I may not so much seek to be consoled, as to—"

"—console," I said. And the words just kept coming. "To be understood, as to understand. To be loved, as to love, for it is in giving, that we receive, it is in pardoning, that we are pardoned..." My voice caught. I couldn't continue.

The priest finished for me. "It is in dying that we are born to eternal life."

I looked up at *The Tree of Life* as the soft northern light streamed through it. "Thank you, Father."

I heard the swoosh of his robe as he left my side.

I hadn't even asked him his name.

Chapter Thirty-Seven

ACCORDING TO SHANE (yes, I was calling him Shane now, a minor concession to Maya's request that I love him), the medical facility at Saint Francis Memorial was state-of-the-art, the staff a team of experts, yet despite all his predictions to the contrary, Maya did not recover. While I'd been walking the labyrinth at the Grace Cathedral on the twenty-ninth of November, the year 2001, Maya passed away. According to Veronica, who'd been at her side, Maya had hallucinated that she was walking the labyrinth, quoting from the Twenty-Third Psalm: *I fear no evil because thou art with me.*

I don't know what brought us all together under one roof at Anne's house. It could've been the magnetic pull of the Victorian. It could've been Antonia finally bending us to her will. It could've been Maya, or just plain need. It certainly wasn't the result of noble intentions on my part—despite reciting the prayer of St. Francis at Grace Cathedral with the mysterious priest.

Lord, make me an instrument of your peace...

It would take time and courage to bury all the misunderstanding and resentment that had built up inside of me over the past months. And I was short on both.

Nessa, the only one among us showing any outward signs of compassion or empathy, regardless of her own suffering, warned us that Shane was beside himself with grief. I couldn't find it in me to care. His stubbornness, his selfishness, and his need for control, had caused Maya's death. How was I supposed to find it in my heart to forgive him, even if Maya had asked me to? I'd never experienced such grief and despair, even after the death of my adoptive father. I thought it would kill me.

Nessa moved into one of the bedroom suites on the third floor so she could make frequent trips to comfort Shane, who'd settled into the attic. To my surprise, and embarrassment, he informed me there was no studio apartment up there, only some second-hand furniture, including an army cot and a lumpy couch from the "good ol' days." Apparently, the fancy furnishings I'd seen there had been a trick of my imagination, or, as Nessa, suggested, something I'd experienced in a waking-dream. She called it lucid dreaming. Veronica called it a "trippy state," like the one Mary Shelley must've been in when she got the inspiration for *Frankenstein*.

Trouble was, Nessa said that lucid dreams usually lasted only a few minutes and when you experienced them, you knew they were dreams. Well, my so-called "trippy state" had lasted more than a minute, and I certainly hadn't known it was a dream. It had felt totally real to me. When I asked Veronica what she'd call my out-of-body visit to her in the basement seven weeks earlier, she said, "Weird."

Of course, I didn't take Shane's word for it about the non-existent studio apartment. I meant to see it for myself in case he was messing with me. So, I took the stairs up there to check things out. Darn. No studio apartment. What I did find, though, was a camel-back couch upholstered in browns and creams, threadbare, but otherwise like the one I'd seen in the borderland of sleep. I also found the same Persian carpet beneath the same glass-topped coffee table, plus a topper appliquéd with orange and black monarchs draped over Shane's army cot. How had I known they existed if I hadn't seen them before?

"Guess that means the cat isn't real either," I said, wishing Maya were here. She'd understand, given her new perspective.

"Shane told me his aunt, Christine, had a cat named Raphael," Nessa said.

Reality warp? Narcolepsy? Hallucination? If Christine and the cat weren't real, how had I known their names and that they'd even existed?

Before Shane disappeared into the attic again to "fall apart in private," he informed us that Anne's idea of the perfect hangout had been the basement. His, the attic. "I didn't want to intrude when I realized you gals were staying here," he said, as though that were an excuse for withholding this information until now. "It was an incredible coincidence, you meeting my sister in Big Sur and she giving you the keys to our house. She'd never set eyes on Maya, and now never will."

Neither would Morgan, thanks to me. I should've called him and told him about Maya when I'd had the chance. If I called him now, he'd drop everything to be here to offer his support. Why put him through that? I was a frigin' mess and had a funeral to help plan.

As far as meeting up with Anne being an incredible coincidence, I didn't agree. Dr. Mendez had told me there are no coincidences, that everything in our lives—past, present, and future—is linked, and that every perceived coincidence, no matter how large or small, is a signal from the Universe to which we should pay close attention.

Our father was happy to move back into the bedroom suite on the third floor. Was he regretting his haste in returning to his rented cottage after Thanksgiving? Did he realize how precious our time together had been and how it would become one of our most precious memories?

Veronica plunged back into the basement, seeking relief from the painful surface waves for a while, which was just as well, because now I had Dad.

Yes, Dad.

After settling in upstairs, he more or less stepped up to the plate and hit the ball. Not quite out of the park, but I wasn't complaining. "I want to take care of Maya's funeral," he announced to me the only listener, revealing a glimpse of the father I'd never known. "It's the least I can do for my baby girl after all my years of neglect. But I'll need your help."

We sat at the kitchen table, the heart of the Victorian, and his offer to see to Maya's funeral soon turned into an emotional deluge. He'd never opened up to me before and likely never would again. All I could do was sit and listen.

"I'm struggling, Marjorie," he said, voice calm, his hands trembling, "not only with Maya's death, but with my dependence on alcohol. Yes, I'm an alcoholic. I can admit that now, thanks to Maya. She helped me see that one reason for my drinking was to keep down the devastating secret I'd been carrying. Talking to her, I could breathe again. It felt like I had a shot at getting my life back and showing my girls how strong I could be.

"Trouble is, now that the secret's out, I find I've spent so many years relying on alcohol to handle life's setbacks, that I'm not sure I can manage without it. I'm willing, really I am. In fact, I haven't had a drink since Maya's death. But it's easier to pick up the bottle than face the reality of how I've ruined my relationship with my wife and you girls. I'm spiraling down, Marjorie, unable to sleep. My thoughts are all over the place, I feel vulnerable and exposed. This time...this time, I want to do things right. I owe that to Maya, and to you and Veronica. Please, don't judge me," he finished with tears in his voice. "Don't' make me do this alone."

Could Maya see him from where she was? I prayed she could. Because the sight of him, sober enough to want to make things right for his wife and his daughters, filled me with hope for his recovery from addiction—and his broken heart.

"You owe it to yourself, Dad," I said. "And just so you know, we're in this together, and together we'll see it through."

❂❂❂

Viewing Maya's body at the mortuary was excruciating for my father and me. We held each other's hands for strength. "Dear God," he said, breaking into sobs. "We can't even see her face."

The bandages covering her wounds took me back to Halloween and how excited she'd been that no one could distinguish between us.

"She looked so much like you," Bob said, lifting a lock of her hair to his cheek, then his lips. It shimmered in his hand like threads of gold.

"What did you do with the mouse totem?" I asked.

"I gave it to Maya in the hospital before she died." He stroked the bandages on her forehead and the top of her head with a trembling hand. "Hope you don't mind."

I turned to my father, touched by his thoughtfulness. Maya had changed him in a way no amount of lecturing or reasoning could. Would his concern for someone outside of himself last long enough for him to enter a drug rehab facility without intervention? "It was the best gift you could've given her. A gift from our mother."

"It was Antonia's most prized possession," he said.

I didn't tell him the totem had returned to me, afraid he'd want it back. I couldn't find it in my heart to part with it again. I remembered Antonia's words: *It will find its way back to where it belongs.* Maybe later, if he checked into the addiction treatment center in Maryland that Maya had referred him to, I'd give it to him for strength. Though looking at him now, I could almost believe he'd no longer need it.

I placed my hand over Maya's. Stiff and cold, it sent shivers of regret coursing through me. Yet, I could've sworn something warm throbbed from its center.

Fighting the urge to cry, I found comfort in knowing the mouse totem had made it full circle, from Antonia to Veronica, Veronica to Joshua, Joshua to me, me to Bob, Bob to Maya, and from Maya back to me. I prayed that in her final hours it had brought her comfort.

"Maya, my sweet, precious sister," I whispered, rubbing her hands, willing warmth back into them. "I miss you so much, but not to the point of wishing we'd never met. I'd like to believe meeting you made me a better person, but I'm beginning to doubt it. Your lessons on forgiveness and acceptance are so far lost on me. I find it difficult to proceed."

"I could sure use a drink right now," my father said.

"Me, too," I said.

He looked at me, brows raised.

"Looks like neither of us has earned our wings yet," I said.

Father placed an unsteady hand on my shoulder. "Come on. We have a big job ahead."

✿✿✿

"You can't hold the funeral service in the small chapel at the grave-yard," Nessa said when my father and I returned to the house and told her of our plan. We'd gathered in the foyer around the table that held the crystal ball. "It won't hold a fraction of the people who'll show up."

"Maya told Veronica and me that she loved the Little Chapel by the Sea," I said. "That it was such a peaceful place to rest."

Nessa moved her hands over the crystal ball, her expression thoughtful, as if part of her mind were engaged elsewhere. "She also loved St. Mary's, and even it may be too small to hold the crowd."

"Crowd?" We were discussing Maya, not some Hollywood super star. "We haven't even put an announcement in the paper."

"Which I think was negligent of you," Nessa said, "though word-of-mouth will do the job. Did you actually believe you could keep her funeral private? Your sister has touched half the people in this town with her singing and community service. Well-wishers will come out of the woodwork."

At my look of surprise, she smiled. "Some of her former patients will even come from out of state."

"But," I said, trying to gather my thoughts, "they'll all need to eat."

My father, who'd been silent until now, stepped in with a no-so-gentle reprimand. "I can afford to provide for my little girl, even though it's a bit late." After all these years, he was trying to make things right. He turned to Nessa in silent appeal. "If you direct me to a suitable caterer, I'll take care of the expenses."

Belatedly, I noticed the current slogan on Nessa's t-shirt. *What you resist, persists.* I touched my face, imaging Maya's birthmark there. If nothing else, she'd taught me that we were part of something greater. That death was not the end. I had to quit fighting what was, let my sister go, so I could accept a different life call. If only I knew what that call was and could find the strength to follow it.

I looked at the crystal ball and saw clouds forming inside. "Can we bury her at dusk?" I asked. "She told me it was the time of day when the mind turns to the spiritual."

I tasted salt on my lips. Instead of resisting what I recognized as tears, I let them flow. "She said the Pacific is then at its most beautiful."

"It'll take some doing," Nessa said, "but I'm sure it can be arranged. The priest at St. Mary's was a close friend of Maya's. He'd do just about anything for her."

I turned to my father and gave him a hug, the kind of hug Maya would've given him, the kind that shows you mean it. "Then I'll leave the rest up to you."

"Nessa," my father said, pointing at the crystal ball with a heart-rending gaze that implied a search for something besides alcohol to heal his aching soul. "What do you see in there?"

She stiffened, but continued to pass her hands over the ball. "Nothing."

"But—"

"I read palms and tarot cards, forms of divination, but not the same as this."

"What's the difference?" he asked.

My question, too. Because not only was I seeing things in the ball, but smelling and hearing things as well. A scent of vanilla, for instance, and the sound of music unrelated to anything I'd ever heard before. No words, just a Harmony-of-the-Spheres type of thing with simultaneous sounding notes of harps, gongs, and singing bowls.

"I only interpret the meaning of physical objects with my physical senses, according to an established set of rules. Sometimes I receive data from the subconscious, but—"

"The ball looks physical to me," I said.

"What one *sees* using the crystal ball does not transmit through the eyes."

"Then how do you explain the billowing clouds I see?" I asked.

"Clouds?"

"And the music I hear and the smell of vanilla?"

Nessa caught her breath. "Do you see, hear, or smell anything, Bob?"

My father shook his head, looking at me as if I were speaking in tongues. "All I see is a clear crystal ball. All I hear is you talking. All I smell is... Actually, I don't smell a thing, except maybe some furniture polish. Have you been doing some housecleaning, Marjorie?"

"Glad someone noticed," I said.

"A crystal ball is only a tool," Nessa said. "With practice and deep concentration, one can use it to attain a receptive mental state capable of receiving information from the deep mind."

The music and scent of vanilla faded as I concentrated on Nessa's words, but the clouds wafting inside the crystal ball like cemetery fog continued to swell.

Nessa cleared her throat. "When you *scry* or gaze into a crystal ball, you send a message to the subconscious that you're seeking information beyond the reach of the senses."

Is that what I was doing? If so, what information was I asking my subconscious to seek?

"The subconscious then accesses this information and makes it understandable through sensory metaphors. Clouds, for instance."

"Of course," I said.

"Like in our dreams," Nessa continued. "It seems like we're actually sensing sights, sounds, and smells through our eyes, ears, and noses, but they're only illusions. Some people actually claim to *see* music and *hear* color."

"Sounds like a trip on LSD," my father said.

Nessa nodded. "LSD leads to a receptive state. That's for sure."

"Or self-hypnosis," I said, my concentration now split between the clouds passing through the crystal ball and awareness of Nessa's eyes on me.

"Which takes practice," she said. "For most people gazing into a crystal ball produces nothing, no matter how much they concentrate, sometimes due to concentrating too hard."

"Their heads aren't in the right place," my father said, "like mine for too many years."

I glanced up in time to see Nessa send him a nod of approval. Dad was a quick study when he wasn't drinking. "The crystal ball can trigger the desired mindset," she said, "but most of us haven't formed the conditioned reflex patterns that allow the ball to act in this way."

"So," my father said, "how does that explain Marjorie?"

Good question, Dad. How does that explain me?

Nessa stared at me as if I were some kind of failed experiment. "My guess is that though Marjorie doesn't necessarily control her extrasensory gifts, she has somehow conveyed to her deep mind that she's willing and prepared to receive that kind of information."

"Are you saying she's naturally clairvoyant?"

"She has experienced many psychic episodes over the last nine months, which makes me wonder... I'd say she probably has a latent gift for scrying. Hearing voices is, after all, the success of the deep mind to communicate important information to the conscious mind."

While Nessa and my father continued to talk, I heard a buzzing in my ears.

"Is telepathy another form of scrying?" my father asked.

The clouds in the crystal ball were parting.

"If deliberate, yes," Nessa said. "Scrying is a deliberate technique of perception."

Figures were materializing from behind the clouds like images on Polaroid film.

"By deliberate, do you mean willing as well as able?" my father asked.

"Yes," Nessa said. "Willingly manipulating your gifts, reaching out into the realm of mystery and the unseen."

I'd reached out into the realm of mystery and the unseen, all right, during my out-of-body experience with Veronica, bridging the physical and mental distance between us. But it was different with the messages from our mother, which arrived unsought and without warning. I had no control over them. But now... I shivered, sensing things were about to change. Like the images in the crystal ball.

"Maya was what we call a 'seer,'" Nessa said. "She saw and heard things that weren't of the physical world. But she balked at willfully accessing that data."

Like the doves in the birdhouse I was the only one able to see?

Dealing with the unknown when hoisted on me was one thing, trying to control it was another. Maybe that's what Nessa so disliked about reading people's minds or forecasting the future—that huge, yet subtle difference between surrender and control.

"It came to Maya naturally," Nessa said, "from when she was a child. Some people believe it's a cliché superstition, but Native Americans are familiar with mediumship via shamans, who experience altered states of consciousness to perceive and interact with the spirit world."

The crystal ball images were sharpening. Were Maya and Antonia materializing inside? If so, what did it mean?

"With Shane's sister, Anne, it's different," Nessa said. "She has no problem with surrender or control. According to her, it takes both. She worked with the crystal ball for hours and, in time, only looked into it for a few minutes before the veil lifted. The interior of the glass would obscure and she'd see any number of things. She did better at dusk, the point of balance between day and night, claiming to be more emotional then, more imaginative. She'd scry here at the same time every day, even wore the same clothing. She'd burn a vanilla-scented candle and listen to celestial music, such as *Om* by the Moody Blues and *Music of the Spheres* by Ian Brown." Nessa looked at me and smiled. "You've already figured that out, haven't you?"

I nodded. Maya and Antonia appeared to be together now, smiling and holding hands. Was this what I could expect in the afterlife? What I could look forward to?

"Anne claims this foyer, as well as the enclosed porch, turret, and attic are receptive to the astral," Nessa said. "That emotional images of the souls of the departed are imprinted on their physical localities."

Maya and Antonia's emotional images were not only imprinted on the localities of this room, but on the locality of my heart.

I love you Sis. I love you Mom. Keep a place open for Veronica, Dad, and me in the circle of your love.

Chapter Thirty-Eight

THE DAY OF MAYA'S funeral arrived shrouded in cold, dripping fog, making lowering my sister's body into the ground and leaving it there almost impossible to comprehend. But what Veronica had accomplished while recharging in the basement brought full meaning to the words of St. Francis.

Where there is despair, hope
Where there is darkness, light
Where there is sadness, joy.

Veronica had contacted the folks at the Guidepost, and it looked like all of them, from those running the place to those in recovery, had shown up at St. Mary's by-the-Sea Episcopal Church to pay tribute to their beloved friend and teacher.

Veronica had also asked the choir to sing one of Maya's favorite songs, and though our sister's strong, clear alto was absent, the grief and joy in the remaining sopranos and tenors (not quite Pavarotti, but good), lifted my heart just the same.

Not too long ago, on a lonely night away from home,
The Lord and I spoke the way we do.
He reminded me of an image,
And of words I've heard a thousand times.
He asked me if I would remind you—and so I do...
The Lord stands knocking at the door to your heart,
A door that opens from within—let him in.

Nessa had been right. The small chapel at the cemetery couldn't have held the crowds that arrived to pay respects to my sister. Neither could St. Mary's. After the pews had filled, people lined the interior church walls. Every nook and cranny not already crammed with wreaths and flowers accommodated Maya's mourners. Loudspeakers had been installed outdoors to accommodate the crowd that now overflowed onto the lawn and courtyard.

Father Al, his face flushed with exertion—or emotion—started Mass late due to the streams of people continuing to gather outdoors. He promised to curtail the service for the sake of those standing out in the cold. "Maya would've insisted," he said.

After readings from the Epistle and Gospel, Father Al asked that we face the truth about death. "Death is not our enemy," he said. "Death inspires wonder. Death makes life possible. Maya is a leaf falling from a tree, letting go, in hope of renewal and revival, a caterpillar transforming and reemerging as a butterfly. Her body has changed, but the observer inside stays the same. Just because her heart stopped beating doesn't mean her soul is gone. It never belonged to her body in the first place. She didn't go anywhere. She is everywhere."

He urged that we accept and forgive. "How do we live up to the gospel message to love one another and grow in compassion? Well, folks, I'll tell you how. Just follow Maya's example.

"Maya's contribution to our community took humility and inner strength. She was humble enough to know one needn't be perfect to make a difference. And her deepest demonstration of inner strength was her love. Look at love long enough," he said, reminding me of Christine's missive during our talk in the sunporch, "and you will become lovely."

The priest paused, either for his message to have a greater impact, or because he felt too choked up to continue.

I believe it was the latter.

"And finally, Maya knew about surrender. When she was stuck, when nothing seemed to be moving along, when people weren't doing what she wanted, Maya took herself out of the way and things always worked out fine. Yes, dear friends, the goal of life is not to win, but to play the game with love."

It wasn't until we were seated in the limousine about to head to the cemetery that I chanced a look at Shane. Despite Nessa's best attempts at comforting him, he looked like a brittle, empty shell. The feel of his cold body next to mine, filled me with regret.

Maya had pleaded with me to understand and love him. In my selfishness, I'd done just the opposite. "It's not about making him happy," she'd said. "It's about saving his soul."

"But how can giving up what you most value in life help save his soul?" I'd asked, angry, confused.

She'd smiled at me. "It'll teach him to love himself."

"What if he ends up hating himself instead?" I asked. Was her consent to surgery worth the risk and the price?

"He probably will, at first," she said.

Maya had been right. Shane looked like he hated himself. And I hated myself, too. Maya's heart of compassion had been her guide. Why couldn't it be mine?

Then came a head-clap of understanding. *We can't direct how the forgiving takes place. Forgiveness is a spiritual act, not one of reason.* I felt myself thawing like the rising of temperature in midwinter. Maya had provided an opening. I would take it from there.

Though trained to be steady during complex surgical procedures, Shane's hand trembled when I took it in mine. He gave me a vacant look.

"It's okay," I said.

He shook his head no.

Something stronger than my resistance to this man, call it compassion, call it a gift from Maya, caused me to put my arm over his shoulder. "Good will come out of this."

"How?" he whispered, his voice hoarse.

"I don't know."

He shivered as if experiencing a sudden chill. "You were wrong in assuming I didn't study up on Maya's condition and didn't consult experts in the field. This was not a life-threating procedure, one I've performed before without mishap or fatality."

I was wrong about many things.

"But *I* was wrong in assuming Maya would be better off without her birthmark. For a reason beyond medical explanation, Maya's birthmark was vital to her well-being…and her life. So why did she let me do it? Sure, I'm overbearing at times, but Maya knew this about me. She was perfectly capable of telling me no."

I thought about what Christine had told me about Maya. *She has learned not only to let go of her ego, but also of herself. She is free from the bonds of space and time.*

Another small window opened in my mind, allowing an insight to slip through previously hidden from me. "If we allow ourselves to believe Maya agreed to surgery because you told her to, then we also have to believe she was weak and easily manipulated. I've seen Maya in action, so know this isn't true. We may never understand her reasoning, but I suspect it had something to do with her selfless love for all of us. And for Antonia. I believe she's leading our mother home."

"Thank you… Thank you for saying that," Shane said.

And with those words, the world appeared less gray.

By the time we reached the cemetery, it was dusk, but no one seemed to mind. People kept arriving and crowded together as if to form a protective wall around Maya's grave.

"We gather here to commend our sister, Maya, to God our Father," the priest said, "and to commit her body to the earth elements."

Commit her body to the earth elements. Dear God.

The call of gulls, with their high *kee-yahs* and low *cow-cow-cows*, caught my attention, while the scripture verses and prayers that followed faded into the background. As Father Al walked around the white casket, first sprinkling it with holy water, then blessing it with incense, the sound of waves crashing against the shore filled all the space in my mind. I thought of our visit to the lighthouse, of our bracing against the wind and Maya's insistence that Shane was as hard to resist as the power of the ocean slamming against the rocks. "He thrills me," she said. "Yet I know if I allow it, he will crush me."

And she had allowed it. But not for reasons I, or anyone else, had imagined.

She had allowed it to help Shane evolve from a self-centered, controlling person to the empathetic and supportive man she knew him to be. Marriage to Shane would never have worked. The difference in their worldviews had been too great. The kindest thing she could do for Shane was to sever their relationship, even if it caused them both pain.

She had allowed it to help Antonia. She'd made it clear during our graveyard visit four weeks ago that she saw death as passing from one dimension to another, where her soul—and Antonia's—would continue to live and to grow. "Death is a transition," she'd said, "not the end of our conscious experience. These people's souls are released from the shackles of their physical bodies and have transcended to the heavenly realm where the body is no longer needed." She would lead Antonia home.

And, yes, she had allowed it to help *me*. Her death—her sacrifice—prevented me from continuing the path I was on, searching, always searching. Cut the excuses. Cut the delays. What I was searching for, like forgiveness, couldn't be found or understood through the mind. All I had to do was look in the mirror to see the person Maya knew me to be and was capable to become.

When the pallbearers—eight of Maya's former patients from the Guidepost—placed their white gloves and boutonnieres on top of the casket, I held back the sobs that threatened, but I couldn't hold back the tears. Dad, who was standing between Veronica and me, clasped my hand, and I leaned my head against his shoulder.

How I ached for Morgan. Why hadn't I called him and asked him to come? He would've dropped everything to be here. In fact, he'd be hurt when he found out we'd buried Maya without him. It was time to include the man I loved in my life. He was not Cliff and never would be. Nor was I the pushover I once was. If I allowed it, Morgan could become the wind beneath my wings, wings I could use to travel the flyways of my life path, assured that he'd always be there to support me. And it was about time I did the same for him. Heaven knows, he could use propping up like everyone else.

The priest announced the Rite of Committal and Interment was over and everyone was welcome to return to St. Mary's church hall for dinner, but no one seemed in a hurry to leave.

Shane, supported by Nessa, stood and walked up to Maya's casket, a spray of orchids, white calla lilies, and green hydrangeas spread over it like wilted angel wings.

From behind us, I heard someone hiss, "Murderer."

"Did you hear that?" Veronica asked.

"Yes," our father and I said at once.

Veronica stood. "We're not standing for that, are we?"

"Maya would've wanted us to give Shane our full support," Dad said.

"Absolutely," I said.

She smiled. "Then what are we waiting for?"

Veronica, father, and I locked arms and walked up to Shane and Nessa, then put our hands on his shoulders. He slumped over the casket and whispered, "I'm so sorry, Maya. You were beautiful as you were."

Help him, a voice prodded.

I didn't need to turn around to know who was speaking.

Tell him I'm happy and want him to be happy, too. Tell him I'm thankful.

I rubbed Shane's back and bent in close to whisper, "Maya's happy Shane, and she wants you to be happy, too."

He shook his head. "I killed her."

How could I make him understand, what I couldn't understand myself?

Tell him to look toward the sunset. I'll send him a message.

"Look toward the sunset, Shane," I said. "Maya's about to send you a message."

His body stilled. "Maya?"

I led him away from the casket and urged him to face the ocean. The fog lifted like a stage curtain swooping up from the center to reveal the theatre platform by the simple pull of a chord. As I led him forward, mourners stepped aside to let us pass. Nessa, Veronica, and Father followed. The ocean shimmered in vibrant yellows, reds, and indigos, while waves crashed against the shore.

A sigh of astonishment arose from the crowd. Then I saw it. "Shane, look!"

Monarchs—hundreds of them—broke free of gravity and flew across the wide, open sky and setting sun, their quivering wings reflecting the fading light like precious jewels.

"A message from Maya?" he asked.

I'd searched for monarchs since the day I arrived in Pacific Grove, and now they were here. "Yes."

When he started to cry, I took his hand and told him the rest of Maya's message. "She said she was thankful, Shane."

He stared at the monarchs as they rushed upward in an explosion of orange and black and flew over us to the cemetery. "Thank you for telling me."

While the flying insects circled and hovered over Maya's grave, I recalled her saying, "In parts of Mexico, people believe the spirits of departed loved ones come on the wings of monarch butterflies." Were Antonia and Maya experiencing the out-of-body freedom I'd experienced while visiting Veronica from the lighthouse beach? And had their spirits found their way to the earthly realm on the wings of the monarch butterflies?

"You're welcome," I said, squeezing Shane's hand.

Like Maya, the monarchs were free of their cocoons, a mystery I'd never understand in my lifetime on this earth, possibly only in my life hereafter. What I *did* understand, though, was what the Grace Cathedral had meant when he said, " go that you can make room for what comes n brief flash in eternity, taking place in the gray s heartache, between *yesterday and tomorrow*. My wc ized, and I was still here, bruised, but undefeatec

Maya was the hero of her story. *And by dying she was born to eternal life.* It was time I stepped forth and became the hero of mine.

Chapter Thirty-Nine

VERONICA INSTRUCTED NESSA, SHANE, and our father to take the limo back to the church hall to join the rest of the funeral attendees for a bite to eat.

"But how will *we* get back?" I asked.

She swept aside my concern with the wave of her hand. "You, my dear, have some unfinished business to attend to."

"But—"

She grabbed my arm and led me toward the Little Chapel by the Sea. "You'll thank me later."

✦✦✦

My hand flew to my mouth. *No, it can't be.*

Whereas one sister had given me the gift of monarchs on the day of her funeral, the other had given me...

Morgan!

He smiled, then frowned at what must have been the mixture of pleasure and pain on my face. "Happy to see me?"

I moved forward in what felt like slow motion until I reached the front of the chapel where he stood. *Gorgeous Morgan.* I'd never seen my cowboy all suited up before. I stepped into his arms, shivering, clinging. "I'm so glad you're here."

He kissed the top of my head. "Me, too."

The door closed behind us as Veronica took her leave.

"Don't be mad at me for not calling you," I said. "I needed to do this on my own, without leaning on you for support. Plus, I was becoming someone you wouldn't like, judgmental, unforgiving, and I didn't want you to see me that way."

"Yet your two sisters still managed to love you."

I pressed my face into the nook of Morgan's neck. Darn, he smelled good.

"I'm so sorry about Maya," he said.

"I wish you could've known her."

"Me, too."

His response, so tender and softly spoken, had me finally taking Maya's advice. "Every time you experience a death in your life, allow yourself to cry."

"Tell me about her," Morgan said.

"I don't...know...if...I can," I said, tears turning into sobs.

"It'll help for you to talk about the person she was."

I lifted my head from his shoulder and looked into his emerald green eyes, edged by a series of small wrinkles that revealed the resonance and vitality that often come with closeness to nature. He was right. Just thinking about Maya sparked the capacity for joy still available to me. "She was amazing, Morgan." I took a deep breath to keep my voice from shaking. "The most giving and unselfish person I ever met. She...she provided support for the newly sober, made them feel heard, accepted, and...and loved. Today's crowd was proof of how many lives she touched with her unselfish service. What will I do without her? It's hard to hold on to the belief that all is as it's supposed to be."

I heard a smile in Morgan's voice. "Sure, you can. It's called faith."

During a moment of stillness, I allowed myself to feel a spark of hope at the prospect of digging out of what currently felt like a deep, dark hole.

"Seems to me, your path is clear," Morgan said.

Clear?

"Why not carry on where Maya left off?"

"You mean with the addicted?"

"With youngsters, instead of adults. They also need to feel heard, accepted, and loved. Speaking of which... Dr. Mendez asked me to relay a message."

"Dr. Mendez?"

"We spoke yesterday when I took Joshua in for his monthly appointment."

"Oh my gosh. Joshua. How's he doing?"

"The doctor is cutting Joshua's office visits down to bimonthly. Apparently, farm life agrees with him.

"That's fantastic. I miss the little guy." *More than you know.*

"He misses you, too."

"So," I said, fighting a new onslaught of tears, "what's Dr. Mendez's message?"

"A friend of his is the principal at West Coast Middle School in Menlo Park."

"I know of the place. Actually, I went to school there."

"They're looking for a part time teacher, and Dr. Mendez believes the job might interest you."

"I abandoned the dream of becoming a teacher years ago."

"Why?"

"I don't know. Guess life got in the way."

"Okay, I get that. You abandoned your dream to survive. But, seems to me, you're past that now."

I'd come to Pacific Grove to meet with our father and discover his secret. To what end? Only to discover that Veronica and I had another sister and then watch her die? There had to be more to it than that. Maya had taught me about love and service, and she'd given me back my mouse totem, a sign that it hadn't yet finished its journey.

Morgan straightened and looked at me. "You've already earned your teaching credential, and the way you reached Joshua when no one else could means you have a special connection with kids. So why not try substituting for a while, see if it agrees with you?"

"Taking on a teaching job would delay our wedding for months," I said, feeling sadness, and excitement, swirl inside like the monarchs sweeping over Maya's grave.

Morgan's dimpled smile made me weak in the knees. "I thought we agreed months ago that I couldn't have all of you."

"But…"

"Consider us married in every way that counts." He kissed me with a passion that promised unending bliss-filled days ahead. "Anyway, we'll still have weekends."

I was where I most wanted to be, within the protective circle Morgan's arms. If I could isolate myself in his world, never have to make another personal choice or decision or take another chance, maybe my life would be safe, stable, and secure.

But if there was a through line in what I'd learned since setting out on my journey nine months ago, it was that I couldn't build my foundation on someone else's back. And that security comes with a price. Maya had opened my heart and showed me that it didn't require special training to make a difference in the world. I had five days a week to put to use all Maya had taught me about love and service.

Weekends would be dedicated to Morgan and Joshua.

Acknowledgments

MY DEEPEST GRATITUDE TO:
My husband and family for their support while I wrote the third book in my "Enter the Between" visionary fiction series.

My line and content editors Judith Reveal, Moira Warmerdam, Marianne Chick, Linda van Steyn, and Theresa Adrian. Thank you for setting me straight when I veered off course.

My critique partners (past and present) for their valuable suggestions: Jo Chandler, Lee Lopez, Dorothy Skarles, Natalia Orfanos, and members of the *Amherst Writers and Artists Group*, directed by Gini Grossenbacher.

My sisters, brothers, and friends, for their faith in my writing. I wish I could express in ways other than words how much this means to me.

Fellow authors and members of the *Visionary Fiction Alliance* for bringing the genre of Visionary Fiction into the public eye.

Musician, singer/songwriter John Wihl for granting me permission to include the lyrics of his song titles *Let Him In, A Mother's Love*, and *Make a Place* in this work of fiction.

Clarissa Yeo of *Yocla Designs* for my wonderful covers and Jonnee Bardo of *Gluskin's Photo Lab and Studio* for my author photo.

You are the best.

Book one of the "Enter the Between"

Visionary Fiction series

Silicon Valley resident Marjorie Veil has been conditioned to ignore her own truth, to give away her power, to subjugate in relationships with others, and to settle for the path of least resistance. But she has many surprises in store, for there are synchronistic forces at work in her life that, if she listens, will lead her to her authentic heart and happiness. The seemingly impossible happens in the wild of the Los Padres National Forest where Marjorie goes on retreat to make sense of her life when she thinks she has gone insane. The innocence of the Native American orphan Marjorie befriends, as well as more mystery and adventure than she bargained for, show her how love can heal in what turns out to be a transformative spiritual quest.

Book two of the "Enter-the-Between"

Visionary Fiction series

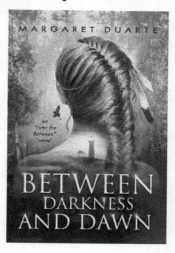

Marjorie Veil is running again. But this time, she's not running from herself. She's running to embrace her past so she may move on with her future. A future that includes a man and an orphaned boy who both love her. But in order to build a life with them, she must have the strength to defy the expectations of her over-protective adoptive mother, and she must be steadfast in deciphering the veiled messages coming from the Native American woman who died giving her birth. Marjorie's quest is the story of the soul trying to break free of its conditioned restraints to live a life of freedom, courage, and authenticity, and focus on what is really important in her precious present moments.

Book four of the "Enter the Between"

Visionary Fiction series

Medicate or nurture; reform or set free? These are quandaries rookie teacher Marjorie Veil faces when she takes on an after-school class for thirteen-year-olds labeled as troublemakers, unteachable, and hopeless. Faculty skeptics warn that all these kids need is prescribed medication for focus and impulse control. But as Marjorie quickly discovers, behind their anti-conformist exteriors are gifted teens, who are sensitive, empathetic, and wise beyond their youth. They also happen to have psychic abilities, which they have kept hidden until now. Can Marjorie help them do what she has been unable to do for herself: fight for their spiritual and emotional freedom?